A Ransom
Conspiracy

A RANSOM CONSPIRACY

A Will and Betsy Black Adventure

David and Nancy Beckwith

ABSOLUTELY AMAZING eBOOKS

Published by Whiz Bang LLC, 926 Truman Avenue, Key West, Florida 33040, USA.

For information contact:
Publisher@AbsolutelyAmazingEbooks.com

ISBN-13: 978-1945772931 (Absolutely Amazing Ebooks)
ISBN-10: 194577293X

A Ransom
Conspiracy

Other Will and Betsy Black Books
by David and Nancy Beckwith

A Hurricane Conspiracy

A Calculated Conspiracy

A Narcotic Conspiracy

A Cosmetic Conspiracy

A Jamaican Conspiracy

Available from
AbsolutelyAmazingEbooks.com

CHAPTER 1

It was a lazy February Sunday. The day was clear with a few billowy clouds in the sky and virtually no chance of rain since it was still the dry season. The weather was a little cool by tropical standards, but not oppressively so if a person swimming wore a t-shirt or wet-suit type top. The afternoon high had been predicted to be 82 degrees. Will and Betsy Black were anchored in two and a half feet of water at Picnic Island near Little Palm Island in the Florida Keys. They looked around them. There were less than twenty-five boats anchored there; when summer came, there could be a hundred or more present on a Sunday like this. A newly arriving boat pulled in and anchored next to the Blacks. Its captain waved and then jumped out to set the anchor while his wife held their boat in neutral.

"B-r-r-r," the man yelled as his body absorbed the initial shock of the cool water.

"Norm," Will yelled back. "It'll be great once you get wet and drink a beer, you weenie."

"I'm a chicken and proud of it. Want to hear me cluck?" Norm yelled back as he finished securing his boat and helped his wife, Catterina, climb down the ladder. "We'll come over in a second and drink our first one with you guys."

"Just one?" Will asked. "The afternoon's still young."

The lyrics to a song written by tropical-rock singer Jim Morris wafted over from an adjacent boat.

A month in Montana, hell I nearly froze.
I guess that my blood is too thin.
But I'm back to my deck shoes with the holes in the toes.

I'm back in the sunshine again.

"That song reminds me," Will said after shaking hands with the new arrivals, "Did you read the weather story in today's *Citizen*? Ithaca, New York surrendered to winter. They replaced their home-page photo on their tourist web site with a picture of the Dry Tortugas and invited people to visit the Florida Keys. They even installed a link sending people to fla-keys.com. They asked people to come back to Ithaca after things thaw out. Then they had to take the Keys link down because it was getting so many hits it crashed their site. Our high today is 82; theirs is an eight-degree high and a minus five low."

Betsy chimed in, "Fat Tuesday was last Tuesday. I talked to some people in Mobile who rode in this year's Mardi Gras parades, and they reported rain and sleet with temps hovering barely above freezing."

"And here we are drinking a beer in the water," Norm said. "My mama didn't raise a dumb child."

Will Black was the branch manager for the Key West office of Reynolds Smathers and Thompson Securities (RST); his wife, Betsy, was the local area president for WB Bank. Even though they were now seasoned Floridians, Will was originally from the Mississippi Delta; Betsy was a native of Mobile, Alabama. They had originally met in Mobile when both were working in the financial district. They had moved to Vero Beach, Florida when Will was offered a promotion and transfer. Their daughter, Lexie, was born in Vero. During their many years in Vero, Lexie grew up, graduated from a private school, and then got her BA on an academic scholarship from the University of Miami. Now she was carving out a place for herself in the corporate world. Vero had been a wonderful place to live and work, but when Lexie left for college and Betsy was offered the presidency of WB Bank in

Monroe County at the same time RST decided to open a Key West branch, it seemed like a no-brainer for the Blacks to move to the lower Keys. Just as it had worked out in Vero, the move to the Keys also turned out to be a marvelous decision.

Norm and Catterina Knoll owned Prestige Boat and Yacht Center. Prestige not only sold various lines of boats but was one of the lower Keys' most complete boat service centers as well. Will and Betsy had originally met Norm when they purchased their Grady-White, which they named Sundance II, at his dealership. Subsequently Will opened an investment account for the Knolls, and Betsy had a banking relationship with them as well. While neither couple would have classified the other as close friends, the Knolls and the Blacks occasionally saw each other socially. When they did encounter each other, the couples seemed to have a lot in common and inevitably enjoyed each other's company.

Will and Betsy now relaxed in the water in their floating chairs. They had a square floating foam raft with a recessed middle designed to accommodate a small ice chest and now had it tethered by a line to the cleat on Sundance II's stern. Two boats down, a man was cooking shrimp shish kabobs on a grill he had set on top of a weighted pedestal made for that purpose. His wife and another couple watched him cook from folding lawn chairs they had set up in the water. Towards the island, a black Lab was chasing a Frisbee being thrown by its owner. A wading man watching the game had a piece of fried chicken in one hand and a beer in the other. Music or parts of conversations were coming from all directions. Betsy and Catt decided to wade up to the island together and explore for shells or rocks.

As Will and Norm sat talking and soaking, Norm

kept looking over his shoulder out towards the channel. Will finally asked him what was of interest.

"Before the girls get back," Norm said, "you mind taking a stroll with me?"

"Sure," Will said. "See someone you know?"

"It's probably nothing," Norm said. "Just a boat I want to see closer. I noticed it when we passed it coming in. It's that one by itself way out there on the periphery."

Will and Norm opened fresh beers, put them in koozies, and slowly started wading in the direction Norm had pointed. They threaded their way over other boats' anchor lines, waving at local people they knew until they got close to the boat, which had attracted Norm's attention.

The boat was a twenty-two foot Grady with a sea-foam green Bimini top. The lower part of the hull was peach colored. It had a horizontal stripe about three quarters of the way up, and was white above the stripe. Norm walked close enough to read the registration numbers on its bow but did not speak to the owner, a youngish man in long pants with a crewcut. His t-shirt said U.S. NAVY. The lone boat inhabitant never looked their way. He was staring into space as if in a trance.

"I thought so," Norm said in a low voice.

"Thought what?" Will asked.

"Wait and minute until we get out of earshot of this boat, and I'll tell you," Norm said, putting his fingers to his lips.

He said nothing more until they waded back to the Sundance II. Betsy and Catt got back from the island about the same time.

Will said, "So, you want to tell me what's going on?"

"I know that boat. I sold it when it was new. Only one I ever ordered around here with that custom color scheme. And the registration numbers bear me out.

That's why I wanted to get close to it. That boat was reported stolen recently," Norm said. He then described it to Catt who agreed her husband was right.

"Is that the one the deputy stopped by your office to ask you about?" Catt asked.

Norm nodded.

"I'm going to call it in to the water patrol," Norm said and quickly made the call from his cell phone. "Then I'm going to wade back over that way to see what happens when the deputies arrive. Anyone want to join me?"

Everyone quickly agreed to come and see what was about to go down. It wasn't long until the recognizable patrol boat arrived. The twin outboard, T-topped, deep-V-hulled boat had SHERIFF MONROE COUNTY emblazoned prominently on the hull. When the man saw the patrol boat approaching, he snapped out of his trance and cranked his engine. Before a word could be exchanged, the man suddenly put the boat in gear. The boat leapt ahead and raced towards the channel churning sand and dragging its anchor. The deputy quickly recovered from his surprise and took up pursuit. When the Grady planed off, the man heaved an ice chest at the pursuing patrol boat. Its captain swerved to avoid being hit. The man then threw a rod and reel at his pursuer, forcing the deputy to maneuver in the other direction. As the patrolman gained ground and closed in on the fleeing boat once more, the man threw a round boat bar-b-q grill off the stern. It bounced off the deputy's bow. The Truman, the boat taking guests to Little Palm Island, came along about that time and was forced to take evasive action as the man pitched a pair of sneakers one at a time. The sneakers hit one of The Truman's passengers. The patrol boat and the Grady-White screamed past Dolphin Marina and ran full throttle under the bridge into the Gulf.

Everyone at Picnic Island stopped what they were

5

doing to watch what little they could see of this unexpected diversion and speculate about what they had just witnessed after the boats had suddenly shot away from Picnic Island.

"I guess you were right about that being a stolen boat," Will commented.

"Told you I knew that boat," Norm said.

"I wonder why a thief would be so dumb as to bring a stolen boat as distinctive as that one out to a place as public as Picnic Island," Betsy commented.

"No one ever said thieves are always the smartest people in the world. Maybe we'll find out why in tomorrow's paper," Will said. "Surely this is newsworthy."

"By the way, there's something of a business nature I was going to ask you about later today," Norm said, "but I don't think it's a good time now. Mind if I come by your office one day next week?"

"Sure," Will said. "By then maybe you can tell me more about what we just saw."

CHAPTER 2

Norm called Will the following Wednesday morning. "Recovered from Sunday's excitement?" he asked.

"Betsy and I are both still wondering about that whole scene," Will said. "It was reported in the *Citizen*, but they were vague about the details. It's like they either didn't know the facts or law enforcement didn't want them to say too much. About all the paper said is that the deputies caught someone in a stolen boat. They did give a name – Eugenio Padron."

"If you have time for lunch today, I'll enlighten you some more," Norm said, "and I also want to discuss that other matter I mentioned to you Sunday at the island. Lunch will be my treat."

"How can I turn down an engagement where the client is paying?" Will said. "Just say where and when."

"How about 11:30 at the Chinese place by the North Roosevelt Winn Dixie?" Norm asked.

"Do I need to bring anything for the meeting?" Will asked.

"Only your ears. And don't forget your brain. See you there."

~ ~ ~

Will and Norm arrived at the restaurant at the same time and walked in together. People sat quietly talking at both tables and booths. They were shown to a booth, and the waitress immediately brought them some fried won ton strips and a sweet-and-sour dipping sauce and both ordered hot tea. Will ordered almond chicken off the luncheon special while Norm decided he wanted Szechwan chicken.

"So is there anything you can tell me about the boat thief that wasn't in the paper?" Will asked.

"Oh, yeah," Norm said. "According to one of my buddies at the sheriff's department, he wasn't a professional bad guy, just a burned out veteran who went off the deep end."

"That accounts for his irrational behavior."

"This poor bastard was a Navy gunner's mate in Afghanistan," Norm continued. "When he came back, his whole world collapsed. He was sending money to his girlfriend to help her with a flower shop. When his hitch was up, they had planned to marry, and he would then be her partner in the business. Unknown to him, she got involved with one of her employees – a former chef, I think. The boyfriend convinced her to try to expand the business into edible arrangements. This was a disaster, and the business went belly up. She never told boyfriend number one that, however, and he kept sending her money. She gave the money to the new boyfriend to pay for his Grady-White boat payments. On top of that, the new boyfriend knocked her up. So this poor sucker gets his discharge not knowing any of this until he got home, and then she admitted it all to him. Then on top of that, she told him she didn't want to marry him anymore because she was in love with the father-to-be of her child."

"Some people..." said Will and shook his head.

"Tell me about it. There's more."

He paused as the waitress served each of them with a cup of won ton soup. Will took a sip and commented that he had never had bad chicken soup in a Chinese restaurant. When they had finished their soup, Norm continued.

"Padron had developed some hearing problems from being exposed to gunfire in the war. He tried to get help through the VA, but five months later they were still processing his claim. Their excuse was being backlogged. Seems that VA applications have gone through the roof after Obama took office. At the same time, the austerity mentality set into Washington. The dumb jerk told the cops that he finally cracked up when he saw on the nightly news that there was a proposal to cut back veteran benefits."

"Damn! Talk about everything that can go wrong going wrong," Will said. "I've read that some of the servicemen have been having problems."

Norm then told Will that Padron's situation escalated when he then couldn't find a job. Since in his eyes he had a vested interest in this Grady-White, he decided just to borrow it and take it to Picnic Island where he could think about his next move. The boat was reported stolen.

Norm paused to sip his tea.

"When Padron saw the patrol boat coming in, he totally wigged out. Well, you know the rest."

"No, I don't," Will said. "What happened to him?"

"He ran the boat aground in the Back Country," Norm said. "He can't afford the bond so he's sitting in jail. We may be reading about this boy for some time to come. I understand the Disabled American Veterans and the ACLU might be getting involved."

The waitress brought their meals, and they ate in silence for a few minutes.

Norm then broke the ice by saying, "But the real reason I wanted to see you today involves my portfolio. I don't want to go into a lot of detail, so you'll have to take my word for my change in emphasis. My investment objectives are changing. I need to position myself for long term growth with as little in recognized gains as I can get away with. I also want to get protection from possible future litigation. I understand annuities will help me fulfill both those objectives."

"Do you have any known litigation on the horizon?" Will asked. "If so, an annuity won't help you with that problem."

"No. I'm just looking down the road," Norm said.

"Is this money that you don't need to maintain your current standard of living? Annuity withdrawals are taxable as ordinary income. Plus there are some other punitive tax features. Is liquidity an issue?"

"No. As I said, I'm looking down the road."

"In that case, I'll work up some proposals on some potential annuity candidates as well as a general list of annuity pluses and minuses. I'll also work up an estimate on the capital gains which would have to be recognized immediately to generate the funds to buy the annuities."

"Thanks," Norm said. "I'd appreciate it."

~ ~ ~

Will called the following day to tell Norm he had materials organized for the two of them to review and invited Norm to bring Catt to the meeting. Norm set an appointment for the following Monday for them to get together.

CHAPTER 3

"Would you agree that Key West is a colorful place?" Will asked Betsy as they were having breakfast at home.

"You won't get any argument from me over that one," Betsy said. "Why do you bring it up?"

"According to the paper," Will said, "Key West added another colorful chapter to its history last night. The cops picked up a fifty-year-old man passed out drunk on Mallory Square who had no ID. He did, however, have a backpack full of school supplies. I'll read you what it says here 'new packs of washable and sparkle pens and pencils, a ruler and an eraser, paint pens, 3D sparkle scent pens, a sketch pad and a pencil pouch.' When asked where he got the items, he said he had gotten them from his wife, but he couldn't remember her name. Each time he tried to stand up he fell back down."

"I don't know if I'd call that a chapter," Betsy said. "Sounds more like a footnote. Anything else about Eugenio Padron? He's closer to a short chapter."

"Not a word."

"I'm glad Norm filled you in on the details. I would have really been wondering otherwise," Betsy said. "He and Catt seem to be a nice and attractive couple. I wouldn't mind getting to know them better. He was even polite when our underwriting refused to expand his credit line recently. You wouldn't believe how some people act when we turn them down."

"That's because he has class," Will said. "The Knolls seem to have it all ... a successful business and each other ... the American dream. I've got my own meeting with him soon."

~ ~ ~

That same morning, the Knolls were also preparing their day. Norm was looking at his pocket Day-Timer, planning his day's schedule at Prestige Boats. He also had a meeting with his accountant. It was tax season. That was never his favorite conference.

"What're you up to today?" Norm asked his wife.

"Oh, nothing special," Catt said as she poured their coffee. "It's food day. I need to go to Publix and GFS. Any errands you need me to run for you?"

"Why don't you rob a bank while you're out," Norm said and laughed. "We could use an extra million or two."

"I'll do that after I leave Publix since the bank's right on the way to GFS."

Norm kissed Catt at the door. She watched him back his car out and waved at him as he drove away before she went back into the house.

Norm's day was relatively smooth. One of his salesmen closed a deal on a large boat with a customer he had been working on for awhile. The worst part of his day was the meeting at the accountant's office. He hated dealing with tax matters. He and Catt did not talk all day, but there was nothing unusual about that. They would have plenty of time to catch up over dinner.

Norm drove home after work. Except for the bad news from his accountant, it hadn't been such a bad day. The accountant had tried again to stress the importance of getting his taxes in order. Certainly not the first time he'd ever heard that. Too bad he hadn't been able to get that credit line expanded at the bank recently, but he'd find another source to tap.

He decided to drop by the Hogfish Bar & Grill on Stock Island for a beer and called Catt to tell her he'd be a few minutes late. She didn't answer. He'd try again in a few minutes. Norm didn't see anyone at the Hogfish he wanted to talk to, so he drank only one draft and paid his tab. He tried to call Catt again. No answer. She probably just couldn't get to the phone. He'd be home in a few minutes. Norm thought about his wife again when Eric Burden's *Spill The Wine* came on Sirius radio.

Catt's always liked that song for some reason. I think it's just strange. Never have been able to figure out what it's about.

Norm sighed. He looked forward to seeing his wife. He was glad they hadn't made any plans for the evening. It would be nice to just have a quiet night at home.

As Norm drove into his driveway he immediately noticed all the lights in the house were out. Odd. Catt's car wasn't in the driveway either. For the first time, he had a vague feeling that maybe things weren't completely normal. He checked his cell phone to see if she had tried to call. No call. Despite the car's air conditioning, he began to sweat and wiped his brow.

Norm parked his car and turned off the ignition. The porch light was on. He thought that he'd sure be glad when daylight savings time returned. He could see a note tacked to the door. Looked like Catt's handwriting. This irritated him slightly. He had just had that door painted recently. She could have taped it on instead of leaving a hole in the door's now pristine surface.

Norm pulled the paper off the door and smoothed out the pinhole with his finger. He then read the note in the gloomy light. His heart almost stopped as he read it.

Dearest Norman,
Why'd she use Norman, he thought. *She never calls me that.*

I have been kidnapped. You will be contacted about ransom. My kidnappers say if you cooperate

*and don't call the police, I will be returned unharmed.
If you don't, I will be killed immediately, and you will
never find my body. Please do as they say. They are
evil people who mean business.*
Love,
Catt

Norm's stomach heaved, and he thought he was
about to lose the beer he had drunk after work. He
unlocked the front door with a shaking hand and
entered the house. He turned on the living room light.
Everything seemed in order. There was no sign of a
struggle. He scurried around the house turning on the
lights one room at a time. The house was in perfect
order. He checked Catt's closet. Her clothes were there.
Then into the bathroom. Her makeup was on the
counter. He could faintly smell the scent from Catt's
Chanel body powder. He went into the kitchen. The
breakfast dishes had been washed and put away. The
coffee pot had been emptied and rinsed. There were no
bags of groceries on the counter.

She said she was going grocery shopping today.

He checked the refrigerator and cabinets. There
didn't seem to be any new purchases there.

Norm paced and finally threw himself into his
favorite chair. He nervously ran his hands through his
hair. The scene seemed so surreal.

What do I do now? I need to think.

But as hard as he tried to think, he couldn't seem
to put together logical thoughts. The knot in his gut just
continued to tighten.

*If I bring someone in on this, am I just signing her
death warrant like she says in the note?*

No matter how hard he tried, he couldn't come up
with a clear plan of action.

I have nothing to go on. I guess I'll have to wait

until I hear from them. Who would want to do something like this to us?

Norm did not sleep the entire night. He didn't eat dinner. His mind was consumed by random thoughts, mostly bad. He paced the house looking for clues. He grabbed a flashlight and searched outside, even shining the light up into the flower beds, but came up with nothing. He wanted to call some of Catt's friends or parents, but he was afraid to call anyone. It might just get Catt killed, and he couldn't live with himself if he caused that. He tried to think of someone who hated him. He hadn't fired anyone recently.

I'm no Rockefeller. There's got to be more profitable kidnap targets out there than us. Maybe this is a cruel hoax. If so, it's the meanest joke I ever heard.

The night seemed endless. Norm left the lights on throughout the house the entire night. It seemed to him morning would ever come.

When the sun finally rose, Norm felt totally wrung out. He looked at himself in the mirror. He was sallow, unshaven and had bags under his eyes. He made some strong coffee. *Maybe caffeine in my system will help me think better.*

He took one sip but then left the rest of the cup to get cold. His desperation was turning into panic. No one had tried to contact him. He called Prestige Boats. His secretary, Donna, answered the phone. She recognized his voice immediately.

"I see you're running a little late this morning, Mr. N," she said cheerfully.

"Have I had any calls?"

"You're good right now."

"Donna, I won't be in at all today," Norm said. "I think I've picked up some sort of bug or something. I've been up all night."

"You didn't look sick yesterday," Donna said.

"It just came on last night," Norm said.

"You pick up food poisoning somehow?" Donna asked. "If so, you'd better get yourself to the doctor. Do you want me to call in and get you an appointment?"

"No, that's all right," Norm said. "I'll take care of me. Just cover for me at work."

"No, problem there," Donna said. "You just get to feeling better, boss."

"I'm sure it'll pass," Norman said and hung up.

OK, that's out of the way, but what do I do now? This waiting is getting unbearable.

Norm didn't have much longer to wait. The house phone rang. Norm snapped out of a semi-trance and ran to answer it. The receiver suddenly seemed as much like an enemy as a friend. He reached it by the third ring.

"Hello," Norm said.

The voice on the other end of the line seemed hysterical.

"Catt!" Norm blurted out.

"Did you read my note?" Catt wailed. "You've got to do what these people tell you to do. Otherwise they're going to kill me."

"Where are you?" Norm said. "What people?"

"Three Latinos," Catt said. "They want $200,000. If they don't get it, they say they'll gang-rape me, murder me and then bury me where no one will ever find me. I don't want to die."

"Where do I go? When?"

"They'll tell you," Catt said. "And if you tell anyone, I'm dead for sure. They told me to tell you you're being watched."

"Are you OK?" Norm asked.

"For now, but I'm scared, darling."

"Have ... th ... th ... they hurt you in any way?" Norm almost stuttered, wanting more assurance.

No response was forthcoming. The phone went dead. Norm thought his heart would stop.

Norm spent several hours thinking what course of action he should take and how he could get his hands on $200,000. His mind kept telling him he should call the sheriff, but he decided if this action led to Catt's death, he would always blame himself for making the wrong decision. Norm, not normally a religious man, began to silently pray for guidance.

CHAPTER 4

Will looked at his watch. It was two o'clock. Norm had been scheduled to meet him at one. Where could he be? After all, Norm had been the one who wanted to restructure the account. He had seemed so hot to trot the other day and knew exactly how he wanted to do it. Will still couldn't understand why Norm's motives were so secretive, but he had been afraid to push too much. Sometimes when a person was convinced he wanted to do something and if you didn't follow their instructions, they'd simply find someone else who would. Will could go on record by speaking his piece and disclose the pros and cons, but after all, in the final analysis, it was Norm and Catt's money, and Will's job was to follow his client's instructions. At least if Will were compliant, he would remain in the loop, and he could try to make sure Norm got the best annuity product available. Then, if Norm decided to go in a different direction down the road, Will would still be part of the equation.

After waiting for an hour, Will called Norm's office. If something had come up, he needed to know so he wouldn't blow his whole afternoon waiting for a canceled appointment. He was a little ticked that Norm hadn't given him the courtesy of a phone call.

Norm's secretary, Donna, answered the phone.

"Donna, Will Black. Is Norm available?"

"Didn't come in today. Called in early this mornin' and said he felt horrible. Said he was going to stay home and try to get to feelin' better. Anything I can do to help you?"

"No, we had a one o'clock appointment today, and when he didn't show, I thought I'd better call and see if he was just runnin' behind."

"He was probably feelin' so bad, it just skipped his mind. I'm sure he wouldn't mind if you called him at home."

"No, I'm not going to disturb him. Just remind him to call me when he's feeling better."

"Will do, and I'm sorry about the inconvenience."

Donna called Norm's home. When Norm answered the phone, she told him of her conversation with Will Black and asked how he was feeling.

"About the same," he said.

"Damn it! I completely forgot about my appointment," Norm said. "I'll call him and apologize. I'll let you know in the mornin' if I'll be in or not."

Donna's call had snapped Norm back into focus. Of course, he thought. Their RST brokerage account. That's where he'd get money. After all he had planned to restructure it anyway. He dialed Will's office.

"Will," Norm said, "Please accept my apologies for standing you up on our appointment. There were extenuating circumstances."

"That's OK, Norm. Donna told me. Just let me know when it would be convenient to reschedule."

"How fast could you get me a check for $200,000?" Norm asked.

"Wow! That's certainly a change in direction. Did someone show you an annuity which seems too good to be true? If that's the case, it probably is. If so, at least let me research it and get back to ya with an objective analysis. If it's a legitimate product, we probably handle it."

"No, it's nothing like that," Norm said. "I'd prefer not to talk about my reasons."

"Norm, please don't think I'm being rude, but you were very vague when you asked me to assemble annuity information for you. Now you're changing directions completely and still don't want to be candid. Is there anything wrong between us? If I'm to be an effective financial consultant, you need to give me the facts I need to work with."

"Can I borrow against the cash values in either of our life insurance policies?" Norm asked.

"I'll have to research how much would be available. I think Catt's policy has more of a cash buildup than yours since it's been in place longer. It's also the larger policy."

There was a pregnant pause in the conversation. Will waited and finally said, "You told me your investment money was long-term money, and that you would not be using it for current needs. Life insurance is not hot money designed for quick release. And there can be adverse tax consequences."

Norm finally broke the silence. "Forget the insurance then. I need cash immediately. I'll fill you in when I can. For right now, let's just say things changed. Just take it out of our portfolio. When can I get a check?"

"Tomorrow, if I can get a next day settlement on the sales. Do you want to know what this is going to do to your taxes before I liquidate anything? If this is a short-term need, maybe we should just temporarily margin the account. Then I won't have to sell anything. All you and Catt have to do is sign a margin agreement. You can pay off the loan when things clear up."

"Can I sign for both of us?"

"No, it's a joint account. I need both signatures."

"Not possible now. You'll just have to sell something. Just use your judgment. What time can I come by tomorrow?"

"Let's say just after ten."

"Can you make it a cashier's check?"

"That would take another day. Why don't you call Betsy at the bank and see if she's willing to not put a hold on the check."

"Would you call her for me?" Norm said. "She's your wife, and you know what to say."

"Sure. I'll have Betsy call you if there's a problem."

"Thanks, Will. I ... uh ... I'll see you tomorrow," Norm stuttered as he rushed to hang up the phone before Will could press him again for more details.

Will sat at his desk momentarily dumbfounded. This was certainly not a turn of events he had anticipated.

Norm waited at home to see what shoe would drop next. As much as he dreaded a call, he wished it would come in.

Will called Betsy and repeated his strange conversation with Norm. She didn't know what to make of it either but agreed to override the hold on the check since she knew the money was good.

CHAPTER 5

Within an hour, Norm's home phone rang again. His heart almost stopped when he heard Catt's desperate voice.

"I ... want (sob) ... come home," she howled. "PLEASE do what you have to do to get these horrible men to turn me loose."

"I don't know what to do yet. Are you OK, honey?" Norm asked.

Catt's tone abruptly changed.

She hissed, "Of course I'm not OK. I'm scared to death. You've got to get me away from these filthy animals. They want to know if you've arranged their money."

"Assure them it's in process. I should have it tomorrow, ... but what do they want me to do then?"

"Norm, if you love me you *must* have it tomorrow," Catt almost barked. "They'll tell you what to do with it then."

A man's gruff voice came onto the phone. "Yeah, then you betta' listen real good ... or you' pretty wife mine."

"When – when will I hear?" Norm pleaded.

"You'll hear what I want you to hear ... when I want you to hear it, and you betta' get it right. NO second chances," the man said as the phone went dead.

Norm spent another miserable afternoon and only slept in spurts that night. If he hadn't been so exhausted, he wouldn't have slept at all.

Norm was at Will's office when it opened to pick up his check. Will told Norm the cashier was just setting up for the day, and the check wasn't ready yet. He suggested they have a cup of coffee while they waited.

He explained that it would take a few minutes to go through procedure since a check of that size had to be approved by the regional operations office.

"I realize you're uncomfortable talking about this, but tell me, Norm. Is this a business-related fire you're trying to put out or a major opportunity you don't want to miss?"

"As I said, I really don't feel comfortable discussing it right now."

"I'm just asking because I have a fiduciary responsibility to you. That's the difference between us at RST and some internet order taker. We care about our clients. You and Catt are not a walk-in doing an isolated transaction but a valued friend and a long-term relationship. You can talk to me. Anything you tell me will never go any further than this office without your permission.

"What makes you and me different is that we both care about our customers and want to do everything we can to do right by them. I'm sure that *your* customers can buy a boat cheaper elsewhere, but they know you'll be there to service them after the fact. My business is built on the same kind of trust."

Norm sat there silently drinking his coffee and looking down. Finally he gave a heave and said, "OK. I really *do* need to talk to someone. I've got a problem."

"Norm, I'd feel honored if you would allow me to be your confidant. Surely, it's not that bad."

"Close the door," Norm said as he sagged in his chair and buried his face in his hands. "Yes, it is that bad. Catt's been kidnapped."

"Oh, my God! Where? When? How?"

"She was gone when I got home from work night before last. The kidnappers had her write me a note and leave it on the door. It said I was going to have to pay to get her back. She said she would be raped and killed if I didn't comply. The note said they would bury her body where I never would find it."

"And you haven't reported this?"

"I was told they'd kill her if I did. She's called twice pleading with me. They want $200,000 to release her. The kidnapper himself got on the phone on the second call."

"You can't handle this by yourself. You've got to bring law enforcement into it."

"I couldn't live with myself if I caused her death by doing something stupid," Norm said.

"Norm, you've got to take the chance. You're out of your league."

"I know, but I'm desperate."

"What are the ransom details?"

"Other than the amount, I don't know yet. They told Catt to tell me to arrange the money, and then they would fill me in on what I'm supposed to do next."

"Do you really think you can take a $200,000 check into Betsy's bank, have it issued to you in small bills without anyone asking questions. There are bank policies and Federal laws."

"I guess I've been too upset to think about that."

"You've got to start thinking with your head not your heart. I know you live in the county and come under the sheriff's jurisdiction, but the Police Chief in Key West, Walter Wanderley, is a good friend of mine. I'll call him if you like and explain the sensitive nature of your problem. I'll give you his private line if you prefer to call, and I'll even take you down there and introduce you personally if you want me to. He'll tell you what to do next and refer the case to the proper place."

"But what if…" Norm started to say.

"There's no what if. You're in uncharted territory. I'm just telling you what I'd do if someone was holding Betsy or Lexie."

Norm continued to sit and stare.

"Norm, please let me take you to the police station, or if you're not comfortable with that, I'll try to get the chief to come over here. No one will know he's coming or why. The longer you wait, the tougher it's going to get to make the right call."

Norm finally agreed to talk to Chief Wanderley if he came to Will's office. Will called and was fortunate. Walter was in. After Will briefly explained the situation to him, Walter said he's be right over.

Despite overhearing the conversation, Norm was silent.

As they waited, sweat broke out on Norm's brow, and he began to fidget and scratch an imaginary itch.

Will tried to fill the dead air.

"Do you have Catt's note?"

"Yes, but it's at home."

More silence.

"Norm, you are doing the right thing. This will do more to turn the odds in your favor than trying to go it alone."

Norm said nothing more.

CHAPTER 6

Within thirty minutes, Walter Wanderley, Key West's longstanding Chief of Police, arrived at Will's office. As usual, he was impeccably dressed in a clean, neat uniform, which looked almost tailor-made for his fit frame. Walter was college educated and was a cop through and through. Law enforcement was the only job he had ever had since he got out of school. He had risen through the system and understood it at every level.

When Will and Betsy had first moved to the Keys, Walter was one of the first people they got to know. Betsy's bank handled most of the banking for both the county and the city including the police department. What had started out as a professional banking relationship had quickly evolved into a social friendship. The friendship had then been kicked to an entirely different plane after the Blacks enhanced Walter's professional standing when they helped him solve the Club Tropic Ponzi scheme.

Will closed the door for privacy and introduced him to Norman Knoll. Walter knew Norm's name from his ownership of Prestige Boat and Yacht Center, but until now the two had never met. Will told Walter again about Norm's discomfort level and about his reluctance to do anything which would make a bad situation worse. Norm numbly nodded in agreement. Walter immediately began to try to put Norm at ease and reassure him before allowing Norm to encapsulate the events which had transpired thus far. Norm hesitantly repeated his story. Walter did not interrupt Norm with questions. He merely listened until he was sure Norm had finished. Then, in an even voice, Walter began to speak.

"Thank you for the show of confidence. You've taken the right first step," he began, "and time is of the essence. While no one can predict the final outcome of these situations, your odds of a successful resolution will improve immensely if you've got law enforcement assistance. We're trained in how to handle these matters and can use our experience to make objective decisions at critical points. Since you live on Sugarloaf Key, you fall under the jurisdiction of the sheriff's department. We have a mutual aid agreement internally authorizing joint efforts."

Walter paused and waited to see if Norman would say anything which might give him a clue as to Norman's frame of mind. Norm, however, just continued to stare at him, saying nothing. Walter and Will glanced at each other, each wondering whether Norm was zoning in or zoning out. When he said nothing, Walter continued.

"They've some very competent detectives on their staff. With your permission, I'd like to contact Captain Dan Hillary. He's more than merely a deputy which is what your initial contact would most likely would have been if you'd just phoned in a complaint. As Commander of both District 1 and the HIDTA task force, he's a ranking, highly trained officer. I'll brief him on the situation before you talk to him. It's very important that some of his people come into your house and assess the crime scene. I'm sure you have already compromised it to some extent. You'll compromise it further if you wait before allowing a trained crime scene investigator access to it. They may be able to get much needed clues from the house, but if you wait, it may become almost totally useless as a source of evidence."

"But if they know I've contacted either of you, they say they'll kill her," Norm protested. He nervously fidgeted in his chair and accidentally kicked the table leg.

"I can assure you this will be handled discretely and in a low key manner," Walter said. "We appreciate the sensitivity of your situation. Let me make a suggestion. I'm rearranging the normal order of events because of the possible dangers to your wife. Give me a house key or allow me to have a house key made. I will then give it to Captain Hillary. One of his crime scene investigators will let himself into your house while you're at work and see what he can learn."

"If ... someone is watching my house, they'll know I didn't follow their instructions," Norm gasped, rubbing his chin nervously. "They said there would be no second chances."

Will put his hand gently on Norm's forearm as a show of support but did not interrupt.

"I can assure you these detectives know how to spot someone watching your house and how to become virtually invisible," Walter said. "They'll check to see if neighbors are present. They will probably enter the home through a back door. They won't be wearing uniforms. They won't leave a car in front of your house that could identify them to a passerby. You've got to trust me. These investigators are professionals who've been well trained on what or what not to do."

"I-I-I-I just don't know what to do. I..." Norm stammered as he shifted in his seat and kicked the table leg again.

Will broke in at this point. "Norm, I hate to interrupt, but that's the point. You don't know what to do. At some point you're going to have to trust someone. The longer you wait ..."

"I know you're both right, but you're not the ones in the hot seat."

"But we're the ones who have your best interest at heart," Will said. "Just remember, she's useless to them dead. You're not going to find a solution with guarantees. Paying the ransom isn't even a guarantee she'll be returned safely."

Walter nodded and continued, "As I said a moment ago, I'm going to suggest to Captain Hillary that we rearrange the normal order of events. I'll brief him on everything I know, but he won't interview you until after his men have analyzed the crime scene. I'll suggest he come to your house after dark through your back door when no one else is around and the two of you can talk privately. Besides the key, I have one other request. Would you allow me to take your fingerprints for identification purposes?"

"Of course," Norm said as he handed Walter a house key.

"Do you need me to copy this key and return it to you?" Walter asked.

"No, it's a dupe I keep in case I lock myself out of the house," Norm said.

"I'll get the ball in motion immediately," Walter said. "Do you have a problem with them installing electronic monitoring equipment?"

Norm shook his head and said, "I hope I'm doing the right thing."

"I'm positive that any other course of action would only decrease your odds of seeing this unfortunate affair come to a successful conclusion. Thanks again for your trust. We're the ones on your side."

Walter then turned to Will, "Will, will you instruct your sales assistant not to discuss with anyone that we had this conference this morning? I wouldn't want people speculating about the nature of this meeting."

"Of course."

CHAPTER 7

Norm left Will's office. He felt a wee bit better, but he was still almost paralyzed by self-doubt. Had he just let the Chief talk him into something he would regret?

Within minutes his cell phone rang. Norm had to force himself to answer it. He heard Catt's almost out-of-breath voice.

"Honey, where are you?"

"In my car in Key West on Flagler," Norm answered.

"Have you been able to make arrangements for my release?" Catt asked. "I'm so scared. I want to come home. Please bring me home, darling."

"I'm working on it, sweet," Norm said. "Have they hurt you?"

"Not yet, but one of them keeps threatening to. I think he's crazy, and he tells me he's killed other people."

"What are my instructions on what to do with the money?" Norm asked.

"They haven't told me yet. They say they'll tell you when you have the money. They just keep telling me what they're going to do to me if you don't come through. They just wanted me to remind you they mean business, and that you're being watched. I love you. Please hurry."

"I just picked up a check from our RST investment account. Now I have to take it to the bank and see if they'll give me cash," Norm said.

"Will they do that today?" Catt asked.

"I don't think so, but I don't know yet."

"They have to. They just have to," Catt said and started crying.

"I won't let you down. You mean too much to me," Norm said as the call was disconnected.

Norm nervously looked into his rear view mirror as

he drove. Catt's words replayed in his head, "you're being watched." He examined the cars at each intersection.

Hasn't that beige SUV been behind me for several blocks now?

He drove slowly. The SUV didn't pass him. He turned onto Kennedy; the SUV turned as well. He turned again by Florida Aqueduct. The SUV kept on going. He circled back to Kennedy and took a right onto Northside Drive. The same SUV was coming up Northside in the opposite direction. He turned into the bank. The SUV turned in as well. Norm's paranoia was getting to manic levels. He parked in the parking lot in front of the bank. The SUV continued around to the back where drive-up lanes were.

Am I losing it? he asked himself.

He waited in his car for the SUV to finish its business and drive around the building to exit the parking lot. He tried to see the driver, but the windows were darkly tinted. He waited for it to turn out of the bank parking lot onto Northside Drive before catching his breath and getting out of his own car.

I don't think I can take it if this is what it's going to be like every time I go somewhere. This sucks.

Norm walked into the bank with an empty briefcase and asked for Betsy. She had been briefed as to the nature of his visit. Betsy closed the door, and they hugged briefly.

"I don't know what to say," Betsy began. "Do you have any idea why you were targeted?"

"Not in the least," Norm said. He then told Betsy how he had found the ransom note tacked to his front door when he got home from work. He admitted to Betsy that even though he was working with the sheriff's department, he was willing to pay the ransom money rather than risk Catt's life.

"I have some bad news for you," Betsy said. "I can't disburse an amount of money this large on notice this short. It's not a 'hold-on-the-check' issue. Will mentioned that to me, and I could overcome that issue. The big issue is that we have to order money in those amounts three days ahead of time. On top of that, you are opening yourself up to being red-flagged by the Federal Reserve. We have to report to the Fed deposits or disbursements over $10,000. They then track this money. If it shows up at another financial institution, it's one thing. If it doesn't, they take that as a sign that money laundering might be occurring. Then they want to investigate further and want explanations as to what is going on. We both know this money will not be deposited with another financial institution."

"Oh, what other options do I have?" Norm said, looking crestfallen.

"I'm going to tell you something off the record," Betsy said. "Many discrete situations remain discrete by going through pawn shops."

"Isn't that expensive?"

"I'm told they can charge anywhere from three to ten percent, depending on their assessment of their risk."

"Do you know anyone in that business?" asked Norm.

"No, I'm afraid not. Never needed them before," Betsy said. "You'll have to research it on your own."

Norm was shell-shocked as he left the bank. The information Betsy had given him was not what he had expected. He thought he'd be walking out with a briefcase full of money.

Norm went back to Prestige Boats and began to look through the phone book. He ripped the page listing pawn shops out of the yellow pages and put it on a clipboard. He told Donna he would be out until after lunch and left. He put a number by each listing in the order of addresses which would require the least amount of backtracking to find. Norm felt slightly sleazy. He was totally out of his element. He had never been in a pawn shop in his life. He walked in each one and pretended to be looking for a Rolex watch. While he was there, he would assess the store and the clerk he was dealing with. Did the store look substantial, or did it look like a shoestring, fly-by-night operation? Could he tell how long it had been in business? Did the employees appear to be lowlifes? None of the stores had enough customers in them allowing him to assess their clientele, but he had already decided it would certainly be low-end.

As he drove from store to store, Norm continued to feel like he was being watched. He never saw anything to confirm his suspicions. It was just a feeling. He wondered again if he really was cracking up from the pressure. He selected two stores from the list which seemed to him to be the best of the lot. Both were in shopping centers on North Roosevelt Boulevard. One of the owners was a rangy, humorless, pale, pockmarked man with tattooed, veined arms extending from his sleeveless black t-shirt. His wispy hair was oiled and combed straight back. He had a least a half-dozen gold chains around his neck. The other man was thick-bodied, round faced and bald. His face smiled a lot, but his eyes were penetrating and steely, making Norm feel he was at the wrong end of the food chain. Both men reminded Norm more of bar bouncers than bankers. What a choice to have to make! Norm decided to go with the heavy-set Mr. Shark-smile. He was the less creepy of the twosome.

Norm showed Mr. Shark-smile the $200,000 RST check. The man nodded and smiled. He did not see checks of this size every day, but he had seen them before. His smile told Norm that he had already tallied the vigorish he would make off a check of this size. It would certainly be his most profitable sale that day. He didn't ask any questions about the proceeds. If this money was being used for an illegal purpose, he didn't want to know about it. All he cared about was verifying Norm's identity and getting Norm's permission to call Will's office to verify the check. Norm phoned Will on his cell phone and gave Will permission to talk to the pawnbroker. Will assured the pawnbroker that the check was not a forgery.

"OK," the pawnbroker said. "This all seems to check out. I'll cash it for you for my usual fee."

"Which is?" Norm asked.

"5%."

"That seems a little high," Norm said. "This is a riskless transaction for you since it's not a personal check but a check issued by a major investment house. I was told 3% was customary for a check such as this."

Mr. Shark-grin momentarily frowned but quickly agreed to the revised terms. He did not want his greed to spoil this sweet deal. Six grand sure beat nothing.

"I don't keep that amount of money in the store. It's going to take until tomorrow for me to get it together," the pawnbroker said.

Norm realized he had no choice but to accept this time frame. Besides, this would give him the opportunity to meet with Captain Hillary. He wanted to hear Hillary out anyway before making a move.

"Fine. I'll have to live with that," Norm said. "I'll see you in the morning to get my money."

He just prayed something didn't happen to Catt in the meantime. It would be impossible to live with that.

CHAPTER 8

Norm was a tangled knot of mixed emotions as he left the pawn shop and wondered what the next shoe to drop would be. Two days ago his life had been more or less in order. His biggest concern had been his frequent unpleasant dealings with his accountant.

Damned IRS! Bastards!

Now nothing in his world seemed to be in order. He went back to his office and pretended to work but neither his mind nor his heart was in it. He kept playing "what if" scenarios in his mind.

About mid afternoon he heard from Catt again.

"Do you have the money to free me?" she asked with a choked voice.

"Yes and no," Norm said. "I have a check, but it will be tomorrow before I'll actually have cash."

Catt pleaded with him to make sure nothing went wrong. She said her abductors were running thin on patience.

Suddenly she screamed. Norm almost dropped his phone Catt screamed a second time. He heard her phone thud onto a floor and then heard what sounded like a scramble. Norm puked on himself as bile he couldn't stop rose uncontrollably in his throat.

"What's wrong?" he panted, now having trouble getting his words out. He heard Catt scramble on the other end. It sounded like she was trying to pick up her phone.

"One of these animals burned me with his cigarette ... and then he slapped me. He's saying you better cooperate and have it by then or else," Catt screeched.

"Or else what?"

"I don't know, and I don't want to find out. Dammit, Norm. Just shut up and do the hell what they want!"

As shaken as he was, Norm tried clumsily to throw out hints for Catt to try to give him a clue as to where she was being held, but she seemed oblivious to his intentions. He asked again what he was supposed to do with the money. She said he would get his instructions only after he had money in hand. Norm was left feeling frustrated, helpless, and totally out of control. He retched again.

After work, Norm went home. He could see no signs that anyone one from the sheriff's department had been there. Everything seemed just like he had left it that morning. He fixed himself a sandwich. A fly landed on it. He didn't care. He didn't even bother with the television set. He couldn't concentrate on it anyway. About seven PM, he heard a soft rapping on his unlocked kitchen door. He started to get up to answer it. Captain Hillary silently let himself in and introduced himself. Hillary turned on Norm's television before continuing the conversation. Then he had Norm repeat what he had told Chief Wanderley earlier. The detective asked some probing questions after Norm had concluded his summary.

"It appears that your men haven't been to my house yet," Norm said.

"Oh, they were here this afternoon," Hillary said. "They examined things thoroughly. They were instructed to leave things just as they found them."

"They did," Norm said. "I couldn't even tell they'd been here. Did they find anything useful?"

"No, unfortunately they didn't, but we had to try. You never know in these cases when you might get lucky. My men did take some digital pictures of your wife from the family photos you had around the house so we can readily identify her later," Captain Hillary said.

"So now what?" Norm asked. He told Hillary that he had arranged for the ransom money the following day.

"In sequential bills?" Hillary asked.

"No, the bank has to order amounts this large three days ahead of time," Norm said. "I was afraid of what might happen to Catt if I didn't comply as soon as possible. To be honest with you, I'm making arrangement through a Key West pawn shop. They said I'll have money in the morning." He told Hillary the name of the pawn shop he was using.

Hillary frowned and asked, "Did you tell the pawnbroker why you needed the money?"

Norm said, "The guy didn't seem to care."

"Figures. And you're supposed to hear from the kidnappers again tomorrow? A judge has finally given me permission to bug your phone. Do you mind if I listen in?"

"Of course not. I've got nothing to hide."

"Then we'll just have to wait and see what happens next and form our strategy then," Hillary said. "I'll also have a man keeping you under surveillance. I know it's going to be difficult, but try to get some rest. Tomorrow could be a big day. I'll let myself out the same way I came in. Many thanks for trusting us. While I can't predict the outcome, I can tell you your odds of successfully getting your wife back have improved with us in the picture."

~ ~ ~

The following morning Norm rose and did his morning essentials. His stomach was full of butterflies as he dressed. As he was preparing to leave home, the house phone rang. It was Catt. She sounded desperate once again.

"Darling, do you have the money yet?"

"I'm supposed to get it this morning."

"When?"

"Shortly after nine."

"They're afraid you gonna try to pull something. They told me to tell you there will be dire consequences if you do. Norm, please do as they say. These're evil men. I just want to come home. Please get me home."

"I'm cooperating, sweetheart," Norm said. "I don't want them to harm you. You mean more to me than money. What do they want me to do with it?"

"They'll tell you after you get it," Catt said. "Darling, remember that black nylon zipper bag that says Princess cruises on it. The one I bought when we took the cruise to Grand Cayman. It's in my closet. Get it out before you leave the house this morning and take it with you. That's what you are to put the money in. You shouldn't have any trouble finding the bag. It's on the shelf."

"I know which one you're talking about. I'll get it," Norm said.

Norm found the bag and threw it on the front seat of his car. He was afraid of wiretaps so he waited until he got to his office before calling Captain Hillary. Hillary assured him his men would be ready when the drop was made.

"Text me the time and location as soon as you get them," Hillary said.

Mr. Alligator-smile at the pawn shop had the funds ready when Norm got there at nine. He still didn't seem curious as to what Norm planned to do with the money. None of his business. He counted the money out. It was $6,000 short. Much of the money was in hundreds. In his desperation to raise cash as soon as possible, Norm remembered he had failed to ask for small bills. He wondered if this would anger the kidnappers. Well, it was too late now. As the pawnshop owner disbursed the funds, Norm realized that the vigorish was leaving him six thousand dollars short of what he would need.

"I forgot your fee was coming out of the money," Norm said. "May I just give you a personal check for that amount?"

"A personal check changes things," the pawnshop owner said. "I gave you the rate I did predicated on my risk. I'll have to charge you ten percent on the funds which carry a higher risk factor."

This "squeeze-everything-out-of-me-that-you-can" attitude irked Norm, but the guy had him over a barrel, so he agreed.

Norm sat in his car in the shopping center parking lot and packed the money into the nylon bag. He was glad not to have to justify this to his accountant. He left going back to his office. As he drove on North Roosevelt, Norm's cell phone rang. It was his wife.

"Is the money in the Princess bag?" she asked. Norm said yes.

"Here's what they want you to do," Catt said. "Take the bag right now to the Rusty Anchor restaurant on Stock Island. Leave it by the dumpster. There'll be a note in a reusable Publix bag telling you where to pick me up. I want this to be over so bad. Screw this up, and I'll never forgive you."

CHAPTER 9

Norm immediately texted Captain Hillary. The text was brief and to the point. "Behind Rusty Anchor – now."

Hillary assembled his backup team before heading for the Rusty Anchor himself.

Norm arrived at the Rusty Anchor first. He walked over to the dumpsters. There was no reusable Publix bag next to either of them. He walked around to the other side thinking the bag might be there instead. Nothing. He raised the dumpster and looked in. The odor took his breath. Nothing. He stirred the garbage around some. Still nothing.

Maybe I got here too early. I'll wait in my car. I'm sure as hell not going to leave the money under these circumstances.

Norm went back and waited in his car with the money. He looked around him and saw no one who even remotely looked like what he thought a kidnapper should look like. A scruffy kitchen employee from the Rusty Anchor threw some boxes in one of the dumpsters. Other than that, nothing. In his peripheral vision he saw Hillary drive by. Hillary didn't appear to look his way. Norm cranked his car and followed Hillary. When Hillary saw him in his rear view mirror, he drove towards West Marine and pulled into their parking lot. Norm checked to see if he was being followed, and when he saw no one, he turned in as well. Hillary got out and went into the store. Norm followed. Hillary paused at a back aisle and looked around to see if he and Norm were alone.

"No one showed," Norm said. "What do we do now?"

Before Hillary could answer him, Norm's cell phone rang. It was Catt.

"I went to the Rusty Anchor like you said. Nobody was there," Norm said.

"They changed the instructions to test you because they didn't trust you," Catt said breathlessly.

"The lying bastards didn't trust me!" Norm said incredulously. "C'mon now!"

"Get hold of yourself. Now they want you to go immediately to Home Depot. You're to put the bag of money in a shopping cart in the back of the garden shop where Home Depot keeps pallets of pavers and then retrieve the Publix bag telling you where I am out of another cart they're leaving there. Then this will be over, my darling. It'll finally be over."

Captain Hillary called his men and told them about the change of plans. Each man climbed back into his unidentified car and headed for Home Depot. Norm took his own car.

Norm had become rattled and impatient. He cursed as he got behind a slow rental scooter being driven uncertainly by an oblivious tourist. He caught the light at the "Y" where US1 and Highway A1A split. He had to keep himself from blowing his horn as he approached McDonald's on North Roosevelt. He certainly didn't want to do that with Hillary within earshot. The traffic turning left into McDonald's' drive-in window had spilled out onto the main street. *Damn it to hell! Can't I get a break? Is the whole world having a Big Mac attack?*

After what seemed to him like an eternity, he whipped into Home Depot's parking lot. Hillary was right behind him. The only parking spot Norm could see was down by Walgreens. Hillary turned the other way and went down closer to Home Depot's lumberyard. Norm grabbed the Princess bag and went in through the garden center; Hillary went in through the main door.

Norm headed for the back of the garden department. He saw an unattended basket, but by the time he got down the aisle, a white-headed man put a flower pot in it and pushed it toward the pallets of potting soil. He saw the automatic doors open to the main store and thought he was just early. This could be his shopping basket being wheeled out now. Maybe he'd get a look at one of the kidnappers. Instead he saw Hillary. When Hillary saw Norm, he immediately turned and reentered the main store. Norm couldn't spot anything that looked like Hillary's men.

Norm turned and made a beeline for the front door of the garden center. In all the excitement, he had forgotten to grab a shopping cart for himself. He put the Princess bag into the cart and nervously rolled it down the aisle while trying to look like a browser. His shopping cart had a defective wheel which kept turning sideways and trying to pull the cart to the right as it bumped along. The bump-bump-bump grated on Norm's nerves farther.

"May I help you find something?" a helpful clerk unexpectedly asked.

"No, thank you," Norm said. "I'm just looking."

He then thought to himself, *how many times have I really needed a clerk and had to search the whole store looking for one?*

Norm paused before virtually every display table and glanced around at his fellow shoppers. He made multiple trips to the back of the store. He looked at every cart he passed. No Publix's bag. He bumped his way into the main store and methodically walked each aisle desperately looking for a cart containing a Publix bag. There was simply no such thing. He got back by the public restrooms in the rear of the store before spying Hillary again. Hillary silently went into the men's room and motioned for Norm to follow. They had the restroom to themselves.

"This whole matter is beginning to really stink. I think you've been bagged a second time," Hillary said.

Norm lost his cool and let out an inadvertent string of expletives. The brief temper tantrum didn't make him feel any better.

"I'll leave a man to watch the garden shop for the next several hours, but I see no reason for you and me to hang around," Hillary said. "The best thing we can do is to wait until the kidnappers contact you again."

"I don't know how much more of this I can take," Norm said. "Sometimes I feel like if we don't end this soon, I'm going to crack up. Do you think the problem is they spotted you or your men?"

"I'm not going to shoot you a line of BS. I don't think so, but I don't know what to tell you," Captain Hillary said. "This is not the way these things usually go. At this point, all I know to do is to ask you to hang in there. We don't have any other logical choice. I wouldn't think it 's going to be long until you hear from someone again."

CHAPTER 10

There was no further contact with the kidnappers that day. Norm was close to being a basket case. When he got out of his car in his garage, he accidentally bumped into an exercise trampoline hanging from the wall. Before he could stop himself, he began to strike it with the stainless-steel martial arts kubatan on his key chain. He punched it until the trampoline's covering was riddled with holes. Norm took the bag of money into the house and brooded each time he looked at it for the rest of the evening.

He waited for a phone call the next morning. It never came. The following day, Norm finally received the call he was waiting for.

Catt sounded frantic. She was slurring her words almost like she had been drinking.

"They say you're not being honest with them," Catt said. "They say you can't be trusted."

"What do they mean?" Norm said. "I went to the Rusty Anchor. I went to Home Depot. I did everything I was told to do. It's not my fault no one showed at either place."

"I don't know," Catt said. "I'm just telling you what they're telling me."

"Who the hell are *they*?" Norm demanded.

"I don't know, and they wouldn't let me say if I did. I just don't want to die. If you try to outsmart them, I will die. Please don't let me die. I want things to be like they were."

"I'm trying, Catt. Damn, I'm trying. I've done everything they asked me to do, and it's gotten me nowhere."

"They say they've lost confidence in you," Catt said.

"They say they won't deal with you again. They made me give them a name of someone I trusted. The only name I could come up with was Will Black. You got the money from him, didn't you?"

"That's partially correct," Norm said. "So what's their latest demand?"

"Will is to take the bag of money over to the Tennessee Williams Theatre on Stock Island," Catt said.

Norm sighed. He didn't want to involve Will Black in this sorry affair.

"And what do they want Will to do after that?" Norm asked.

"In Tennessee Williams Theatre's parking lot, there's a concrete street light. Sort of to the left when you're facing the box office. There are some low palms and some Jamaican caper plants around the pole. The capers have been trimmed into a ball. They want Will to put the bag of money under one of those bushes. They'll pick it up there."

"And what about the note telling me where to find you?" Norm asked.

"That's the change," Catt said. "They'll let me call you and give you my location only after they're sure they've gotten the money and no one has followed them. They say they can't trust you again."

"So they're stacking the deck totally in their favor," Norm said. "What if I refuse?"

"Please don't say that," Catt pleaded. "In that case, I'll be killed, and they say you'll never find my body. Do you want that to happen? Please do what they say."

"I guess I don't have any choice," Norm said. "When am I supposed to do this?"

"Tomorrow morning before the box office opens at ten," Catt said. "And don't stick around. They say if they see you there, they won't pick up the ransom."

CHAPTER 11

Captain Hillary had heard every word of Norm's latest conversation with his wife. He called Norm and told him to meet him at the Wendy's on the out-parcel in front of the original Key West Publix.

When Norm arrived, Hillary was sitting at a corner table drinking a cup of coffee.

"Do you really want me to trust these people?" Norm asked. "We're talking about $200,000. That's a lot of money. I don't have another $200,000 if this doesn't work out."

"Have you got an alternative suggestion?' Hillary asked. "We still don't have any clues to the perps' identities since they have never once directly gotten on a phone call that we've monitored. Your wife's done all the talking. That in itself is unusual."

"So you're saying I have no choice," Norm said.

"There'll be men covering the drop site," Hillary said. "They'll be able to see everything that happens and then follow the pickup men. Hopefully, you're going to find out where to find your wife, or my men can follow the pickup men to where she's being held. Then the job will be to nab the suspects and recover your ransom money."

"They must've seen some of your men at Home Depot," Norm said. "Otherwise why are they saying they can't trust me?"

"This surveillance should be fairly elementary," Hillary said, ignoring Norm's comment. "Right in the middle of Florida Keys Community College's campus. Students will be going back and forth constantly going to classes and other places. We've got one problem, however. Stock Island and the college are under the jurisdiction of the Key West Police Department. I'm going to have to get hold of Chief Wanderley and let his people handle the situation. He's got a very competent staff. Also, we've a very good working relationship with them. He should have some investigators who look young enough to pass as college students, and who won't look out of place. Plus they can park a car discretely in that large parking lot and leave someone in it. Once the kidnappers pick up the money there's only one road leading back out to US1. Maybe they'll lead us to where your wife is being held. I think this drop site favors the good guys."

"I hope you're right."

"Does Will Black know of his prospective involvement?" Hillary asked.

"No. I haven't seen him since I picked up the check at his office the other day. He does know about Catt's abduction though. He was the one who convinced me to call Chief Wanderley who then called you."

"Let me visit Chief Wanderley and explain the situation to him. He can then decide how to approach Black and ask his involvement. Since they're friends, it'll probably play better coming from him anyway," Hillary said.

After talking to Hillary, Walter called Will and told him he needed to discuss a matter of some urgency with him. He told Will what had transpired thus far on the Knoll case and said he would consider it a personal favor if Will chose to help. He asked Will to keep the matter confidential for the time being. Will did not hesitate to come on-board. After all, Walter had certainly helped Will and Betsy on more than one occasion. Will spent the remaining part of the day making sure he had cleared his calendar for the next morning and telling Barbara he would be running late. Walter asked Will for his spare car key.

The following morning Walter had one of his men put the Princess bag full of money in the back seat of Will's car while he was having an Egg McMuffin and coffee at McDonald's on North Roosevelt Boulevard. Walter did not want to risk being seen delivering the bag to Will's office or to ask Will to risk keeping the bag overnight at home.

Walter called Will on his cell phone while Will was in McDonald's.

"The money bag is locked on the back seat of your car," Walter said. "Let me just remind you one more time. Your role is simply to deliver the bag and make sure it's concealed under one of the Jamaican caper bushes. Don't hang around after you deliver it. Just leave. My men will take over from there. Don't look for them. I doubt if you could identify them anyway. Take my word for it, they'll be there. Do we understand each other?"

"Absolutely. I'm to drop it off and leave. You'll keep me posted afterwards?"

"Of course, and thanks, my friend."

Will had no trouble identifying the group of shrubs. It was behind a curb and consisted of three precisely manicured Jamaican capers and some saw-palmettos. The concrete light pole rose in the middle of the clump just as he had been told it would. The capers were wiry feeling, but there was plenty of room to slide the bag underneath them. Will deposited the bag as he had been instructed to and left. Walter was right. He never saw anyone looking like cops. There were simply loads of students hustling from one class to the next.

A few minutes after Will had left the parking lot, a young man on a scooter came by. By all appearances, he was a student. He rode by the clump once and circled around and came back for a second look. He stopped his scooter, picked up the bag, and seemed to look at it to see if it had a name-tag on it. He shrugged his shoulders, secured it behind him and left. He exited the parking lot onto College Road heading for US1. Some of Walter's men drove out behind him. When they got on College Road a slow Waste Management truck plodded along. The scooter driver looked to make sure there was no ongoing traffic coming in the other direction and darted out, passing the garbage truck. Walter's men tried to follow but a curve suddenly loomed ahead. When they pulled out a second time, a car was coming. The last they saw of the scooter was it disappearing around a curve. When they arrived at US1, the scooter was nowhere to be seen.

"Damn it to hell," said the detective. "Do you think the driver went into Key West or back towards Big Coppitt?"

"Shit if I know," his partner answered. "He might have gone to the intersection and then gone south on Stock Island."

"Boss is *not* gonna like this," the first detective said.

"Of all the times for a stinking garbage truck to be out on College Road," the second detective answered.

"No shit! What do we do now?"

"First thing we better do is put out an APB on that scooter. Do we have a tag number?"

"No, unfortunately. It was obscured."

"Figures. Chief's not going to be a happy camper."

CHAPTER 12

A ndy Gerber was getting by. It wasn't easy, but it was better than returning to Chicago and his mother's dysfunctional life. He had a small scholarship to Florida Keys Community College, a manageable student loan, and a part-time job bussing tables at the Hogfish Bar & Grill on Stock Island. He had moved in with Debbie, one of the waitresses who worked with him, and they lived on her sailboat docked at Safe Harbor Marina. He had a scooter to get Debbie and him all the places they needed to go economically. It was sometimes a struggle, but he was young and felt his life was moving in the right direction.

Andy had had some trouble as a teenager in Chicago. He had gotten caught shoplifting. Since he had only been fifteen at the time, however, he had just been classified as a first time juvenile offender. The judge had let him off with a slap on the wrist. When he got out of high school, he decided to leave Chicago. His mother's boyfriend had made it clear that now that Andy was eighteen, he would prefer Andy to move out. Andy's mother didn't seem to care one way or the other. Andy had somehow wound up in the Florida Keys. He got a small needs-based scholarship to FKCC. Behind her boyfriend's back, Andy's mother cosigned on his student loan. Anything to keep Andy out of Chicago and insure her life was a peaceful one.

As Andy Gerber passed the bag Will had deposited in the bushes, he was preoccupied. He sighed at his dilemma.

My textbooks for this semester sure seem to be expensive and as usual, I'm short on money.

When Andy saw the bag in the bushes, it flashed

through his mind that the bag might contain textbooks. Even if he weren't taking the same courses as that that student, Andy thought maybe he could sell them as used books and use the money to offset his own book bill.

Andy circled the parking lot once, looking to see if there would be any witnesses. Coast seemed to be clear. On the second pass, he stopped, grabbed the bag, and secured it to his scooter. Andy took off on College Road heading back to US1. He didn't know he was being tailed and as was his habit, passed the slow-moving Waste Management truck on College Road. When he got to US1 he crossed the highway, got on McDonald Avenue and headed for Safe Harbor. Andy would have been rattled had he known he had been observed, but as it was, he was totally unaware he had both inadvertently stumbled into a police sting and then accidentally eluded a tail.

Andy took the bag to the boat. Debbie was at work at the Hogfish. He threw the bag on the bunk and unzipped it. He was shocked at what he saw. The bag wasn't full of books. It was stuffed with cash. Andy felt through the bag. There was nothing in it but bundles of money. What in the world had he stumbled on? He wasn't sure what to do next. Andy re-zipped the bag and went up on the deck to think. He hadn't counted it, but there was a lot of money there. Enough money to get him through school. Maybe enough money to pay off his student loan.

As Andy sat on the boat deck, a multitude of issues flashed through his brain. Who would put that much money in a nylon bag and leave it under a bush? Should he turn the money in? He was pretty sure no one had seen him. There might be a reward. Should he keep the money instead? If he kept it, should he quit his job bussing tables, so he could concentrate more on his studies? No, people would then wonder what he was living off of. Could someone trace the money to him? He had seen TV whodunits about marked bills. Was anyone looking for him right now? Where should he hide the money so it would be safe? Should he tell Debbie, or just keep it all to himself? He thought he could trust her, but what if she let something slip. If things between him and Debbie didn't work out, he would have the money to move somewhere else. After all, he was living on her boat. It would be a nice insurance policy to know he wasn't totally at her mercy. Was there anyone he *could* trust? Who knows! He didn't think he'd ever seen that much money in his whole life.

It would be several hours before Debbie finished her shift at the restaurant and returned to the boat. That should give him some time to find a hiding place for the bag and think this thing through. Andy walked around the dock and looked for a prospective hiding place for his newfound windfall while he tried to work all these issues out in his mind. He couldn't find anywhere that seemed secure enough. Maybe his locker at the restaurant. A definite no. He would have to find a place to hide it on Debbie's sailboat. The bilge was out of the question – too wet. Maybe one of the aft lazarettes. No, she might go in there for something. Where was someplace she would never have a reason to go? Of course! The anchor locker in the bow. It had plenty of room, and the bag should stay dry. If he put the bag under some of the anchor line, it should remain hidden even if Debbie did open that door. Perfect! Now he could think this out at his leisure.

Andy held out one bundle. After all, a guy needed a little walking-around money.

Andy had a final thought as he stowed the bag in the anchor locker.

I'd better get some zip-locks as insurance that the money will stay dry if I'm going to use the locker as a permanent hidey-hole. And I'd better get rid of that incriminating Princess bag.

This could be my lucky day.

CHAPTER 13

While Andy Gerber was congratulating himself over the fortuitous fluke which had provided him with a Princess cruise ship bag filled with cash, the police were trying to decide what their next tactic should be to recover the ransom money, nab their suspect, and deliver the victim safely back to her husband. They dreaded reporting the unexpected turn of events to either the police department or to Norm.

Norm remained at his home in Cudjoe Gardens waiting for the phone call which would tell him where to go to find his wife. A sheriff's deputy was assigned to stay with him for the remainder of the day. Listening devices had been activated on all Norm's phone lines. Now all everyone could do was wait. Each time the phone rang, he jumped to answer it. An hour later Norm had still not heard from the kidnappers. His phone jingled. It was Captain Hillary. He asked to speak to the deputy on duty. They spoke briefly and hung up.

"The Captain'll be here shortly," the deputy said.

"Did he give you any information?"

"No. He just said he wanted to talk to you when he gets here," the deputy said.

Hillary arrived within half an hour.

"Did the cops catch the assholes?" Norm asked desperately. "Please tell me they got them and got Catt back. I haven't heard from anyone."

"I wish I could say so," Hillary said.

They sat at the kitchen table. He then told Norm blow by blow what had happened at Tennessee Williams Theatre.

Norm squinted and in disbelief rubbed his

forehead and face with his cupped open hand.

"You mean to tell me they lost my money and the pickup man as well, and we still don't know anything about who he is or where my money went?"

"Not at the moment, but both the police department and the sheriff's office are working on it."

Norm went ballistic. All of his pent-up emotions gushed forth. He began to scream expletives and slam his fist on the kitchen table. He called the cops stupid, incompetent, lame-brained and every other name that came into his mind.

Captain Hillary sat silently until he was sure Norm had vented.

"I understand your frustration. I feel the same way ... Mr. Knoll, screaming at each other will get us nowhere."

"No, you couldn't," Norm interrupted. "And why haven't you been able to trace Catt's calls?"

"Because she's not using her cell phone. The one she's using has had the GPS disconnected," Hillary said. "Sometimes unfortunate unforeseeable things just happen. A scooter's small and nimble. It can pass in a small opening on a two-lane road like College Road. The police couldn't risk harming the public by trying to plow through both a garbage truck and ongoing traffic in an attempt to keep up with it. And it wasn't the detective's fault that a jacket was hanging down obscuring the license plate. Sometimes these things just happen. We have to take the situation as it stands right now and deal with it. We can't undo what happened before."

"I could never come up with $200,000 all over again. That's a lot of money," Norm said.

"You shouldn't have to," Captain Hillary said. "The kidnappers got what they demanded. Now they have no further reason to hold your wife. Now we just have to

58

wait for 'em to contact you again."

"I hope you're right," Norm said. "If Catt comes to any harm, I'll sue the whole sorry lot of you."

"This futile argument is getting us nowhere," Hillary said. "We're *all* on your side, and we're doing everything possible to get your wife back unharmed. But we'll need your continued cooperation if that's going to be the case. Please keep working with us, not against us. That's the only way we'll ever get this whole grimy affair resolved. We shouldn't take action for the sake of taking action. If we're to outsmart them, we're going to have to use our brains not our heart."

Hillary then told Norm to stay put by the phone for the rest of the day. The odds favored the kidnappers calling back. He said he would leave the deputy there so if something did happen he and his men could respond promptly.

"That's all we can do for now," Hillary reiterated. Norm didn't know what to say. He just felt drained and helpless.

"This can't be happening," he yelled at no one in particular after Hillary left. "Why me, God? The deputy didn't respond or try to defend the police department's actions. He felt like everything constructive that could be said had already been said between Hillary and Norm. Sometimes silence was the most logical rebuttal. As Hillary had clearly stated, they would simply have to wait and see what shoe dropped next.

CHAPTER 14

For the rest of the day, Norm Knoll was a bundle of nervous energy. He knew subconsciously that his actions were manic and irrational, but he couldn't seem to help himself. He paced. He flipped on all the local news shows to see if they were reporting about Catt even though he knew there was very little chance that the media was aware of his situation. He turned on US1 radio at the top of each hour. He checked the in-box on his e-mails constantly, but he didn't respond to any. He cleaned up the kitchen and the bedroom.

If Catt comes home today, he told himself, *I don't want her walking into a dirty house after everything she's been through.*

Norm tried to read but instead found himself just staring at the pages and not comprehending a word on them. He kept checking the mail even though he knew that it didn't normally get delivered until after mid-afternoon. All the while, he had virtually nothing to say to the sheriff's deputy on duty. The deputy patiently watched Norm pace and fret, but he said nothing unless Norm addressed him. He was almost invisible. He felt sorry for Norm but knew there was nothing he could do to relieve Norm's stress. Each disjointed, nervous event only added to the tension each refused to acknowledge but knew was increasing exponentially. The deputy periodically called in and told Hillary that there was nothing new to report. There had been simply no contact from Catt's abductors.

When the deputy's normal shift got close to its conclusion, he broke the silence.

"I guess we're not going to hear from anyone today about your wife," he said, breaking the silence.

"What do you think that means?" Norm asked. "Does it mean she's dead?"

"Not necessarily."

"Well, what then?" Norm demanded.

"I'm not qualified to give you a meaningful answer," the deputy said. "I'd suggest you ask Captain Hillary about that.

About that time, Captain Hillary pulled up in Norm's driveway.

Norm tried again to get some assurance that things would still turn out all right."

"Anything I'd say right now would be just guessing," Captain Hillary said, "but something we don't know about must be amiss. I'm sure it won't be long until we find out just what that something is."

"I'll be a basket case by then," Norm said. "In fact, I think I already am."

The deputy looked at Hillary and nodded slightly when Norm was faced away from him. Hillary's eye contact told the deputy he understood his message.

"I'll have someone check with you throughout the evening," Hillary said, "and you know what to do if you get a call. I'll be by here first thing in the morning. Is there anything else we can do for you before we leave?"

Norm shook his head.

As promised Hillary came by the next morning. As he and Norm sat drinking coffee, Norm's house-phone rang. Norm jumped up to answer it. It was Catt. She was more hysterical than ever.

"Why didn't you bring the money yesterday?" she demanded. "Do you want to get me killed – you cheap SOB? Is that what you want? They checked several times during the day, and the money was never there."

"But we did take it over there," Norm said. "To the penny. And Will Black put it exactly where you told him to. It was in the Princess bag. Someone picked it up.

Someone driving a scooter. I thought it was your kidnappers."

"Bastard! I don't believe you. You're lying," Catt screamed. "How do you know someone picked it up?"

"I had somebody watching," Norm said.

"So you brought the police in on this. They told you not to do that. They'll kill me for sure now."

"No, not the police," Norm lied. "Will Black had someone assisting him."

"I don't believe you," Catt said. "You hate me. Caromba."

"I don't hate you; I love you," Norm said. "That's why I've done everything they demanded. I wanna see you home safe."

"Then you've got to do what they tell you to do. You have to."

"Darling, I don't have any more money," Norm said. "I virtually drained our investment account to come up with the first $200,000."

The phone line went dead. Norm's knees buckled. Hillary caught him before he could crash into the furniture.

When Norm had settled down, Hillary helped him to the couch.

"Norm just continued to moan, "Oh, my God. Oh, my God."

"When he finally stopped hyperventilating, Norm asked, "So what should I do now?"

"I don't know," Hillary said and sighed. "I'll have to consult my people and decide what we can logically do next."

"I'll kill those mothers if I get a chance. I swear I will."

"Don't talk like that," Hillary said. "You'll only make matters worse. I'm going to pretend I never heard you make that statement. Something'll happen to break this case when you least suspect it to. We're overdue for a break."

CHAPTER 15

The break Dan Hillary was referring to happened just as unexpectedly as he had predicted the following day. A car had been seemingly abandoned on Garrison Bight. When the patrolman on the Bight beat saw it there three days in a row, he became suspicious and checked the registration. The car was registered to a Norman and Catterina Knoll. He had heard through police station gossip that there was some situation afoot with a Mrs. Knoll, but he didn't know exactly what the situation was. He reported his find to his supervisor who was very aware of the case. His supervisor called Chief of Police Walter Wanderley. Walter immediately called Captain Hillary and told him Catt's Beemer had been found parked next to the dumpster on the east side of the bight. He then ordered that the car not be touched until he authorized it. Walter jumped in his car and headed for Garrison Bight. The patrolman was waiting when he arrived. Hillary arrived moments later.

"Been here long?" Hillary asked.

"Just got here," Chief Wanderley said. "I haven't even had a chance to debrief the patrolman yet so your timing is perfect. We can talk to him together."

"Do you know how long the car has been here?" Walter asked.

"We think a couple of days," the patrolman said.

"And why wasn't it towed?" Walter asked.

"It had a parking sticker on it," the patrolman said.

"Is it locked?" Hillary asked.

"No."

Walter put on some throw-away gloves and opened the door. The heat from the closed up vehicle

65

immediately hit him in the face. Nothing seemed out of order in the car. An empty Wendy's coffee cup was in the cup holder. Otherwise it was clean. He checked the glove compartment and found an owner's manual, some wadded up napkins, and a SunPass. They hit the button to pop the trunk. Once again – clean. The spare and jack looked factory fresh.

"I'll get one of my investigators to dust it for prints," Walter said to Hillary, "and we'll see what else they might find. I'll keep you posted on whatever they turn up."

"Thanks," Hillary said.

"I'll also get my men started on interviewing the people who live and work here to see what they can tell us," Walter said.

"Since I'm already here and have been involved so heavily in this case, would you mind if I canvassed the area myself?" Hillary asked.

"Of course not," Walter said. "The MOU between our departments covers both of our backsides."

"Thank you for the professional courtesy," Hillary said. "I'll keep you apprised if I find out anything which will help either of us to put this matter to bed."

Hillary's first interviews turned over no facts of significance. People just seemed to be intent on minding their own business and not interfering in any one else's.

As he was mulling who to talk to next, Hillary heard familiar Ray Charles' lyrics

My bills are all due and the baby needs shoes and I'm busted

Cotton is down to a quarter a pound, and I'm busted

He turned and saw a tricycle approaching. Mardi Gras beads and other assorted trinkets dangled from every side. Each tire had multicolored spokes. Lights twinkled all around the trike. Behind the seat was a pyramid of bungee-corded plastic water bottles advertising Fat Tuesday on Duval Street. A compact CD stereo system was hooked to a car battery in the basket on the rear. Speakers were attached to the handlebars. A leather pouch hung from the handlebars to give the rider a place for his stuff. Riding the unusual tricycle was an elderly black man with a snow-white handlebar mustache. He wore cargo-shorts and a faded generic t-shirt. On his head was a baseball cap with a floral design that said "Dry Tortugas or Bust." When he saw Hillary, the man's eyes lit up in recognition.

"Narley Gristle, as I live and breathe," Hillary said. "What are you doing here?"

"I live on my houseboat here on the Bight," Narley said.

"You got a houseboat on the Bight?" Hillary asked incredulously.

"Shore do," said Gristle. "I inherited it from my dear ole daddy."

Narley Gristle was well known to the old time Conchs. He had been born over on Petronia Street and was a third generation Conch. The seventy-four year old had 16 children, 16 grandchildren, and 8 great grandchildren. He was a favorite subject for tourists to photograph since he was always patient with them and beamed when they asked to take his picture. He would tell out-of-towners tall tales of Hemingway, Tennessee Williams and Shel Silverstein.

"You got time for me to ask you something?" Hillary asked.

"For you, all the time in the world."

About that time Narley's stereo began to play Eddy Grant's *Electric Avenue*.

"Do you know the people who own that Beemer?" asked Hillary pointing to Catt's car.

"No, but I noticed that it's been there most of this week," Narley said.

"Have you ever seen the driver?"

"Uh, Huh. A couple – white couple – kind of young looking," Narley said.

"White gringos or white Hispanics?"

"Now that you mention it, I think I did hear one of them use Spanish. The woman yelled something at the man."

"Did she seem to be in distress?"

"Nah, just kind of momentarily pissed at him. Like she was frustrated about something," Narley said. "But then she grabbed him by the arm, and they walked off together."

"Did you see where they went?"

"Nah, not really."

"But you don't think she was being held against her will?" Hillary asked.

"Didn't seem that way to me. They seemed pretty tight."

"Like they knew each other?"

Yeah. Think I saw 'em another time eating a Whopper over at Burger King on Roosevelt."

"Do you know where they're staying?"

"Not a clue," Narley said. "Unless there appears to be trouble, I try to stay out of white folks' business."

"I understand," Hillary said. "The car has a residents' parking sticker on it."

"That may or may not mean anything," Narley said. "Kind of like having a handicapped sticker. Not everybody I've seen with one looked handicapped to me."

"Would you let me know if you see them again?" Hillary said and handed Narley his card. By this time Hillary could hear Elvis' cover version of *I've Got A Woman* coming from the tricycle speakers.

"You betcha. What's up?"

"Can't comment right now, but I'd sure like to find those two."

"I hear you. You take care now," Narley said.

"You too, and thanks. By the way, Elvis is a bit of a departure from your usual repertoire, isn't he?"

"I don't discriminate. I play all the brothers," Narley said.

"I've been told there are three kinds of people in the world – Elvis fans, Beatles fans and everyone else," Hillary said.

Both men laughed.

CHAPTER 16

Walter Wanderley phoned Norm Knoll at his office. "Mr. Knoll, I've got some news to report to you."

"Good or bad?" a distraught Norm almost hyperventilated into the phone.

"Not great, but I guess it's better than it's bad," Chief Wanderley said. "We have found your wife's car, but we haven't found her yet."

He then told Norm about finding Catt's Beemer parked on Garrison Bight. He did not tell Norm about her possible companion.

"Do you know why she would've been over there?" Walter asked.

"Don't have a clue unless she was going to eat at that Thai place," Norm said.

"I don't think that was it," Walter said. "The car was found on the southeast side of the Bight. That's about as far away from the restaurant as you can get. You can't walk from that side to the restaurant. Does she have any friends who might live on one of the houseboats moored there?"

"Not to my knowledge."

"The car has yielded some prints, but we haven't been able to match them up with anyone in a current data base," Walter continued.

"So where does that leave us?" Norm asked.

"I really would hesitate to guess," Walter said, "but as we have told you, clues will most likely continue turning up. This is just the first one. I'll keep you posted."

"Thanks," Norm said and hung up.

Norm called Will and told him that the police had found Catt's car. Norm felt the desperate need just to talk to someone, and Will was the only person who knew what had been going on. They talked about all the events which had transpired.

Will Black got the next phone call relating to the case as well.

"Is my husband trying to get rid of me?" Catt Knoll said in a stressed voice. "Is everyone purposely trying to get me murdered?"

"He's trying to get you back," Will said. "They found your car. Where are you? You still OK?"

"For the moment, but I won't be OK long unless you come up with the ransom money. Why didn't you just pay them like you were supposed to?"

"I did pay them," Will said. "I left it under the bush in front of the theater just like I was instructed to. They should have it. It was all there."

"Liars! Liars!" Catt screamed. "Y'all are going to get me killed."

"You've got it wrong. Can't you see they're scamming you to try to get more?"

"Then you've got to get more money," Catt said. "You've just got to."

"Your account here doesn't have that much more money left in it," Will said. "You need to talk to your husband. I don't have the authority to release money, even if it was here."

At that time, a frustrated Latino man came on the line.

"You and her husband better figger out a way to get us our money," he said gruffly. "I'm going to disfigure this bitch. Nobody'll want her when I get through with her."

"Mister, I'm telling you like I told her, there isn't that much money here, and even if there was, I'm not empowered to disburse it without the owner's permission. I'll go to jail. I ..."

The angry Latino man interrupted him in mid sentence, "Then you got a real problem, asshole. I'm going to slice this bitch's tits off for a start."

"It'll accomplish nothing," Will said. "I'm telling you, the money isn't here. You're going to have to settle for what you already got."

"Which is nothin'. Nothin's not enough," the man said, and the line went dead.

CHAPTER 17

Andy Gerber's life had changed dramatically over the last two days. It wasn't apparent because outwardly he was the same FKCC student he had been two days ago, but in Andy's mind, he was rich. He pulled the Princess bag out several times while Debbie was at work and looked at his windfall again in private.

Do you know how long it would take me to make this much money?

He packed the bills in quart size zip-locks to protect them from moisture before putting them in a Gordon Food Service zippered cold-food bag and then putting it back in the anchor locker. He even splurged on heavy-duty freezer bags instead of the less expensive sandwich bags. Boy, was he glad he had chosen the route which he had that day to go to class. He checked each time he returned to the boat to make sure his fortune was still there.

With the bundle he had kept out for walking around money, Andy took Debbie to Sunset Key. She had always talked about wanting to go there. He told her she could order anything she wanted off the menu. When she questioned him about his generosity, Andy was vague with her and told her he felt he owed her a few good times. It was a perfect evening until they returned to the boat and found their air conditioner had quit working. Debbie spent the rest of the evening worrying about where they would ever get the funds to repair it. Andy was not concerned, however. He knew he could get it fixed or replaced the following morning after Debbie went to work, and for once he knew exactly how he would pay for it. He would surprise Debbie and take care of the matter while she was gone.

When Debbie returned from work, a new air conditioner was humming.

"Andy, you got it fixed? Must not have been much wrong with it," she said.

"No, quite the opposite. The compressor was totally shot. This is a new unit," Andy said.

"But where'd you get the money?" she asked. "They cost thousands of dollars. We don't have that kind of money."

"I had a little put back," Andy said.

"Seriously," Debbie said. "Did you rob a bank or something?"

"Oh, all right," he said. "I got the money from my grandmother. Don't worry about it. At least we won't be sweatin' all night long."

Debbie was confused and not totally convinced. How did he get it from his grandmother that rapidly? She wasn't local. She lived in Chicago. Or was it just a coincidence that she sent Andy some happy money? It wasn't like her, and it wasn't Andy's birthday. For the moment, she decided not to make it a bone of contention, but the matter continued to bother her. She hated to think of Andy as a liar even if his heart was in the right place. She didn't bring the matter up again until the following day, her day off.

"What's your grandmother's mailing address?" Debbie asked. "I've written a thank-you note to her, and I'd like to get it in the mail."

Andy was evasive.

"Sweetie, you don't need to do that. She doesn't expect a thank-you."

"It's the polite thing to do," Debbie said, "and it's also the right thing to do."

"She asked him about it an hour later. He made an excuse about not having time to look for it.

"Why don't you give me her phone number, and I'll

just call her and thank her in person," Debbie said.

Andy hesitated but finally said, "Sweetie, I wasn't quite honest with you. Nana didn't send me the money."

"Then where'd you get it?" Debbie asked.

Andy broke down and came clean on the whole story. Debbie sat and listened. She was mortified.

When Andy finished, Debbie finally spoke. "Andy, that money doesn't belong to us."

"Well, I guess it does now," he said sheepishly.

"How much is it?" she asked.

"I don't really know. I haven't counted it. Enough to fill a nylon zipper bag."

"Andy, students don't carry that kind of money in a zipper bag and leave it under a bush. I think that's illegal money."

"Nobody saw me take it. ... I'm sure they didn't," Andy said.

"Do you realize who you could be dealing with?" Debbie said. "That's probably dope money or something."

"Then they won't go to the police, and we can just keep it. We deserve it more than some scummy dope dealer."

"Dope dealers aren't just scummy; they're ruthless people. They kill people over money. Is that money worth dying for?"

"Of course not, but..."

"But nothing," Debbie said. "You've got to turn that money over to the cops. I've seen TV shows where drug smugglers not only kill people but usually torture them to death before they do."

"But I'll get in trouble."

"Just tell them you found it, and that you're doing the right thing. I'm sure they'll understand. You might even get a reward. Let's go right now before you start having second thoughts."

Debbie and Andy continued to argue for the next half hour before Andy surrendered to her point of view. As bad as he hated to, he'd either have to take her advice or she'd never let him forget about it. But he wasn't going to give back what he had already spent. He was determined to get something for his trouble and to keep the walking-around money he had taken out of the bag as well. After all, Debbie didn't even know about it, and the cops didn't know how much had originally been in the bag. While Debbie was taking a shower, he hid this secret windfall in a rolled up sock.

Andy and Debbie cleaned up and changed into presentable clothes. Andy retrieved the bag, and they took off for the police station. He drove his scooter, and she rode behind him, holding the zipper bag. When they arrived at the station, they asked for a detective. One came out, introduced himself, and escorted them back to a cubicle.

"When I was on campus a couple of days ago, I accidentally picked up a bag that didn't belong to me," Andy said. "Now that I know it's not mine, I wanna do the right thing and turn it in."

The detective opened the bag and knew exactly what it was. He quizzed Andy about the details of the find. Andy was scared and gave evasive answers that he thought wouldn't incriminate him.

"I'm not in trouble am I?" Andy asked nervously. "I just wanna to do the right thing."

"No, you're not in trouble," the detective said, "and I congratulate you for bringing the money in."

"Do you know who it belongs to?" Andy asked. "If no one claims it, would it belong to me?"

"No, we don't know who the owner of the money is," the detective lied. "And yes, I guess it is always possible that if no one claimed it, it could be returned to you … but understand that's highly unlikely."

"Do you think it might be drug money?" Debbie asked.

"I'd really rather not comment, not knowing any more than I do at this juncture," the detective said, "but once again I want to thank you for being a good citizen. Not everyone would have been as honest as you two."

"Is there a reward?" Andy asked.

"If there is, I'll be sure you get it," the detective said. "I assume you will be available if we have any further questions on the matter?"

"Of course."

"Then, we'll be in touch."

After Andy and Debbie left the police station, the money was counted and logged in, all $190,000 of it.

The detective walked down to Chief Wanderley's office and reported the morning's events to him.

"So it took two days for this guy to bring the money to us which is $10,000 short," Walter said. "And I don't remember it being in zip-locks."

The detective smiled knowingly and nodded.

"Did you bring this matter up with Mr. Gerber?" Walter asked.

"No, we didn't count it until after they had left the building."

After the detective had left his office, Walter called Captain Hillary and told him the latest turn of events.

At the same time as Andy and Debbie's meeting was going on at the police station, Norm Knoll received a phone call on the private line in his office.

"Norm, do you have the damned money?"

"Darling, I told you I don't have that much money, and I can't put my hands on it," Norm said. You've got to convince them that as much as I want to cooperate, I simply don't have it."

"Bull-shit! You cheap bastard! ... Asshole!"

There was no more pleading. No more argument.

Catt Knoll simply hung up on her husband. Norm sat there staring at the dead phone, not knowing what to think. Had he just signed his wife's death warrant? When he finally regained his composure, he dialed Captain Hillary.

Captain Hillary told Norm that his money had been recovered but it was $10,000 short. Apparently the kidnappers had told the truth after all. He asked Norm if he should squeeze Andy for the shortfall. Norm told Hillary he felt so beaten down and was so sick of problems he simply didn't care. He could replace $10,000, just not $200,000.

"I'm just relieved they didn't keep it all," Norm said.

Hillary asked Norm what he wanted to do next.

"Pay the pricks, of course," Norm said. "I wanna get my wife back."

They waited the rest of the day, but once again there was no further communication from the kidnappers."

CHAPTER 18

The following morning Betsy Black was going through some mail when Margaret came in and told her she had a phone call.

"A woman's on the phone for you," Margaret said. "I shouldn't say this, but she doesn't sound normal."

"Betsy, this is Catt Knoll," a shaky voice said when Betsy picked up the phone. "I'm Norm Knoll's wife. He owns the boat company. Do you remember me?"

"Of course, I know who you are," Betsy said. "We've been worried to death about you."

"You've got to come get me," Catt rattled on. "I've escaped. I ran away. You've got to come get me before they catch me again. I don't want to get caught again. I don't think I could take it. You've got to come get me. Please."

"Catt, please settle down," Betsy said. "I can't come get you unless I know where you are."

"Don't you know where I'm calling from?" Catt said. Betsy could hear desperation in Catt's voice. "Come get me. Please. And come alone. Please, before they find me again."

"No, I don't know where you are, but if you'll tell me, I'll be right there," Betsy said. "You just stay put. Why'd you call me instead of the police?"

"Because you're a woman, and I knew you'd understand? I don't want the police involved."

That comment made no sense.

She must be disoriented.

"You've been kidnapped. The police are already involved. They'll meet us wherever you are and take you to the police station or the hospital," Betsy said.

"No, I said I don't want'm involved," Catt almost

81

screamed into the phone.

"Catt, they need to be involved. After all, a crime's been committed," Betsy said.

"No, I just want to go home," Catt said. "Unless you promise to come alone, I'm won't tell you where I am."

Betsy tried to reason with Catt, but finally reluctantly agreed to Catt's terms. Catt told Betsy she'd be waiting in The Restaurant Store on Eaton Street.

"I've got to go out," Betsy told Margaret as she hurried to leave her office. "Be back."

"Where to?" Margaret asked.

"Don't have time to explain," Betsy said. "Call Norm Knoll, and tell him to call me on my cell phone."

Betsy arrived at The Restaurant Store within minutes and entered the store. She started at the front door and walked down the aisle closest to the window. No one. She headed for the back of the store, looking down each aisle as she went. No sign of Catt. Then she spied Catt Knoll in the back corner by the electronic appliances with a *Conch Color* magazine held up to hide her face. Catt rushed over and hugged her.

"We need to get out of here," Betsy said. "My car's in the parking lot out front."

They walked rapidly towards the entrance of the store. No one seemed to be paying them any attention. Betsy pushed open the front door and a rush of hot air hit them in the face as they left the cold building. Betsy pointed to her right towards Strunk Ace Hardware.

"My car's this way."

"Take me home," Catt said. "Please."

At that moment Betsy's cell phone rang. She paused to answer it. The call was from Norm. Betsy quickly told him where they were and that Catt was insisting on being taken home. He asked if Catt was physically injured. Betsy said it didn't appear so. She was just a psychological mess.

Norm said, "I'll meet you at home."

Once they got in the car, Catt broke loose with a torrent of tears.

"It's OK," Betsy said to reassure her. "It's almost over now. You're going to be safe."

As they drove, Betsy looked at Catt closer. She appeared to be in pretty good shape for someone who had been until that morning held by kidnappers. She seemed freshly bathed, her hair was tied back and her clothes didn't look nearly as rumpled and disheveled as Betsy would have expected. If Betsy hadn't known better, she would have thought Catt was in her Saturday morning errand-running outfit. Betsy looked around the parking lot. She drew a relieved deep breath. There was no sign of Catt's kidnappers. She wasn't sure what she would have done if she had seen thugs closing in on her car.

Betsy drove towards Cudjoe Key. She kept looking in her rear-view mirror to see if she was being followed. The coast appeared to be clear. She turned by the sheriff's sub-station. Catt looked at Betsy in panic thinking Betsy might turn into it instead.

"We live on 3rd Avenue," Catt said. "Take a left when you get there. We're the third house down on the left."

Catt produced a house key when they drove into the driveway of the ground-level home. *Strange,* Betsy thought. *She's still got her house key and the presence of mind to get it out.*

They went in, and Catt collapsed on the sofa. Betsy just stood there wondering what she was supposed to do next.

Within minutes, Norm Knoll arrived. He rushed into the house.

Catt jumped up off the sofa and ran to hug him. Both began to cry.

"I can't believe you're home," Norm said. "We've been frantic about you. Where've you been?"

"I just can't talk about it right now," Catt said and began to cry again. "Just hold me."

As Norm held Catt, Betsy slipped out into the front yard and dialed Walter Wanderley. She told the woman answering the phone that it was urgent she talk to the chief. He immediately came on the line.

"Walter, I'm in Cudjoe Gardens, and I have Catt Knoll," Betsy said.

"What?" Walter said. "Why didn't you call me before now?"

"Catt wouldn't let me," Betsy said. "She said she wouldn't tell me where to find her unless I came to get her alone."

"That's odd," Walter said.

"She doesn't know I'm on the phone with you right now. I'm in her front yard."

"Where in Cudjoe Gardens?"

"Take a left on 3rd Avenue. Third house on the left."

"I'm on my way," Walter said. "I need to call the sheriff's department."

"Would you just come alone for now?" Betsy said. "I don't think she can handle too many people descending on her right now. I don't know how to explain it. You'll see what I'm talking about when you get here."

"OK, it'll just be me," Walter said.

"Thanks," Betsy said. "I think you'll see it's the right move at this juncture."

"I hope you're right," Walter said. "This is not the way we're supposed to do things."

"Take my word for it. You're going to be a big enough shock for her. By the way, her husband is here."

"How come?"

"Because I called him," Betsy said.

"You called him," Walter said, "but you didn't call me?"

"Like I said, this is a highly unusual situation. I can't put my finger on it, but something's off. You'll see when you arrive."

"I'll be there in twenty to twenty five minutes," Walter said.

"I'll call you if there's a change before you can get here."

Walter drove into the Knoll driveway within twenty minutes. Betsy listened for him and went out to greet him when he arrived. The Knolls didn't seem to notice. Walter had wisely not arrived with his siren blaring, staying low-key. As they were walking into the Knoll living room, Betsy announced Walter's arrival.

"Catt, Norm, Chief Wanderley's here," she said.

"You told me you weren't going to call him," Catt said.

"I told you I wouldn't call him from The Restaurant Store," Betsy said. "You need to talk to him. This's a serious criminal issue. The police and the sheriff have both had a lot of people looking for you over the last few days."

"I told you I don't want to talk to anyone," Catt said.

"At some point you're going to have to," Betsy said.

"Darling, talk to Chief Wanderley," Norm said. "We all want to know more about your ordeal. Don't you want us to catch the people who did this to you?"

"No. Not today. I'm not talking to anyone today."

"We also need to have you evaluated medically," Walter said.

"Not today," said Catt in a petulant, almost childish voice.

"The sooner we do it, the sooner we'll catch these creeps. Timing is crucial," Walter said. "They're felons who deserve to pay despite our recovering the ransom money."

"You got the ransom money back?" Catt said, almost snapping out of her stupor.

"Yes, isn't that good news?" Norm said. "I thought you'd be thrilled."

"But you said it had been stolen, and you couldn't get any more. You lied," Catt said. "If I hadn't escaped when I did, I might have died."

"The guy who accidentally took the money was honest enough to bring it back," Norm said. "This all happened after I talked to you last. I was going to tell you if I talked to you or them again and make fresh pickup arrangements, but, thank God, here you are. Now I don't have to give the money to those creeps, and I have you back in once piece as well."

Catt just stood there saying nothing. Finally she said, "Eh, eh..." She cleared her throat. "I'm glad."

She turned to Walter and Betsy and said, "I don't wish to be rude, but would you mind leaving me with my husband. I'll be all right."

"Mrs. Knoll, are you waiving your right to medical attention?" Chief Wanderley asked incredulously.

"Yes. Now please leave. Go! I thank you both for everything you've done, but I'd just like to be left alone with my husband now."

When Betsy and Walter had gotten back out to the front yard, Walter whispered to Betsy, "You're right. This is a most unusual situation."

Betsy said, "I thought you'd understand when you got here. See why I couldn't explain it on the phone?"

"If I were in her shoes, I'd be hell-bent-to-leather to see my abductors apprehended and prosecuted to the full extent of the law."

"I would too," Betsy said. "I can't explain her attitude."

"I'm not sure how to explain this to Dan Hillary,"

Walter said.

"I'll leave that up to you. Maybe the woman's just in shock. What can I say? After all, I'm just a drafted volunteer."

CHAPTER 19

Police Chief Walter Wanderley wasn't the only law enforcement officer being surprised by the day's events. Captain Dan Hillary's day took an unexpected turn as well. It began when his cell phone rang.

"Captain Hillary."

"Captain Hillary, Narley Gristle, the psychedelic tricycle man. I come into possession of some information about that black Beemer which I think you'll find interesting."

"Oh, yeah? What's that?" Hillary replied.

"Druther tell you in person," Narley said. "Could you meet me at Strunk Hardware's parking lot? I'd rather talk there than at the Bight."

"Sure. When?"

"I'm not far from there now."

"Give me 20 minutes. I'm on Lower Sugarloaf."

When Hillary arrived, he looked around but didn't see Gristle's colorful ride. Within sixty seconds, though, he heard the familiar lyrics to Wild Cherry's *Play That Funky Music* and knew his information source had arrived. Narley was grinning and drinking coffee out of a Styrofoam go-cup.

"Wassappening?" Narley said, reverting to street talk. Hillary smiled at Narley's speech flexibility.

"Oh, just another day with the Gestapo," Hillary said. "Thanks for calling. What's up?"

"Well, I put mah ear to the ground ... you know, that good old coconut telegraph shit, and I think I found out something you'll find interesting."

"I'm all ears."

"They's this person ... kind of a temporary resident on the Bight," Narley began.

"You mean like a snowbird?"

"Naw, she local all right. Just don't pay no rent."

"Like a homeless person?" Hillary said.

"You're very perceptive. Well, this person seen the people you axed me about leaving the parking lot one day. They kissed and hugged to the embarrassin' point before they got in that ride and drove off together."

"Do you know who was driving the car?" Hillary asked.

"I was told the woman was," Narley said.

"Very, very interesting," Hillary said. "Would your source talk to me?"

"Uh, uh! Ain't no way! She don't like no cops or any other 'thority figure for that matter, and she don't like getting involved ... strictly believes in staying under the radar screen," said Narley. "That's why I axed you to meet me down here. She didn't know why I was axing, and I don't want her to know. If I got a reputation for axing questions for the po-lice, nobody would ever trust me enough to tell me anything again."

"I understand the code of the street," said Hillary, "and you know I'd never do anything to ruin your credibility with your fellow residents. Did she know if they were live-aboards at the Bight?"

"Didn't know that, but I might be able to find out."

"I'd appreciate it. Man, I owe you one. Thanks."

"Don't forget old Narley, if the cops ever start to hassle me."

"You know I won't."

CHAPTER 20

As soon as he returned to his office, Walter Wanderley called Dan Hillary.

"Dan, we got Mrs. Knoll back."

"Where is she? She OK?" Hillary asked.

Walter told Hillary the strange story about how Betsy Black had picked up Catt at The Restaurant Store and then carried her to her home on Cudjoe. He described the tearful reunion with her husband and told Hillary about Catt's refusal to speak to anyone concerning her case. Hillary agreed that this was not how he had expected to resolve this case.

"Walter, there is absolutely nothing normal about this case," Hillary said. "Continuous phone calls coming only from the victim instead of the kidnappers, the multiple half-assed disorganized attempts to try pry the money out of Mr. Knoll, the stupid way the wrong person ended up with the ransom money and the almost bizarre way the money was turned back in after it was considered to be lost. Now the victim is turning up in The Restaurant Store of all places and then refusing to clarify her whereabouts with anyone. None of it makes much sense. And now I'm about to tell you another saga equally bewildering."

Hillary then told Walter about his meetings with Narley Gristle.

"You're right. This case still has more holes in it than a leaky bucket. I wouldn't call Gristle conventional by any stretch of the imagination," Walter said when the captain had finished, "but I've always found Gristle to be principled and reliable."

"Same here," Hillary said. "Narley had nothing to gain by making up a story about a complete stranger.

Don't forget. I originally sought him out; he didn't seek me out."

"So what do we do now?" Walter said. "We shouldn't just let it drop. This investigation has been a budget buster and could become a PR nightmare. If it's a farce, someone's going to pay. If it's not a farce, then the perps need to be brought in and held accountable."

"I couldn't agree with you more," Hillary said. "Since you've already tried with her, why don't you let me take a swing at the ball? I'll do it first thing in the morning after we've given Mrs. Knoll all night to maybe regain her senses. Perhaps I can force a come-to-Jesus meeting with the woman. Maybe I can scare her husband by telling him just what this investigation has cost the taxpayers and potentially cost him if we can prove collusion. If he sees himself as being possibly on the hook for the tab, he might just talk some sense into her."

"Maybe she'll get her equilibrium back overnight. What I heard her say today could have been the irrational thinking of a person who's temporarily in shock and just couldn't deal with the matter anymore after everything she had been through - kind of like battle fatigue. We've managed to keep this whole affair out of the press so far. Let's continue to hold our cards very close to the vest until we can figure out just what the hell is really going on."

"Agreed. If you hadn't brought the topic of media discretion up, I was going to bring it up with you," Hillary said. "We don't need to complicate matters by having a third party looking over our shoulder in public."

"Good. Then we're on the same page. Good luck," Walter said. "And if it's feasible, if you make headway about getting her to open up, I'd like to participate in the interview. This is still very much of an open case, and

I intend to treat it as such until all the questions are answered."

"I don't have a problem with that. In fact, I would welcome your input and assistance into this screwball affair. The only reason that I would leave you out is if it appeared that Mrs. Knoll would perceive us as ganging up on her and that fact would end up queering the whole interview. Why don't we try visiting her together?"

"I was hoping you'd ask," Walter said. "And I think going through the husband is probably a good idea. He's been very straightforward with us both so far."

Captain Hillary and Chief Wanderley did not call the Knolls the next morning; they simply took a chance and went by the Knoll home on Cudjoe unannounced. Norm answered the door.

"Mr. Knoll, how is your wife this morning? Would it be possible for us to meet with her and debrief her about the events of the last few days?" Hillary asked.

When Norm hesitated and mumbled about seeing if she was up to having visitors, Hillary said, "Sir, it's extremely important that we debrief her as soon as possible. I know you wouldn't want us to have the mistaken impression you that you were interfering with an active investigation. I would hate to have my superiors think that you were. There could be both criminal and economic consequences, and I think you two have suffered enough. Both of our departments are determined to apprehend these culprits."

Norm relented, "Come on in, gentlemen. We were just having coffee, May I fix you a cup?"

Walter and Dan were shown into the Knoll's kitchen where Catt sat at the table. After exchanging pleasantries, Captain Hillary asked Catt to summarize the events of the last few days for them.

Catt took a sip of her coffee, sighed and began.

"I went to Ben Franklin over by GFS to buy some

garland to make a wreath to dress up our front door. I bought what I needed and got back in my car. One of the kidnappers was hiding in the back seat. He pulled a gun on me and forced me to drive to Garrison Bight."

She stopped to wipe away tears as if talking about the incident were depressing her once more.

"He took me aboard a boat moored there," she choked out.

Catt almost wiped her eyes on her sleeves but then reached for a napkin. She knocked the napkin-holder over. Hillary caught it before it spilled napkins on the floor. Catt took a deep breath before continuing.

"They gagged and tied me. They made me call my husband and demand the ransom. When they didn't get the money promptly enough to satisfy them, they took turns raping and sodomizing me. One stuck his ... his foul smelling thing ... in my mouth. It made me almost throw up. I had to pretend to enjoy it because otherwise I was afraid they'd kill me. After awhile they got overconfident and began to leave me alone. I managed to get loose and then walk over the bridge to The Restaurant Store. That's when I called for help."

"Why didn't you walk over to US1? There were a lot of stores closer to you than The Restaurant Store? Like Miami Subs, for instance."

"I don't know. I guess I just wasn't thinking clearly. I just wanted to get as far away from those evil people as possible."

"And how did you get a telephone to call for help with?"

"It was a Radio Shack model they had bought for me to call Norm on. I saw it and took it with me."

"Your abductors were two men?"

Catt nodded.

"Can you describe them?"

"They were Hispanic."

94

"Could you be more specific?"

"Oh, I don't know. Young. Dark complexioned. Kind of average looking."

"That's not much to go on. Could you identify them in a picture or a lineup?"

"Probably. Do I have to do it today?"

"The sooner the better."

"Where's the cell phone?"

"I don't know. I'll have to try to find it. Do you need it?"

"Yes, we do."

The questioning continued. Walter and Dan asked her questions about the boat and whether it was permanently moored at the Bight. They asked her about a multitude of things and issues. Her responses were mostly vague and not very helpful. They insisted on escorting her in to Lower Keys Medical Center so she could be examined for possible venereal diseases, AIDS, and vaginal and rectal damage. Catt resisted, saying she was fine. Instead of the affair becoming clearer, it just got odder and odder.

Walter and Dan wondered silently why Norm was not more insistent that Catt give them more pointed, specific answers to their questions. He now seemed unusually unruffled by the events which had transpired. When he did contribute, his statements were calm and composed instead of being emotional. He seemed a whole different person from the nervous-wreck he had been while the authorities had been searching for his wife. He only became proactive and agitated when the topic of possible venereal diseases was brought up. At this point he insisted Catt comply and submit to an examination. He told her she was being selfish if she did not make sure she would not accidentally pass a disease on to him in the future. She agreed to submit to the exam only if it were performed by her regular gynecologist.

Captain Hillary called Catt's gynecologist and set up an appointment for him to see her. He insisted on talking to the doctor directly and stressed that the exam had to be done that day. The doctor agreed to work her in that afternoon.

"Thanks you for allowing this exam. We might get DNA, and it will be crucial information for us to have in any upcoming trial," Captain Hillary said. "Now, will you accompany me to my office so we can officially record the information concerning your kidnapping? May I have the clothing you were wearing during the abduction so I can have it tested for DNA?"

"I'm sorry. I didn't know you'd want it," Catt said. "I washed it. It was so nasty I couldn't stand to have it around."

Once again Catt resisted going to the sheriff's office to look at pictures of known local felons until her husband insisted she comply. Hillary called Norm aside and told him that they would also like to connect her to a lie-detector machine for the debriefing. Norm told Catt about this request.

Catt began to cry. "You just don't believe me. You think I'm making all this up," she said as she sobbed. "Instead of getting out there and catching these horrible people, you're wasting your time grilling me, the victim."

Hillary told her the lie-detector test was a procedural matter and that they merely wanted to make sure her remembrances and responses were as accurate as possible. This would be very important in their attempts to apprehend the culprits and then seek to prosecute them. Norm snapped out of his malaise and angrily insisted she cooperate. Catt capitulated and agreed to the voluntary lie-detector test.

CHAPTER 21

As Walter Wanderley reached for his phone, his private line buzzed.

"Walter? Dan."

"You must have ESP. I was just picking up the phone to call you," Walter said. "Do you have anything from the doctor on our mystifying Mrs. Knoll?"

"As a matter of fact I do. You got time for me to come over?"

"Come on."

"Be there in a few."

Captain Hillary drove straight to the Key West Police Department. Walter got them both a cup of coffee.

"So what about the doctor's report?" Walter asked.

"I'll come back to that in a moment," Dan said. "First, let me tell you about the polygraph. She flunked it bigger than hell."

"Why am I not totally surprised?" Wanderley said. "After what you told me about your Narley Gristle interview, I had an intuition that things were not totally as she portrayed them. Does she know she failed?"

"No."

"How about her husband?"

"He doesn't know either."

"OK, we'll come back to this in a moment. Do you have the doctor's report?"

"Yep," Captain Hillary said. "He can find no rectal or vaginal bruising ... or bruises anywhere else on her body, like from rope burns on her wrists or legs from being tied up. He sees no signs that she's been through any unusually rough sexual activity recently."

"And the good Mrs. Knoll *accidentally* destroyed

any DNA evidence we might have gotten from her clothing by washing them."

"Uh, huh," Hillary said. "And the only fingerprints on the Radio Shack cell phone were hers. We showed her mug shots, but she wasn't very helpful in identifying a suspect. She just kind of looked bewildered. She wasn't consistent in just what the perps looked like. I would think if you spent that much time with your abductors, their image would be imprinted on your brain permanently."

"Hmm! Are you starting to think what I'm starting to think?" Walter asked.

"I thought that before I came over here. Something ... or should I say someone ... doesn't add up," Hillary said. "That's why I didn't just want to report this to you via phone."

"And your suggestion?"

"Let's keep all these facts to ourselves for the moment," Hillary said. "We'll tell her we're still waiting on results, but in the meantime we'll hit her with what Narley told us and watch her reaction."

"Should we do it in front of her husband?"

"I don't see why not. He's a part of this whole equation. I've also wondered about some of his reactions at times recently. They seemed inconsistent to me. I'd like to see how he's going to react to this," Hillary said. "The car was in your jurisdiction. What'd you learn from it?"

"I just got an idea. We'll set up an interview on the pretense of releasing her car back to her now that they've finished searching it for clues," Walter said.

"Did they find any clues of significance?" Hillary asked.

"We got some prints, but we don't know who they belong to," Walter said.

"One person or more than one?"

"Only one person," Walter said.

"But she said she had two abductors."

"Another inconsistency," Walter said.

"We've definitely got to put this dizzy dame on the spot if we hope to learn the truth."

"Don't you mean amateur femme fatale? My gut is beginning to say that truth is a fleeing thing with this woman."

"I agree. She has an undisclosed agenda which we don't understand. Do you think the husband suspects as much?" Hillary said.

"If he hasn't, he's bound to start wondering soon if all has been kosher with his wife – unless he's totally brain dead."

"When do you want to put your plan into play?" Hillary said.

"Nothing to be gained putting it off."

CHAPTER 22

Walter called Norm Knoll and told him they had finished examining his wife's car and would like to schedule a time to return it. Norm said he would like to get it back as soon as possible.

"Why don't we plan on my bringing it out to your house after work this afternoon? Since you have your own car to drive home, I'll have a patrolman drive Mrs. Knoll's car. I'll follow, and I can bring him back to the station afterwards. That'll keep us from having to make double trips and make things more convenient for you," Walter said.

"Did you learn anything from the Beemer?" Norm asked.

"I'll share all that information with you when we get to your house."

"What time?" Norm asked. "Catt's definitely going to be glad to get her car back."

"Make it easy on yourself," Walter said. "You know when it's a good time for you to leave work."

They agreed on a time, and Norm told Walter he would call him as he was leaving work.

They all arrived about the same time at the Knoll residence on Cudjoe Key. Catt was in a bright sundress and appeared to be in good spirits. Walter thought as they greeted each other that if he hadn't known what he did, he would never have guessed anything had been amiss. Walter wondered if she were on some type of upper.

"I'm really glad to get some transportation back," Catt said. "I was starting to get cabin fever, and there's some errands I need to run."

"Did the car produce any clues which will help you

catch these creeps?" Norm asked Walter.

"We got some fingerprints, but we don't know who they belong to yet," Walter said. "Interviews were conducted with residents and workers on Garrison Bight. They proved to be more enlightening than the car was."

"Oh, yeah," Norm said. "In what way?"

Catt looked puzzled but remained silent.

"We had reports that a couple was seen using the car on several occasions."

"So you got a description?" Norm asked. "Two men?"

"Not exactly, a man and a woman. But according to the witnesses, this couple seemed to be a normal, friendly, somewhat amorous couple. Both people were seen at different times driving the car. On one occasion they had what appeared to be a brief argument; on another occasion they briefly kissed in the parking lot. There was also a report they were seen eating burgers at Burger King on North Roosevelt," Walter said.

Catt's sunny smile had by this time turned into a frown. Worry lines began to form on her forehead. Norm silently stared out into space as he digested Walter's comments.

"Did they say what the woman looked like?" Catt asked uncertainly.

"As a matter of fact, they did have a rough description," Walter said. There was a pregnant pause as his comment sank in.

"Well?" Catt asked nervously.

"Oh, just a general description of the woman. White, attractive, youngish but definitely an adult. Average height. Nicely dressed."

Suddenly Norm jumped up and turned. He waved his extended index finger from his balled up fist at his wife. His face was flushed.

"Were you up to no good, you two-timing no-good bitch? Answer me right now. I demand to know," he yelled. "If you put me through this so you could have some sleazy affair, I'll get even. You'll regret the day you ran around on me. And don't think I'll forget. I'll make your life so miserable you'll wish you'd never been born. Your good life's gonna come to an end. I want to know the truth – now."

Catt feinted to avoid Norm's waving fist and tripped over a chair. She then appeared to faint dead away. As she fell, she cracked her wrist on the coffee table. It appeared to possibly be either sprained or broken. The wrist began to swell. Catt began to talk incoherently. Walter tried to help her up.

"You can finish your family discussion later. Right now we need to take your wife to the Lower Keys emergency room," Walter said. The patrolman helped get her into the patrol car. Norm followed in his own vehicle.

Catt continued to thrash and babble in the emergency room and talk about how she didn't want to go home. Each time Norm came in the room, she shrank back away from him. Her blood pressure soared, and she gasped for breath. The doctor finally sedated her and recommended she be admitted for observation until she seemed coherent again.

Walter left Norm at the hospital with his wife. He and the patrolman drove back to the police station. He called Hillary on the way.

"We had a very interesting meeting with the Knolls," Walter said. "When I arrived, Mrs. Knoll was little Miss Sunshine who was more likely to have spent the last three days on a tennis court rather than being tied up on a boat as a hostage. It was like she had never had a stressful moment in her life, but that changed when I told her that a woman and man had been spotted at the

Bight driving her car, *and* that people watching them had concluded the woman seemed to be a willing participant, *and* that the couple seemed to observers to know each other very well. Mrs. Knoll's husband went ballistic at that point and accused her of having an affair. He said he wasn't going to let her get away with it and almost threatened to divorce her. Then she became afraid of him, fell down, sprained her wrist, and began babbling bull-shit until we took her to the hospital. I don't know if it was an act or not, but she's in Lower Keys Medical Center for the night under observation."

"Almost sounds like she might have been on a controlled substance. I wish I'd been there," Hillary said.

"The thought of a happy-pill crossed my mind. The sudden mood swing makes me wonder even more. Like we both said, this whole case is beginning to smell like rancid fish."

"So what do we do now?" Hillary asked.

"Why don't you visit Mrs. Knoll at the hospital in the morning, and we'll decide after that. Let's see what's going to happen between her and her husband."

"But we still don't know who the mystery man or men are?"

"That's correct," said Walter, "but we may not be far from finding out."

CHAPTER 23

Captain Hillary went by Lower Keys Medical Center to visit Catt Knoll the following morning. As he took the elevator up to third floor and looked for room 315, he wondered what to expect. He had learned by now to expect the unexpected in his dealings with her. He gently rapped at her door and was granted admission. Catt was watching one of the morning television shows. They exchanged pleasantries, and he inquired about her condition. She said she would be going home later that morning. She seemed to want to keep him on small-talk as long as she possibly could. After several minutes of verbal dancing, Hillary cut to the chase.

"Chief Wanderley and I have been sharing notes on your case. There seem to be some discrepancies which have us both concerned."

Catt looked at him nervously but said nothing. Hillary sat silently waiting for her to speak. He was determined to say nothing until she spoke first. He thought he could almost hear the wheels turning in her brain as she debated with herself what to say. The bed creaked slightly as Catt nervously shifted her weight. Hillary patiently waited. After what seemed to Catt like an eternity, she finally broke the silence first.

"I may have misrepresented some of the facts in my case, but it wasn't my fault," Catt said. "I was forced to do so."

"We suspected that there was more to your case than what appeared on the surface," Hillary said. "Would you be more specific?"

"I come from a small, close-knit family," Catt said. "I was the oldest child. I have a brother, Paulie, who is four years my junior. I've always felt responsible for him. He works on a boat in Miami. They take people out snorkeling and diving on the reefs. The boats he's worked on take people down to the Bahamas. Paulie's had trouble making ends meet on what he makes. Several years ago, he met a local on Allens Cay in the Exumas who offered to sell him some marijuana and cocaine. He persuaded Paulie that the boat jobs gave him the perfect setup to sell drugs to the tourists and talked Paulie into selling marijuana to some of the tourists he meets through his work. It seemed like an easy way to make money since tourists sometimes asked Paulie where to buy drugs anyway. Things went along smoothly until some of the local dealers who were connected with the syndicate decided they didn't want to compete with Paulie. To make their point, some of them caught Paulie outside a bar and beat him up pretty badly. They broke several of Paulie's ribs and fractured his shoulder. He had to continue to work while he healed, however, and ended up becoming addicted to his pain medications."

"Did he get his pain medications through a licensed physician?" Hillary asked.

"Initially he did," Catt said, "but after he healed, his doctor wouldn't prescribe them for him anymore. By that time, he'd become addicted. That's when he began to buy his pills illegally from the dealers who had caused him to need the pills originally."

"So what happened next?" Hillary asked.

"Paulie's habit began to eat up all his income, and he began to buy drugs on credit," Catt said. "Before he knew it, he was in way over his head."

"Not uncommon."

"So Paulie came to me and told me his problem. He said these people were going to beat him up even worse if he didn't come up with the money he owed them. I told Norm what was going on and pleaded with him to help. He agreed to bail Paulie out one time but told me he would never do it again. If Paulie ever got back in trouble, he'd be on his own," Catt said.

"What does all this have to do with your abduction?"

"I'm leading up to that," Catt said. "Paulie called me last week. He said he had been laid off of the most recent boat he'd been working on and had no money coming in. On his last trip before he got laid off, the syndicate hired Paulie as a drug mule to bring in some cocaine. After the layoff since he no longer had an income, Paulie kept the dope and sold it himself. He told the syndicate that had had hidden the dope in some boat equipment but now couldn't recover it since he was no longer allowed on the dive boat and had had to give his key to their storage locker back. His syndicate contact called him a liar and told him they either wanted their coke or the street value of the drugs. Otherwise they would maim or kill him. Paulie called me for help. He said he needed $200,000. I told him Norm said he would never bail him out again. The next thing I know I've been kidnapped, and the kidnappers are asking my husband for $200,000."

"That's quite a story," said Hillary. "So who kidnapped you, the syndicate or your brother?"

"They were people my brother knew," Catt said, "but I didn't know that at the time. I only found out when Paulie came to see me at Garrison Bight."

"So the man you were seen being friendly with at the Bight was your brother?"

"That's right. You're not going to tell Norm are you?" Catt said with pleading eyes. "He'll never forgive me even though I wasn't part of the kidnap conspiracy. I only found out what was going on after the fact. I didn't want to get Paulie in trouble. He's my family. He's the only brother I've got. I don't even know for sure if he was part of the scheme, or if his friends were just trying to help him out. Paulie said things are going to be fine now, so I escaped so Norm wouldn't have to pay the ransom."

"This is all pretty far-fetched," Hillary said.

"I just didn't know what to do," Catt said. "You've got to help me. I wasn't completely truthful because I didn't want to get Paulie's friends in trouble. After all, their intentions were very honorable. They were just trying to help a friend who was in a jam and didn't know any other way to do it."

"Mrs. Knoll, I'm a law enforcement officer who has taken an oath to enforce the law. Laws have been broken here. I sympathize with your dilemma, but I can't become your accomplice. I have to report my findings to both my department and to your husband."

"But Norm'll kill me."

"There may be unpleasant consequences, but I don't think your husband is a murderer. Will you work with a sketch artist to try to come up with a picture? Laws have been broken."

"I don't know. I hate to get them in trouble for just trying to help Paulie," Catt said hesitantly.

"Would you rather they were in hot water, or would you rather it be you in trouble instead?"

Catt's face turned red. She almost stammered a reply, but nothing came out.

Hillary left Catt's room shaking his head in disbelief. As he walked down the hall, he ran into Norm Knoll.

"Mr. Knoll, may I have a few minutes of your time? Why don't we go down to the cafeteria for a cup of coffee?"

They took the elevator down to the first floor. Hillary put some money in the honor-system bucket by the food line. They each got a cup of coffee out of the machine and took a table in the far corner. Since it was mid morning, they had the cafeteria to themselves.

"What can I do for you?" Norm asked.

"Mr. Knoll, does your wife have a brother named Paulie?"

"Yes, she does. Paulie Lopez. He's younger. Her only brother. Is he involved in this?"

"Have either of you had to intercede on his behalf in the past?" Hillary asked.

"He had some debts a few years ago which he couldn't manage. I helped him pay back the money he owed."

"Would you mind being more specific?"

Norm then told Hillary pretty much the same story Catt had told him in the hospital room.

"What's this got to do with my wife's current situation?" Norm asked.

Hillary repeated what Catt had told him.

"That worthless son of a bitch was behind this! I thought he'd finally gone straight. I'll nail his sorry ass to the cross this time. I'll prosecute to the limit. I don't care who he is," Norm said loudly. The Cuban food service worker looked at them with a startled expression.

Hillary grabbed Norm's arm. "Calm down. She didn't say Paulie instigated the kidnapping. She just said it was done for his benefit."

"Then go get the sorry mother-fucker and make him tell you who these jerk-wads are," said Norm.

"It's not that simple. These people aren't local. She said they are all from Miami."

"Then extradite them back or whatever it is you do to people. One of his Miami running mates moved to Key West. I understand he works somewhere on Duval Street."

"What kind of work? Work on a boat?"

"No. Bartender, I'm told."

"Do you know where?"

"Rick's, I think," Norm said. "I never had anything to do with the sleazebag. I just know he came down from Miami, and every time Paulie comes to see us, he also looks this guy up as well."

"You ever hear a name?"

"I even saw him once. I think Paulie called him Raydel. A muscle man – steroid freak - works out with weights."

"Since the only identity we have is your wife's brother, I'd like to get her to work with a police sketch artist so we can get an idea of what the perps look like."

"I'll tell her to. I'll tell her to cooperate or else. I can't believe her shitty family put me through this."

"Does she have other family in the area?" Hillary asked.

"Her parents are still in Cuba."

"I didn't realize she was Cuban," Hillary said.

"What the hell do you think Paulie stands for? Norm said. "Pablo, that's what. Catt's maiden name was Lopez."

"Thanks, Mr. Knoll. You've been a big help. I'll keep you posted as matters develop."

As they left the cafeteria, Hillary heard Norm mumbling to himself, "If my wife's going behind my back to help that sorry brother, oh, is she gonna pay."

Hillary pretended he hadn't overheard this comment.

CHAPTER 24

"Do you enjoy escapist fiction?" Captain Hillary said as he sat in front of Chief Wanderley and took his first sip of a cup of coffee.

"On occasion." Walter said. "Now let me guess the story line. A tornado picks Mrs. Knoll up and transports her to the Land of Oz along with her little dog, and she keeps saying 'I want to go home.' Did I get the plot right?"

"Close, except she doesn't have a dog," Hillary said, "but she could credibly star in a fantasy story. Our latest version of her abduction involves Mrs. Knoll's baby brother, Paulie. Paulie is a ne'er-do-well deckhand or something who lives in Miami."

"Some of the loveliest people I've ever met seem to come from Miami," Walter said sarcastically.

"Well, Paulie wasn't exactly a model citizen. He supplemented his meager income by bringing dope up from the Bahamas and was selling it as an independent until the local dealers informed him that Florida is not a right-to-work state for drug peddlers. They had a serious discussion with Paulie which resulted in his admission to the hospital. Paulie then became addicted to his pain medication. Of course, the syndicate was sympathetic and provided him with the pills at street price. When Paulie's debts became so massive that he can't keep the syndicate current, Mrs. Knoll convinced her husband to bail him out, and Mr. Knoll agreed to do it on a one-time basis."

"This is getting good. I take it once wasn't enough?"

"You're warm," Hillary said. "They then began to use Paulie as a drug mule in exchange for future pills. He picked up drugs for them on his trips to the

Bahamas and brought the drugs back in on whatever boat currently employed him. But then Mr. Paulie managed to get himself laid off."

"He got caught?"

"I don't think so. She never made that quite clear. I think he may have just been a marginal deckhand, but for whatever the reason, he lost his job. Paulie continued to have monetary obligations so, being the Einstein that he apparently is; he stole his last drug shipment and sold it himself on the street. He told the syndicate boys that the drugs on were either on the boat or in the boat-owner's office or warehouse, but he now couldn't recover them since he had lost his boat and office privileges. He said he no longer had access to the keys to anything."

"I'm sure his associates bought that story lock, stock, and barrel."

"Not exactly. They told him they either wanted their drugs or their street value. Paulie called his sister, Mrs. Knoll, for help, but she was afraid to ask her husband for the money."

"And what he needed to get slick just happens to be $200,000?" Walter asked.

"Gee! How did you ever come up with that number?" Hillary said and smiled. "Now I know why you make the big bucks as big chief conch-blower. This is where the story gets foggy. According to Mrs. Knoll, the next thing she knows, she's been kidnapped by mystery men who she later learns are her brother's sympathetic, dumb-ass friends who want to come to his aid, and they ask for ... ta ta ... $200,000."

"Oh, give me a break!"

"I ain't finished yet. Mrs. Knoll met with her scum-bum brother and mistakenly inferred from their conversation that he had his problems under control and would be OK going forward. So she decided to save her husband's money and escaped at her first opportunity."

"You're right. This woman left Kansas behind and took off for Fantasyland a long time ago."

"Since interviewing Mrs. Knoll, I met with the husband. He confirmed the part of the story where he had bailed his sorry brother-in-law out who he said had sworn never get in trouble again. He then accidentally told me something I didn't know about Mrs. Knoll – she's Cuban and her parents are still alive."

"I guess that explains some of the closeness Mrs. Knoll has with her brother. Cubans often come from tight-knit families," Walter said. "Did you tell Mr. Knoll what you learned from his wife?"

"Not entirely. I saw no reason to tell him everything we know at this point."

"I agree. Is she going to cooperate with us in identifying her abductors?"

"I honestly don't know."

"I'd sure like to be a fly on the wall when this stink-bomb drops on the Knoll household."

"Mrs. Knoll seems *very* worried about that issue as well," Hillary said.

"Why don't I try to see if she'll cooperate with a police department sketch artist?"

"Can't hurt," Hillary said. "I tried to impress upon her that she's broken laws herself and could be held accountable."

"Good. By the time I talk to her, she ought to have had time to think about that issue. I'll re-emphasize her liability as well. I'm sure Mrs. Knoll's husband should also pressure her to cooperate, and she can't very well refuse without coming completely clean with him."

"I agree. Keep me posted. Not bad coffee here, by the way. Not as good as at the sheriff's department, but not bad."

"We try," Walter said.

CHAPTER 25

Narley Gristle saw his window of opportunity to safely cross US1 and peddled vigorously over it onto Palm Avenue. As usual, his elaborately-decorated three-wheel tricycle attracted attention, and he could see the people driving on US1 poking their passengers as they nodded or pointed in his direction. The stereo speakers on his bike broadcast Barry Cuda's cover medley of Fats Domino's *Hello Josephine*. He smiled back at the drivers or pedestrians who made eye contact. Narley loved spring in Key West. Whereas the hustle and bustle from the tourists irritated some locals, it invigorated Narley and made him feel alive. He also loved the eighties temperatures and lower than usual humidity that was a product of still being in the dry season. He knew when this period was over they would be into the wet-season, steamy, nineties temps which would not subside again until October. Also making Narley feel good was enjoying the company of one of his young granddaughters, Carroll Anne, who he was babysitting that morning. Carroll Anne was in the passenger seat behind him. She was thrilled to be on an outing with her grandfather.

Once across the highway, Narley slowed his bike and peddled leisurely toward Garrison Bight. By this time Barry was singing *Rockin' Pneumonia*, the second half of the medley. Narley veered off the main street into the long, thin parking lot adjacent to the Palm Avenue Causeway. Dan Hillary heard Narley approaching. By this time, Barry Cuda was singing another Fats Domino tune, *I'm Walkin'*. Hillary had ridden down to Old Town looking for Narley, and when he didn't find him there, took a chance on catching up with him at the Bight. Each man waved as he recognized the other.

"Good morning, Captain Hillary," Narley said as he braked his bike. "I'd like to introduce you to my granddaughter. Carroll Anne, say hello to Captain Hillary. To what do I owe the pleasure of a second visit from the sheriff's department in such a short period of time?"

"I was hoping you might clarify a certain matter for me," Hillary said.

"I'll certainly try, but before I do, would you mind if Carroll Anne and I eat the fried chicken sandwiches I just picked up at Dunkin' Donuts while they're still hot. I also bought a dozen fresh donuts. May I offer you one?" said Narley.

"Don't mind if I do," said Hillary. "I guess you know we cops have a legendary weakness for donuts. By the way, who was that you were playing on your bike as you drove up?"

"That was Key West icon Barry Cuda. He gave me a couple of his CD's. One day I was riding down Greene Street and saw Barry rolling his piano towards Sloppy Joe's. He had his hands full with it so I asked him if I could help him bring the rest of his things on my bike. When we got to Sloppy's, he gave me two CD's as a thank-you. Nice guy. Now he always waves at me when he sees me, and I help him whenever I can."

"Don't you like how the locals still look out for one another in this town?" commented Hillary.

"That's partially why we still call it paradise," Narley said. "Now what can I do to help our finest today?"

"I have two pictures and a drawing I'd like you to look at," Hillary said. "Are either of the men the person you saw with this woman. She's the owner of the Beemer which stayed parked here for several days?"

Hillary showed Narley a picture of Catt and then one of her brother, Paulie. His picture had been taken by the Miami-Dade sheriff's department when Paulie had gotten in some trouble a few years earlier.

"I don't think I've seen him before," Narley said after he examined it.

"What about this person?" Hillary showed Narley the police sketch which Catt had assisted the artist to draw.

"Now this one's looking somewhat more familiar," Narley said. "The two pictures aren't the same person are they?"

"Not to my knowledge."

Narley finished his sandwich and wiped his mouth on a napkin. "Would you mind sitting here for a few minutes with Carroll Anne while I do something? Have another doughnut while you're waiting."

"May I have a doughnut too?" Carroll Anne asked her grandfather.

"Of course you can," said Narley. "I bought these sweets for my sweet. Just don't eat them all. Granddaddy don't want to have to explain that to your mother when she gets back."

Narley took the three pictures and walked down the dock. He came to a permanently moored houseboat. It had hanging baskets all around the awning-covered deck. A large chainsaw-carved pelican fashioned from a palm tree trunk and some lawn chairs sat on the deck. Narley shouted, "Permission to come aboard."

The occupant inside the cabin shouted back, "Come on aboard, Narley." Narley opened the door and disappeared into the interior of the boat. He vanished for between five and ten minutes before he opened the door and came back out onto the deck. He called out, "Thanks, dear thing," to the person in the interior. "You've been a wonderful help."

Narley walked down a couple of slips and repeated the process. Hillary could hear him say, "You're a good man" as he stepped back onto the dock afterwards from the second boat. He began to walk back towards Hillary and Carroll Anne.

"I thought so," he said as he walked.

"Who's this drawing supposed to be?" Narley asked Hillary after he sat down again.

"I don't know. That's what we're trying to find out. Just who it is."

"Well, both the people I talked to agree it looks like Raydel Medina. Been a sometime, on-again-off-again Bight resident. Cuban guy. Big steroid-looking guy – weight lifter. That was my first impression too when I looked at it, but I wanted another opinion before I said anything which might cause Raydel problems."

Hillary perked up at the mention of the name Raydel Medina but didn't let on his recognition to Narley.

The second time that name's come up – once with Norm Knoll and now with Narley.

"What do you know about this Raydel?" Hillary asked.

"Lives down here from time to time," Narley said. "Never owned anything. Doesn't have that kind of money. Probably never will. The kind of person who wants to big-shot when he's flush. But he's rented houseboats from time to time, and I think has lived with ... and maybe off of ... some women here as well. I think he's kind of volatile. You know, beats some women up every once in a while. Thinks he's a stud. I understand some women get turned on by the muscle-man type."

"Does he live down here right now?"

"I think he might be."

"Was he seen with this woman?"

"Both people said they think this was the woman they saw him with. The two-some stood out because they seemed unusually lovey-dovey."

"Hmm! Does Raydel work?"

"I think he might work at Rick's on Duval," Narley said.

"Do you know if he's ever been arrested?"

"I honestly wouldn't know."

"Thanks my friend. You've been a big help," Hillary said. "And before I forget, you have a lovely granddaughter."

Both Narley and Carroll Anne beamed at the compliment.

"Yeah, I do. I'm a lucky man," Narley said as he gave Carroll Anne a big hug. "Now, young lady, you ready to keep on exploring with granddad?" She nodded enthusiastically.

Narley loaded her back into his trike's passenger seat and drove away. Frogman Henry's *Ain't Got No Home* was playing on the bike stereo.

Yes, you do, Hillary thought. *Young lady, you've got a good home and a good family to boot. A lot of people would trade places with you. I'm sorry they broke the mold when they made your grandfather. Really too bad. We could use more like him.*

CHAPTER 26

Captain Hillary decided to follow up on the information he had gotten from Narley Gristle and see if he could locate Raydel Medina. First he placed a courtesy phone call to Chief Wanderley.

"Walter, it looks like the drawing your man drew in the Knoll case may have produced results. I got a lead when I showed it to Narley Gristle."

He then went on to explain what he had learned from Gristle.

"I'll follow up and see if Medina still works at Rick's," Hillary said.

"I wish you luck, my friend," Walter said. "Anything I can do to help?'

"At the moment, I don't think so," said Hillary, "but if something comes up, I'll give you a shout."

Rick's Bar at 202 Duval Street is Key West's largest entertainment complex and features eight different venues under one roof. To many, it is the heart of the Key West party zone. Different bars cater to different clienteles – from acoustic tropical rock in Rick's Downstairs to loud live hard-rock in Durty Harry's to DJ.s spinning dance music in Rick's Upstairs.

Hillary walked in and asked to speak someone in management.

"I think the manager went up to the Crow's Nest," the waitress said. "Go on up and ask someone for Mr. Harrington."

Hillary thanked the waitress and headed up. The Crow's Nest was an upper deck bar which overlooked the wild crowd below it in Durty Harry's. It gave its patrons a bird's eye view of Durty Harry's live rock band each evening. This time of day it was quiet and mostly empty since there was no entertainment going on below. He saw a man he estimated to be in either his late thirties or early forties talking to a bartender. He took a chance that it was Mr. Harrington.

"Mr. Harrington?" Hillary said. "Captain Dan Hillary, Monroe County Sheriff's Department. May I have a moment of your time?"

Harrington immediately became mildly defensive. "Is there something wrong, Captain?"

"No, not at all," Hillary said. "I just need some information. May I talk to you in private?"

"Is that table over there private enough?" Harrington pointed to a table in the corner. "May I give you a complimentary beverage?"

"Yes, that'd be fine," Hillary said, "and yes, a diet Coke would taste wonderful."

The bartender drew a fountain diet Coke for Hillary. He and Harrington walked over to the table.

"Do you have an employee by the name of Raydel Medina?" Hillary asked.

"Yes, as a matter of fact, we do," Harrington answered. "Has he done something illegal? Is there an immigration issue? I know he's Cuban, but I know for a fact he's not an illegal."

"No, nothing like that," Hillary said. "We just think he may have some information which might help us on another matter we're involved in."

"Well, he's a bartender in The Red Garter ... that's our adult entertainment lounge. As a matter of fact, he's on his shift right now."

"Would you introduce me to him and give him a coffee break for a few minutes so I can talk to him privately."

"Certainly. We pride ourselves in cooperating with law enforcement. You sure there's no problem?"

"Not at this juncture. I just need him to help me

clear up a matter."

Harrington took Hillary into The Red Garter and introduced him to Medina. The muscle-bound Medina looked uneasy as he motioned Hillary to a table by the wall. He reminded Hillary more of a bouncer than a bartender.

"Do you know a woman by the name of Catterina Knoll?" Hillary asked.

"Don't ring a bell with me," Medina said without pause.

"Are you sure?" Hillary said. "I've got reports that you were seen with her on Garrison Bight."

"Positive. I don't know nobody by that name. Besides that, I haven't been over to the Bight in weeks."

"Here's a drawing made by a police photographer from descriptions given by people on the Bight," Hillary said. "I'd say it has a striking resemblance to you, don't you think?"

"That could be a lot of people."

"Would this picture help your memory?" Hillary said as he produced Catt's photo. Raydel looked at it hurriedly before sliding it back to Hillary.

"This lady drives a blue BMW. Witnesses say they saw both you and her driving it and walking around the parking lot holding hands," said Hillary.

Raydel was silent.

"Another witness says he saw you two eating burgers at the Burger King on North Roosevelt."

"OK, so I know her," Raydel said. "She told me her name was Kimberley. I met her in the bar. There's no crime in picking up a girl in a bar, is there?"

"No crime in picking up a girl," Hillary said, "but there is something wrong when that girl goes missing."

"I didn't do nothin' to that girl. I was nothin' but good to her. She's the one who was hot- to-trot for my bod. Ain't nothin' wrong with getting a piece as ass from an adult, is there? You know, two consenting adults and all that jazz."

'Like I said, people are free to have affairs, but this girl was seen in your company after she'd been reported to be kidnapped. Her husband is looking to press charges against someone."

Raydel was starting to sweat. "She didn't tell me she was married."

"This could get very sticky if you can't tell me something to convince me and her husband that we're wrong in what we're assuming. Do you know what the penalty for kidnapping is? People get sent away for a long, long time, and Starke is no country club. More often than not, people leave there in a box. I'd hate to risk Starke if I didn't deserve it."

Raydel fidgeted and mashed his fist into his open palm. Hillary said nothing more. He just let the silence envelop Raydel like a woolen blanket.

Finally Raydel spoke hesitantly.

"OK, I'm gunna to level with you. Her name wadn't Kimberley. I've known all along who she is. You see, I'm a friend of her brother, Paulie's. He lives in Miami. We used to work on a boat together, and Paulie occasionally sold some controlled substances. I didn't ... I'm clean ... He did. Well, Paulie got in some trouble ... you know ... trying to compete with the cartel. They don't like that ... Then Paulie got in too deep ... I don't know why I'm tellin' you all this."

"Because you don't want to take the fall for something Paulie might have done," Hillary reminded him.

"Well, Paulie started branging in drugs for the cartel from the Bahamas ... tryin' to get square with them. Then he lost his job and couldn't do that no more. But he still owed them money. And he wanted to get his parents out of Cuba. His sister went to her husband to get the money ... $10,000 passage fee each ... and he wouldn't give it to her. So her and Paulie decided to solve two problems at the same time. The cartel agreed to help Paulie come up with the money for a boat if he'd use it to brang drugs in for them until they was paid back. They'd get their money back for the boat plus the vig and also the other money he owed 'em. Paulie'd get a boat. You know ... I win, you win ... everybody wins. His sister was still beatin' him up about gettin' their parents out of Cuba so the cartel agreed that on the first run Pauli could pick 'em up, and then after that voyage, he'd start to move merchandise. But Paulie didn't have the money for his half of the boat. So's he and his sister decide to pretend like she's been kidnapped, so's he can get the money he needs out of her husband. He says the husband got money so he'll never know the difference. He come to me and asked me if his sister can live with me a few days. I says sure. Why not? So's she moves in. But then she and me find out we get along pretty good with each other. You know ... that man and woman thing. She likes my bod."

He flexed his muscles and poked his index finger into his fist.

"So's next thing I know we're in the sack together. I didn't kidnap nobody; I just gave a friend's sister a place to crash for a few nights. That ain't a crime, is it?"

"Have you ever heard of being an accessory?" Hillary asked.

"No. I ain't no accessory. I didn't find out until later what they's up to."

"It's not my job to argue that point. My job is to uncover the truth," Hillary said. "Thanks for giving me some fresh insight into this situation. I won't forget that you've been very helpful in helping me clarify this muddled picture."

"I do got evidence which will clear me, but Catt

don't know nothin' about it, and I got it hid where nobody else can find it," Raydel said as Hillary was leaving. "Paulie may be my friend, but he ain't a good enough friend to go down for. And his sister sure as hell ain't."

"And may I ask what that evidence is?" Hillary asked.

"You can ask all you want, but I'm going to keep it secret in case I need it."

CHAPTER 27

"Oh, what a tangled web we weave when we practice to deceive," Captain Hillary said when Walter Wanderley picked up his phone.

"Ah, words of wisdom from another notable Walter," Walter Wanderley responded, "Sir Walter Scott. I presume you are quoting him for a reason."

Hillary then brought Chief Wanderley up to date on the Knoll affair.

"You got any thoughts on this whole thing?" Hillary asked.

"No, you just hit me cold with it, and I need to think it through," Walter said. "But that explains one thing I forgot to tell you about. We told Mrs. Knoll that the polygraph had had a problem the first time it was administered to her and convinced her to take it again. Well, she flunked it the second time as well."

"As Jim Nabors used to say on Gomer Pyle, 'Surprise, surprise, surprise!'. We both certainly now know why," Hillary said.

"And as Ray Stevens used to say, 'Yeah, we do.' Since you're on a roll, why don't you go back to Mrs. Knoll with this latest revelation," Walter said. "I think it's time you got tougher and more specific."

Hillary made an appointment with the Knolls.

Hillary began by asking Mrs. Knoll if she had recovered from her ordeal. She responded that she was getting better each day. He then asked if she had recalled any additional facts since his last interview with her which could further help in apprehending a suspect. She shook her head. Norm quietly let his wife lead the conversation.

"Just to help insure that I have the events clear in

my head, may I summarize and encapsulate our conversations thus far?" Hillary began. "You originally stated you had been abducted from Ben Franklin's and forced to drive to Garrison Bight. At Garrison Bight you were forced to call your husband and demand a ransom. When things did not move forward at the speed your abductors wished, you were then sexually abused. You said you willing participated because you feared for your life. You described your abductors as swarthy and average looking. You subsequently failed to be able to identify your abductors from pictures of known felons. Finally you failed to pass a polygraph test given to try to verify your reports."

He paused and let his synopsis sink in with both the Knolls.

"Now let's move on to your next report in which you said fear led you to misrepresent facts in your initial interview. In this version of events your brother Paulie became involved with some unsavory people in Miami and needed your assistance. Your husband did not agree to help Paulie solve his problems so some of his well-meaning friends abducted you to try to raise money to help Paulie out of his jam. The kidnappers had no intention of harming you and only wanted to pressure your husband to help Paulie, but you didn't know that at the time they made you call and demand a ransom. And then when you did learn the truth, instead being an accomplice to the fraud, you ran away and returned home to your husband. Another reason you gave for distorting facts in your first interview was that you felt the need to protect your younger sibling. Once again a second polygraph test failed to validate your story."

He paused again. Neither Knoll said a word.

"Now, let me move forward once more. We've been conducting some interviews of our own. The first was with residents of Garrison Bight. They reported seeing a woman answering your description with a man. They identified you as being the woman in a photo we showed them. The man, however, did not answer the description you gave in your first interview. He was not an average looking man but one who had the physique of a body builder. They were able to identify him as a sometimes Bight resident and said his facial features resembled the drawing you made up with the police artist. We were able to locate this person and interview him."

Catt was beginning to look uncomfortable and stare at the floor. Norm looked as if he would explode at any moment. Both remained silent, but Norm flashed hateful looks at his wife. Each time he looked at her, she refused to make eye contact.

"This individual had a different recollection of the events surrounding your abduction. His version of Paulie's problems more or less concurred with your story, but then the tales part ways. According to this person, while you and Paulie both had overlapping agendas, you each had different priorities. He says Paulie had indeed had problems with drug abuse. And he had indeed sold drugs illegally. And yes, he had problems with the cartel. This agrees with what you told me at the hospital. But then the stories diverge. He says you wanted to get your parents out of Cuba, that you had tried to get your husband to pay for their passage over, but Mr. Knoll refused. You and Paulie then came up with a plan, which would not only get your parents into the country but would solve Paulie's problems with the cartel at the same time. He would enter into a partnership with the cartel to buy a boat. They would give him the down payment on the boat and in return, Paulie would use the boat to haul illegal narcotics for them. As a bonus, they would look the other way as he used the boat to transport your parents to the U.S. But Paulie couldn't come up with his part of the money for the boat, and you knew your husband probably wouldn't lend it to him. So you and Paulie decided to get the money with a phony kidnapping scheme. This guy says Paulie sequestered you on his houseboat to give you a place to live for the duration of scheme."

Catt was looking more and more like she had her foot caught in a mousetrap. Norm was turning redder by the minute.

"Is this version accurate so far?" Hillary asked. "Shall I continue? Do you have anything you wish to contribute or confess?"

Catt was quiet so Hillary continued.

"Then some unexpected things happened. First, after you moved onto the houseboat, you found you were actually attracted to Paulie's friend and that the feeling was mutual. The other unexpected event was that the ransom money was not delivered as planned but was picked up by an anonymous party. Your husband couldn't amass that much money a second time so, unaware that the money had been recovered, you and Paulie decided to throw in the towel – scrap the plan – and you would return home, pretending you had escaped from your abductors."

By this time Norm was standing, glaring hatefully at his wife. "I can't believe you'd..." He couldn't finish his statement and walked from the room.

"You're wrong – he's lying – you can't prove any of this," Catt said as she sobbed. "They're lying because I wouldn't go along with them."

"But we've got other people collaborating parts of the story, people who saw the two of you holding hands in the Bight parking lot and having lunch together in Key West," Hillary said. "We'll be getting official statements from them. Are you sure you don't want to be truthful with us now?"

"I didn't! I swear I didn't!" Catt said. "I swear I was kidnapped. I wasn't part of the plot. I was the victim ... just like I told you."

"One person says he has hard evidence contradicting that assertion that he's willing to turn over to us," Hillary said, continuing to pressure Catt.

Norm walked back into the room. "I warned you about that sorry, good-for-nothing brother of yours. I told him I was through with him. And of course, I'm not going to participate in illegally smuggling your parents into this country. Catt, I told you and I meant it, I'm not going to risk everything I've worked so hard for by getting involved in illegal harebrained schemes with that brain-dead brother of yours. God-damn it Catt, why would you do this to me? I warned you ... I warned you to stay away from that worthless brother. He's no damned good ... I'll divorce you ... God-damn it woman, how could you do this to me?"

"But I didn't, darling," Catt screamed. "You've got to believe me. This is all made up. They can't prove a thing. Who are you going to believe, your wife or other people?"

"Sounds like they've made a pretty damned good case," Norm said. "I'll get you for this, Catt. I swear, I *will* get even."

Hillary thought for a moment Norm was getting ready to lunge at his wife. He involuntarily put his hand on Norm's forearm.

"Do you wish to make a statement, Mrs. Knoll?" Hillary asked.

"Of course not," Catt screamed. "It's lies. It's all made-up lies."

"I'll be back to you," Hillary said as he let himself out the front door. "It's better all around if you have something to disclose that you do it in a voluntary statement. Under Section 837.05 of the Florida Statutes, giving false information to law enforcement is a third degree felony punishable up to five years in prison. Do you want to risk serving time in prison and then be classified as a felon for the rest of your life?"

Norm grabbed his car keys and headed out of the house.

"Where are you going?" Catt asked.

"I don't know," Norm said.

"When'll you be back?" Catt asked.

"I don't know that either. I may not come back."

"Norm, you've got to believe..."

Norm slammed the door before she could finish. Catt immediately called Paulie.

CHAPTER 28

"Wanna to go to Dade County with me?" Captain Hillary asked.

"If you're asking me for a date, I'd better clear it with my wife first," Walter Wanderley said.

"I hope to have a date all right," Hillary said with a laugh, "but not with you. I'm hoping my date will be with Mrs. Knoll's brother, Paulie Lopez. By the way, I think I've worn out my welcome at her house."

Hillary then told Walter on a blow-by-blow basis what had happened on his last interview with Catt Knoll.

"My mama told me a long time ago that the only people mad at you for speaking the truth are those living a lie," Walter said. "I wouldn't have guessed Mrs. Knoll's motivation to bring her folks into the country. This case is like peeling a banana. If we keep peeling, we'll get to the fruit."

"And it looks more and more like this fruit's gonna to be rotten," Dan said. "She still refuses to admit that she was an accessory to this crime. I told her I'd get to the bottom of it with or without her help, and I intend to do it."

"Go for it," Walter said. "Do you have Paulie's address in Miami?"

"I think so."

"When are you driving up?"

"First thing in the morning," Hillary said. "If I have to run all over town to chase him down, I'd like to have as much day as possible to do so. Besides, today before I go, I need to make a courtesy call to the Miami-Dade sheriff's office to let 'em know I'll be doing some investigative work in their area."

Captain Hillary drove to Miami the following morning. He got Paulie's last-known address from the Miami-Dade Sheriff's Department. The trip was largely uneventful except for a close call by a pedestrian at mile marker 99.6 in Key Largo. He saw a pedestrian crossing US1 from a hotel almost get hit by a motorcycle traveling north on the Overseas Highway.

Now I understand what all the controversy is about with this crosswalk, he thought. *FDOT really should probably change these yellow blinking lights to red ones.*

The address given to Hillary was 107 Grand Avenue in Coconut Grove. He had no problem finding the house. It was a small, one-level, 1930ish yellow, wooden, clapboard-sided, shotgun house nestled on a small lot between identical peach and lime-green shotgun houses. The house was built on one-foot-high brick piers instead on a concrete slab. It had a small unscreened porch and window-unit air conditioners hanging out of every side window. Hillary thought it looked like so many other old houses he had seen over the years.

Probably doesn't rent for much up here in the Grove, but houses like this are dear in Old Town Key West. Location, location, location, he thought to himself.

There was no sign of anyone being home. He walked up the irregular brick walkway onto the bare porch and knocked on the door. As he expected, there was no answer.

On the porch of the peach-colored house next door, Hillary saw a man in a white tank-top and faded gym shorts weaving palm fronds. He was sitting on an aluminum-framed lawn chair. The sagging nylon webbing was frayed and almost broken in places. He had a solid snow-white goatee and long bushy white sideburns protruding from a topless palm-frond hat. His tanned scalp showed through his thinning hair. He was tapping a sandaled foot to Captain Harry's *Bahama Breeze* which was playing on a boom-box he had set on the two-by-four railing. Next to him were a pile of palm fronds. Behind him was a rusty grocery cart containing more supplies. On the floor were several hats and bowls he had obviously completed that morning. He shouted at Hillary as his fingers continued to work the fronds, "You looking for Paulie?"

"Yes," Hillary said, "I am. Is this where he lives?"

"Yep," said the man. "Haven't seen him for a couple of days."

"Has he been gone?" Hillary asked.

"Dunno. I just live next door."

"Do you know him very well?"

"Just enough to speak," said the palm weaver, "but he might be gone on a trip. Saw somebody pick him up, and he had a carrying-bag in his hand. He might be out on a boat. He works on a dive-boat, you know."

"When did he get picked up?"

"Dunno. Yesterday, I think."

Hillary thanked the man for his help and gave him a business card. He then walked over to the lime-green house and rang the front door bell. A thin woman with a paint brush in her hand came to the door. He judged her to be either in her late twenties or early thirties. Her shoulder-length brunette hair was in a plethora of natural unkempt curls. She was barefoot and wore a midi-length, blue, flowered sun dress.

"May I help you?" she said with a little uncertainty in her voice.

Hillary identified himself as a Monroe County sheriff's detective and asked if he could come in. The woman told him her name was Eileen Hudson as she ushered him into her small, rustic living room. An easel was set up and had a partially completed bright pastel tropical painting on it. It was obvious she had been working on it when Hillary had rung the bell. Hillary asked her about Paulie.

"I don't know him very well," Eileen said, "and I try to keep my distance from him."

"Any particular reason?"

"Why do you ask? Is he in trouble?"

"No," Hillary said. "He's just someone who we think might be able to give us some information on a case we're working on."

"And you came all the way up from Key West?" Eileen mused. "It must be important."

"Back to Mr. Lopez," Hillary said. "What can you tell me about him?"

"At first I just thought he wasn't my type, you know, loud ... coarse and vulgar ... Latin. I live a low-key life. I'm not a partier. My main interest is my art. But then ... I don't want to cause him trouble ... there was something more. He had an inordinate amount of traffic coming and going. People who seemed to be party types or sometimes not the most savory ... I had a feeling there was more going on than what I saw ... I probably shouldn't be telling you this since I have nothing concrete to base my assumptions on, but I began to be concerned about having him as a neighbor. I came down from New York to try to get away from disreputable people."

"You're wise to be observant," Hillary said. "Have you seen Mr. Lopez recently?"

"Not for the last day or so. I just heard some big-talking going on between him and this large muscular man which led me to believe they had some big deal going together."

Hillary gave Eileen Hudson his card and asked her to call him if she thought of anything new or if she saw

Paulie again.

Hillary's next stop was the Miami Beach Marina where Paulie's former employer, Wreckreational Divers, docked its dive boat. He made an inquiry at the marina office as to the Wreckrational's owner's name. Fortunately for him, the boat was not out at sea.

"Mr. Seasless, I'm Captain Dan Hillary, and a detective with the Monroe County Sheriff's Department May I have a moment of your time?"

"Monroe County. That's a first," Seasless said. "What could I have possibly done to offend you boys? By the way, just call me Buster."

"Not a thing," Hillary said. "I just need to ask you about one of your former employees. By the way, Wreckreational Divers. Very imaginative name."

"Beats the hell out of Seasless Diving," Buster said with a laugh.

"I see your point."

"Now, who's of interest to the Monroe County Sheriff's Department?"

"Paulie Lopez. Do you know where I might find him?"

"I just had to let Paulie go," Buster said.

"Do you mind if I ask why?"

"He misrepresented himself to me when I hired him. He told me he was rated by PADI as a Master Scuba Diver and that he'd passed six specialty diver courses. He said he didn't have the paperwork, but he'd get it for me. I bugged him for months about the issue, but he always had some excuse. So I investigated myself and found out that he was only certified by PADI as an Open Water Diver and had no specialty certifications whatsoever. Do you know what my insurance company would've done to me if they had found out? Can you imagine the liability if a paying customer had either gotten hurt or killed, and that fact had come to light? I'd be out of business, my friend. So as soon as I found out he was a bald-faced liar, I ran his butt off. I also spread the word around the dock with some of the other owners so he wouldn't show up and bag one of them. I also told PADI he was misrepresenting himself."

"Do you know where he is now?"

"Don't know and don't give a damn. I hate a goddamned liar. But I can tell you this; he probably won't find a job on any dive boats around here again unless he gets his shit together. We're a pretty small close-knit community, and I can guarantee you, his sorry little ass is blackballed. Besides that, I didn't like the looks of some of the people I saw him hanging around with. In fact, you aren't the first one down here looking for him the last few days. Some scurvy looking wetback came by here a few days ago asking about Paulie. I'm positive he was carrying a concealed pistol. Got kind of shitty with me when I told him I didn't know where Paulie was and didn't want to know."

"Thanks for your help, Buster. If more industries took self-regulation seriously, life'd be easier on all of us."

After stops at a few more marinas, Hillary gave up looking for Paulie's new employer. Paulie didn't seem to be working any of the boats in the area.

After learning the name of the Paulie's landlord, Dan and the landlord returned to the Grand Avenue rental house. The landlord let him in. There were no clothes in the closet, and the bathroom had been stripped of Paulie's personal effects.

Paulie seemed to have vanished.

CHAPTER 29

Dan Hillary was disappointed about his lack of results in Miami but not totally surprised by Paulie Lopez's apparent flight.

At least, he thought, as he drove back, *I may have proven Paulie has reason to feel guilty about something.*

He had confirmed with Paulie's landlord that the rent was not past due, confirming it was not an eviction issue resulting from Paulie's unemployment.

And he didn't even bother to get his deposit back, Hillary thought. *If I had cash-flow problems from being unemployed, I wouldn't have left that money sitting on the table. He must have really been in a hurry to clear out – like he knew someone might be looking for him. I wonder if someone gave him a tip that he might be in trouble.*

Hillary decided his next mission when he got back home would be to revisit Raydel Medina. Unfortunately, it was so late when he returned. He had to defer this investigation until the following day. He decided he would pop in unannounced at Rick's during Raydel's normal shift for the follow-up conversation. He hoped Raydel would give him what he needed once and for all so he could prove Catt Knoll's complicity in her own abduction.

Hillary entered Rick's and headed for The Red Garter. Mr. Harrington saw him come in.

"Good afternoon, Captain Hillary," Harrington said pleasantly. "Back to see Raydel again?"

"As a matter of fact, I am," Hillary said. "I promise to make it as brief and unobtrusive as possible. I just need to clarify some of the items we discussed the other day."

"Oh, I don't mind," Harrington said, "but he's not

here."

"Isn't he supposed to be on shift right now?" Hillary asked.

"Yes, normally he is, but we haven't seen him today or yesterday. Haven't heard from him either. I'll walk up to The Red Garter with you, and we'll see if he communicated with one of the other employees."

When they entered The Red Garter, Harrington motioned one of the waitresses over.

"Rachel, have you heard from Raydel today?"

"Not a word, and Zach's bitching because he's having to hold down the bar all by himself again. It's not busy now, but when things pick up later, he's going to need some help."

"Let me see who I can get up here," Harrington said.

"When you saw Raydel last, did he indicate that he might need some time off?" Hillary asked. "Was he sick or anything?"

"No, everything seemed to be fine until towards the end of his shift when some friend of his showed up. The guy was drinking draft beer at the far end of the bar, and they were talking. Seemed to know each other pretty well. I'm not sure what they were saying, but Raydel got a little agitated a couple of times. I assumed they were planning to go out barhopping or something when he got off work. This went on until Raydel's shift was over, and then they left together. He didn't say anything about needing any sick days," Rachel said.

Hillary showed Rachel Paulie's picture. "Was this the guy?"

"Yeh. That's him. Are they in trouble?"

"I just need to get some information from each of them on a matter I'm dealing with," Hillary said. "Would you either give me a call, or tell Mr. Harrington, so he can call me if you see either of them again?" He gave Rachel his card.

"Certainly."

Hillary thanked both Rachel and Harrington for their time and turned to leave Rick's.

Rachel called out to him, "Deputy, I just thought of something else. After Raydel and that man left yesterday, another man came in looking for him. Kind of a swarthy man. Tough looking. One of these people who give you the creeps when he looks at you. He asked Emma ... She's another waitress ... for Raydel. I heard Emma tell him Raydel had gone for the day. Then he just turned around and left. Didn't stay for a drink or nothing."

Harrington motioned Emma over and introduced her to Hillary. She repeated the same thing Rachel had said, adding that the guy also inexplicably creeped her out as well. Hillary asked if the man had left a business card. Emma said no. Hillary gave Emma his card and then walked out with no further discussion. Next stop, Garrison Bight.

Hillary sat in his car for a few moments and jotted down the time and some notes to himself while things were still fresh in his mind.

So I've got competition. Someone else is interested in this twosome. Surely it's not a plainclothesman from KWPD, he thought. *Just to be on the safe side I better call the Chief though and check.*

He dialed Walter Wanderley's number.

"Walter. Dan. Quick question. Did you send someone over to Rick's to question Raydel Medina?"

"No, you said you were running with that ball, so I'm just letting you run with it. Why do you ask?"

Hillary brought Walter up-to-date on his unsuccessful trip to Miami looking for Paulie Lopez and now his failed effort to interview Raydel Medina again locally.

"You're right," Walter said. "Someone else is

stirring this pot. I wonder who? Maybe it's some of Paulie's old drug dealer buddies or one of his contraband customers."

"Could be."

"And you say you got a description indicating Raydel had been in Miami as well as another description that Paulie was in Key West. Maybe they've both decided to take a hike."

"This damned deal just keeps stinking to high heaven more and more," Hillary said, "and by-God, I'm going to douse it with air freshener if it's the last thing I ever do."

"I hear you and totally agree."

Hillary drove one block over to Whitehead Street and took it until he could pick up Eaton. This led him to Palm Avenue, headed for Garrison Bight. He saw Narley Gristle's familiar trike on Eaton. Actually, he heard it before he saw it. Narley was posing for a picture for some tourists.

Keep searchin', searchin' every night and day

If we gotta keep on the run, we'll follow the sun-ah, wee-ooh

"Narley, I need to talk to you," Hillary called out the window.

"You still workin' on that same case?" Narley asked. Hillary nodded. "Can it wait till I get back to the Bight?"

"Of course."

"Meet you there."

Hillary beat Narley back over to the Bight parking lot, but Narley wasn't far behind. Narley parked his tricycle, sat on the bench, and unwrapped a fish taco.

"Gotta eat these things while they're hot," he said and smiled. "Got another one I'd be willing to share."

"No, thanks," Hillary said. "I'm not going to take your lunch. Dig in. Have you seen Raydel the last few days?"

"Matter of fact, I have," Narley said after he had swallowed the bite of fish taco in his mouth. "Saw him yesterday. With some Cuban looking fellow. Looked like they were taking off on a trip together. Made a couple of trips carrying things to the Cuban's truck. That's when I finally figured out which houseboat he's currently renting."

"So he made a couple to trips with his stuff?" Hillary said. "Look like he might have been leaving for good?"

"It didn't look like he was just taking his clothes to the Margaret-Truman laundry mat."

"Do you remember what the Cuban was driving?"

"F-150," Narley said. "Dade county tag. Last thing they did was to load Raydel's scooter in the back before they left."

He paused and took a swig of his bottled water.

Hillary waited for Narley to continue. "Then something strange happened. Not too long after they left, this tough looking dude ... I mean killer-looking tough ... came in here. He asked me where to find Raydel. I pointed out the houseboat to him but told the guy Raydel wasn't home. He went over to the boat and with this heavy metal rod on his key ring, broke out the glass in Raydel's front door and let himself in. He looked around real quick, didn't see what he was looking for, and climbed back in his car and drove away. It happened so fast, I didn't even have time to call the fuzz. He also gave me this look as he was leaving which said 'you don't want to get involved.' I got the message."

"Show me which boat Raydel was living on," Hillary said.

"Lemme finish this fish taco, and I'll walk you over there. I wasn't sure which boat it was when we talked last week, but I do know now. You sure you can't tell me what this is all about?"

143

"I'm really not at liberty to say, but man, you've been a big help. I'm not going to forget that."

They walked over to the houseboat. Just as Narley had said, the front window was broken. Hillary snapped on some disposable rubber gloves, let himself in, and looked around. The houseboat definitely looked abandoned. He asked Narley to try to keep people off the boat until it could be examined thoroughly. Then he called his office, requested a fingerprint expert, and waited for the person to arrive. Within twenty-four hours, four sets of fingerprints were confirmed – Catt's, Paulie's, Raydel's and those belonging to an unknown fourth person.

CHAPTER 30

Will Black was attempting to get some of his non-market related phone calls returned before the market opened. He combed the list before him and placed a priority number by each name on it to establish his calling order.

"Mrs. Sexton. Will Black. Just wanted to let you know that I've journaled $10,000 per your request to your granddaughter, Jane's, account. That's a very generous birthday present. I'll be sending you a written acknowledgment so you can enclose it with her birthday card. Glad to do it. Call any time."

Barbara poked her head in the door. "Norm Knoll's here to see you."

Well, so much for getting these callbacks done, Will thought, but to Barbara he said, "Show him in."

Barbara showed Norm in and offered him some coffee.

"Sure. Thanks," Norm said. "Black. Decaf if you have it." Barbara left and headed towards the office kitchen. He waited for Barbara to leave before continuing the conversation.

"I'm glad Catt returned home safely," Will said. "Is she OK? Have they caught the culprits?"

"Thanks for asking, and thanks for helping out. She seems to be fine. And no, the authorities are still looking for her abductors."

Norm mentioned nothing to Will about any of the conflicting episodes which had happened since Catt's return home.

After Barbara returned with the coffee, Norm said, "What would it take to get my wife's name off my investment accounts?"

"Different procedures for different accounts," Will said. "You know she will have to voluntarily relinquish her interests. These changes are not something that can just be arbitrarily done. I've got to ask you this, Norm. You're not in the first stages of getting a divorce, are you?"

"No, nothing like that," Norm said. "It's just that these recent events have made me reassess some matters. I think it'd be best for all going forward, if I was the sole person controlling the family's finances. I've always been the primary decision maker anyway."

Will started to bring up the topic of duress but decided not to. He did not know what was going on currently at the Knoll household, and it was apparent that Norm did not wish to candidly discuss it with him.

"Well, let's start with the joint account," Will said. "I'll have to set up a new account in your name only which will require the usual new account documents. Catt will then have to sign a letter of authorization to journal the assets from the joint account to the new single account. I can set up the single account with a "transfer on death" or TOD provision which would re-register the account into her name in the event of your death. Without this provision, your will is going to be the determining document directing the distribution of the funds."

Norm questioned Will about TOD's and finally settled on just a simple single account in his name. Will then moved on to a discussion on Norm's corporate accounts, explaining to him how an attorney would need to redraw the papers to change the officers of the corporation. Finally they discussed Norm's IRA. Will explained to Norm a spouse's right to be the primary beneficiary of an IRA account, and how that spouse had to voluntarily surrender that right. He also briefly covered the tax consequences.

Norm listened and then asked Will, "Make sure I understand this right. The beneficiary has no rights to control anything until I die. Am I correct?"

"That's correct."

"Then we'll leave the IRA as it is," Norm said. "Give me the papers which will accomplish the changes we discussed with my other accounts, and I'll see that they're executed and returned to you."

"We *are* on the same page about these changes being voluntary on her part?" Will asked. "If there's a problem, I can't be put in the position of taking sides."

"They will be voluntary. I assure you," Norm said. "Do they have to be notarized?"

"Nope, just signed."

After lunch, Will was walking past Barbara's desk when she motioned to him."

"Your wife's on line one."

When Will picked up the phone, Betsy asked, "You'll never guess who I got a visit from?"

"Publisher's Clearing House saying you have the winning number?" Will asked.

"Not quite, Norm Knoll."

"That was going to be my next answer," Will said. "So'd I. Wanting to consolidate ownership of his accounts to himself only?"

"You win the Lotto," Betsy said. "He also wanted me to put lower limits on Catt's credit cards and change the safety deposit box to his name only. What's going on?"

"He didn't seem to want to talk about it," Will said. "I just told him what it would take and what the ramifications were. He did tell me straight out that there are no divorce proceedings currently in play."

"I asked the same question and got the same answer."

"Why don't you call your old buddy, the police chief,

and see if you can learn anything. I don't want to get caught in the middle if these two start taking pot-shots at each other."

"I think I'll do just that," Betsy said. "See you tonight, my love."

Betsy didn't have to call Walter. She saw him walking across the bank lobby.

"You in a hurry, or have you got time to visit?" Betsy asked as they walked into her office.

"I'm never too busy not to give you a few minutes. What's up?"

"The Knolls."

"What're they up to now?" Walter said.

"Oh, Will and I both got a visit from Norm today."

"Should I ask why?"

"I'll tell you briefly in complete confidence off the record." She paused and waited for Walter to nod his assent. "Norm wants to be the sole owner and have sole discretion over the family's finances."

"I'm not surprised," Walter said.

"So what's going on?"

"I wish I could be as candid with you as you have been with me, but I'm limited in what I can tell you. There's an active investigation going on. It's being conducted primarily by the sheriff's department. Let me just say, there are a lot of conflicting stories going on concerning every phase of Mrs. Knoll's abduction and her return. Nothing seems to be what it appears to be. We're still trying to get to the bottom of just exactly what the real truth is. And I don't know just when that will be. We're having trouble finding some of the parties who could possibly provide us with the answers. I'm not surprised Mr. Knoll has gotten antsy and is taking measures to protect himself."

"You can't be more specific?"

"No. I really can't," Walter said. "Let me just say,

that just as Mr. Knoll has taken steps to protect himself, you should do so as well. I would document each meeting you have with him in case you need to verify the information later."

"Should I apprise the bank's attorneys of the situation?"

"I wouldn't go that far yet. Just make sure you dot all your i's and cross all your t's. The same goes for Will. Let me just say this. Right now Mr. Knoll looks like he might be the true victim."

CHAPTER 31

As Catt Knoll turned off *The Young and The Restless*, she wondered what the next episode in her own life was going to be. Things had not been normal in the Knoll household since that last meeting with Captain Hillary. Since Norm still had no concrete proof of her complicity, he had only tightened the screws on her. He found more and more excuses to work long hours. When he finally did get home, he had normally already stopped somewhere for dinner before he arrived. Once there, he gave Catt the silent treatment and had started to sleep in the guest bedroom. It was as if he were waiting for the next shoe to drop before he took further action. At least he hadn't threatened her out loud with divorce yet. However, since she knew she was on shaky ground, Catt didn't want to give her husband an excuse to go ballistic again. So she had readily agreed to sign the papers he had brought home concerning their financial accounts. She had not even looked closely at the documents to see what she was signing. At this point she was simply trying to keep peace in the household until all this blew over. She could fight that battle later if Norm began divorce proceedings. At least, she thought, she had given Paulie a heads-up so he could lie low for awhile, and without Paulie's input, she was sure the cops wouldn't bring a case against her. She mainly regretted that she would not be able to help her parents leave Cuba and move to Florida. She shook her head in retrospect. Paulie had seemed so certain that by working together they could not only solve his current dilemma but would get their folks out of Cuba as well, but Paulie had always been such a dreamer.

Catt's phone rang. When she answered, she heard

her mother's voice.

"Catterina, when will our arrangements be finalized?" her mother asked in Spanish. "Madre," Catt answered. "We've run into an unexpected problem about your birthday." Catt purposely kept the conversation ambiguous in case her mother's phone had been tapped by Cuban government censors. "We don't know if we will be able to attend the party."

Her mother sounded deflated and audibly sobbed. It tore at Catt's heart. She wanted to tell her mother that the money to buy the boat had not worked out, but she knew it wasn't prudent to be as specific as she wished on an open phone line.

"We had so counted on seeing you," her mother said. "I got a package from your brother, Juan Paul."

"What is it?" Catt asked.

"He sent me an envelope," her mother continued. "He told me not to open it. He just wanted me to hold it for him. He said he'd get it back if he needed it."

Catt began to wonder. *What would Paulie have sent our parents? He hasn't said anything to me. He must be hiding something. I better find out what it is.*

"He told me about that," Catt lied, "but he told me since then that he has now decided he didn't want to burden you, and that I should keep it for him instead. He asked me to get you to mail it here. Would you mind returning it to me?"

"If he's changed his mind, why wouldn't he tell me himself?" Mrs. Lopez answered.

"He's just so busy with his job, he asked me to take care of the matter for him," Catt said. "In fact, he gave me a note. I'll be glad to send it to you."

"That's not necessary," Mrs. Lopez said. "I know you wouldn't tell a fib to your Madre. I raised you better than that."

"Yes, Madre, you did," Catt said. "I'm sorry to put

you to all that trouble. I'll gladly reimburse you for any postage. It's just that Paulie thinks he may need it sooner than he originally thought."

"That's not necessary, dear. I'll send it to you right away. It really does make more sense for you to hold it since you see him frequently."

Catt sighed in relief after she hung up the phone. Talking her mother out of the package had gone smoother than it might have gone. Madre could be pretty hardheaded at times. She really wanted to find out just what Paulie would take the trouble to send all the way to Cuba. Paulie probably wouldn't tell her folks she had lied about the matter, and if he did, she'd apologize later and convince her family that it was all a big misunderstanding. The important thing right now was to find out just what Paulie was hiding from her and the world.

Within the next week, the package from Catt's mother arrived. The contents only added to the mystery. All the envelope contained was a key and a brief note. The note said, "Box 41722, the Coconut Grove Post Office on 3191 Grand Avenue."

What could this mean? Catt pondered. *I need to find out ASAP.*

She called Norm at work.

"Honey, I need to make a run up to Miami to pick up some of Paulie's things," Catt said. "I hope to be back by the time you get home tonight, but in case I'm running late, I want you to know where I am so you won't worry."

"Why can't that sorry brother of yours take care of his own stuff?" Norm asked.

"I don't know, sweetheart. I haven't talked to him. I just got a call from the man who owns the house saying he's renting the house to someone else and someone needs to take care of Paulie's things. Don't worry. It's nothing big. He said it was just some personal items."

"How'd he get your phone number?"

"I don't know. Paulie may have listed me as next of kin to contact in an emergency when he rented the place. I didn't ask. I just need to take care of it for him."

"Are you lying to me again?"

"No, of course not. Why would I?"

"I thought it was a natural question to ask a natural born liar. I've got another call."

Norm abruptly hung up the phone.

Catt just sat and stared at the phone for a few moments before she told herself, *I definitely need to get on up there and get this over with.*

Catt drove to Miami and went directly to the post office. She had no trouble finding Paulie's box and opening it. The only item in the box was a manila envelope. She took the envelope and left. She saw a Pollo Tropical and realized she was hungry. Catt ordered grilled chicken with black beans and rice. As she ate her meal, she opened the envelope. It contained a diary. She started reading and almost choked on her food. The diary gave a blow-by-blow account of Paulie's drug dealings. He told where the dope came in from and on what boat, how much, who was involved, who they reported to, who he sold it to, how much he got etc. etc. etc. It was a law enforcement officer's dream book if he were trying to build a case or if he were trying to dismantle the cartel's local operation.

My God, Catt thought, *No wonder Paulie was trying to hide this. No wonder he sent the key to my mother where he was sure no one would ever track it down. This was Paulie's ace in the hole if things went bad. And now it's mine. This will be my bargaining tool if Hillary or Wanderley try to build a case against me. This is exactly what I've been looking for to keep my ass out of trouble.*

As Catt drove back to the Keys, she had an occasional conscience attack. What would using this book do to her brother? Was she trading his freedom for hers? Finally she rationalized the whole affair to her satisfaction in her mind. She wouldn't even be in this mess if it hadn't been for Paulie's harebrained scheme. She wouldn't be in trouble with her husband. She wouldn't be in possible trouble with the law. She wouldn't have had her credit cards restricted. She wouldn't have had to sign all those damned financial papers she didn't understand. And maybe if Paulie hadn't been such an incompetent, her parents would be in Florida right now. Yes, this whole thing was Paulie's fault, so she should feel free to use this diary any way she wished. She bet herself the sneak was going to use it only for his own benefit anyway. Why else would he have tried to hide it from her?

I did my duty. I gave him a heads-up so he could go on the lam. If he's smart, he's gotten out of the country. Now it's every woman for herself. And I'm not going to tell Norm about it either. This is now my ace in the hole.

Catt suddenly felt more secure about her future. She did wonder just where Paulie was. She hadn't talked to him since the day she called him and told him he needed to lie low.

CHAPTER 32

Catt worried on the way back about just what she would say to Norm if he wanted to see what she had picked up while in Miami. This turned out not to be an issue. When Catt walked into their empty house, a note was scotch-taped to the refrigerator door.

> Catt
> *I have decided to move out for awhile while I try to sort matters*
> *out. I have taken an efficiency apartment. If you need to call me,*
> *call me at the office or on my cell phone. I will continue to pay*
> *your expenses. I need some time alone to think.*
> Norm

I guess I should've seen this coming, Catt thought. *I hope my trip to Miami wasn't the catalyst that pushed him over the edge. I'm still glad I went. That diary is going to be very important before this whole affair is over.*

Catt Knoll's life changed dramatically over the weeks following the day Norm informed her he was moving out. She expected him to call periodically or to return to get his clothes, but this did not happen. She was simply on her own. The house suddenly seemed big and empty. Being a first generation Cuban-American, Catt had never felt totally at home around the gringo friends that Norm had chosen for them to associate with since they'd been married. She would have preferred being around her Hispanic family and their acquaintances. She had never been one to cultivate a cadre of girlfriends so there no one she felt comfortable using as a sounding board. She now felt very alone.

Catt wondered how Norm planned on paying her expenses until things were right between them again. When the regular bills came in, they had been prepaid on WB Bank's internet bill-pay service. Norm had not had the billing addresses updated. Maybe there was hope they could work things out. He simply estimated the amount of each bill from its historical levels, rounded it up to an even number, and paid it. Most of the bills showed slight credit balances. None were past due. The only surprise she got was one day when one of her credit cards was declined in a store. The store told her she was over her limit. When she got home, Catt called Betsy concerning the card.

"Betsy. This is Catt Knoll. There appears to be a problem with my Visa card. It was declined today at Publix."

Betsy told her she would check, see what the problem was, and call her back. Betsy knew that Norm had requested a reduction in the card's limit but thought Norm should be the one to tell his wife and explain his reason. She didn't want to risk getting caught in the middle of a potentially explosive domestic situation, especially one she was totally in the dark about. Catt had been too embarrassed to tell Betsy that Norm was now living in an apartment. Betsy never thought to ask.

Betsy called Norm's office immediately.

"Norm. Betsy Black. I feel funny about broaching this sensitive topic, but circumstances are forcing me to do so. Did you apprise your wife that you had lowered the limits on her credit cards?"

"Uh ... I don't guess I did," Norm said. "Is there a problem?"

"As a matter of fact there is," Betsy said. "Catt just called me and told me that her WB Visa card had been refused by Publix. To refresh your memory, you lowered the limit on that card from $10,000 to $5,000."

There was a pause. Betsy waited for Norm to speak first.

"Betsy, I'm going to be candid with you," Norm finally said. "After Catt's recent purported abduction and some other matters which have occurred, I've decided she is not always as responsible as I would like her to be. I decided to control her spending by keeping her cards below their limits by a stipulated amount each month. I can't be there with her all day every day, so this regulates her spending. I decided that the maximum I want her to charge on that account each month is $2,000 so I'm keeping the debit balance at $3,000 and paying off whatever she adds to that amount each month."

"Don't you think you should have told her that?"

"Well, I guess I was hoping it wouldn't become an issue," Norm said. "Things have been tense, and I knew it would probably cause an argument."

"Norm, please don't interpret this as my meddling in your affairs, but she needs to know. How can someone play by the rules when they don't know what the rules are?"

"Well, there's one other thing," Norm said. "I'm not living at home. I've taken an apartment until we can work out matters between us."

"Is this your way of saying you are getting a divorce?"

"No. We haven't taken any steps in that direction. We're just in a cooling off period. Would you tell her for me?"

"Norm, I really don't feel comfortable with that. You two should be talking to each other," Betsy said.

"I know, but it will go over better coming from a neutral third party. I'll tell you what. I'll pay down that card another $500 through bill-pay today. That should get her through to the end of this month, but after that, she simply has to learn to live on a budget."

"OK, I'll call Catt and tell her what you told me. I wouldn't do this if I didn't know you both," Betsy said, "but I'm going to tell her to call you if she wants to discuss it any further."

"Thanks, Betsy. I won't forget I really owe you one. I'll handle matters going forward. I promise."

"I'm going to hold you to that promise, Norm. I hope you two can work matters through. Will and I have always thought you were such a nice couple."

Against her better judgment, Betsy called Catt back and paraphrased her conversation with Norm. She couldn't tell whether Catt was deflated or just embarrassed that her dirty laundry was now known. She didn't scream, cry or argue. She simply seemed to capitulate and accept matters for what they were.

Within days, Catt got the dreaded but half-expected phone call from her mother in Cuba.

"Catterina, I received a phone call from your brother asking if I had received the package he sent me," Mrs. Lopez said in Spanish. "I told him I had gotten it and had forwarded it to you in accordance with his wishes. He almost sounded surprised I didn't still have it. You did receive it, didn't you? You are saving it for Paulie, aren't you?"

"Yes to both questions, Madre," Catt said. "I'm sure he just forgot. He's had a lot on his mind. Did Paulie say where he was calling from?"

"What do you mean, where was he calling from? You told me he was up there with you."

"Oh, he is most of the time, but his job does take him out of town."

Catt wasn't sure her mother had bought her cock-and-bull story, but since her mother didn't make an issue of the matter, Catt really didn't care. The important thing was she had control of the diary and could use it if and when it became necessary as a bargaining chip.

CHAPTER 33

While Catt Knoll was thinking about where her brother might be, Paulie Lopez was thinking about his sister as well, glad that she did not know where to find him. Paulie Lopez and Raydel Medina were "vacationing" on Isla Margarita, off the Venezuelan coast.

The day Catt had called him, Paulie had immediately driven to Key West. He went over to Rick's, ordered a beer, and talked matters over with Raydel. Raydel did not disclose to Paulie that he had talked to Dan Hillary and had implicated both the Lopez siblings. This would have sent Paulie into a tirade and probably ended their friendship. When Paulie suggested they leave Key West together with the windfall money he had gotten from selling stolen cartel drugs, it seemed to Raydel like the best way out of the bad situation he had created by trying to buy time with the detective. If he and Paulie left the country together, Raydel might avoid another conversation with the detective, and Paulie might never find out Raydel had ratted him out. By the time Raydel got back to Key West, *if* he came back to Key West at all, maybe this would be a closed case, and he would never have to pay for his part in the conspiracy. It really didn't matter to him if Catt Knoll took the blame for all of them. After all, what could they do to her for plotting to kidnap herself – put her on probation? So what! He had regarded Catt as being a convenient short-term sexual diversion from the get-go. Until now he simply did not have the money to go on the lam. Yes, Paulie's proposal simplified things for him greatly. It was a lot simpler, he reasoned, than sticking around to face the music.

Paulie told Raydel he planned to fly from Key West to Cancún. If they hurried, they might make the 3:16 Delta flight. If not, American had one at 7:45 that night. Paulie and Raydel rushed over to Garrison Bight to get Raydel's basic necessities for the trip. They cleaned the rest of his things out of the houseboat and dumped them at the Salvation Army Thrift Shop on Flagler Avenue. He sold the truck and the scooter for cash, and they took a cab to the airport. By the time they got to the Key West airport, it was too late for the Delta flight. They nervously killed time at the Conch Flyer Restaurant and wandered aimlessly through some of the airport gift shops. The American flight left Key West without incident, and they arrived in Cancún before 10:30 PM. Raydel asked Paulie what their next stop was. Paulie admitted he was still formulating a plan. The following day Paulie and Raydel went to an internet café. Within the hour, Paulie announced their destination –Venezuela.

"Since Venezuela is a Spanish speaking country, we would fit right in," Paulie told Raydel. "It's had an extradition treaty with the United States since 1922, but it's riddled with ambiguities and contains an extremely limited list of extraditable offenses. According to what I've just read, even when the treaty does apply, Hugo Chavez rarely cooperates. It'll be perfect. Con Viasa Airlines has a direct flight today going from Cancún into Del Caribe Gen S Marino Airport in Caracas."

"Sounds good to me. Let's do it," Raydel said enthusiastically. "Then what do we do?"

"I'll figure that out when we get there."

For the first couple of days, Paulie and Raydel just hung out in Caracas. They explored local restaurants and, of course, the local bars. Paulie did not talk much to locals since he wanted to remain as invisible as possible as he plotted their next move. He did, however, pick up local real estate and tourist brochures and read them avidly.

A couple of days later he announced to Raydel, "I've got our plan mapped out. We're going to rent an apartment on Isla Margarita."

"Isla Margarita? Where the hell's that?"

"It's an island about twenty miles from here. It's got beautiful beaches and everything else we need. No one'll ever think to look for us there. And the main city, Polamar, is large enough and touristy enough for us to feel right at home. We'll take the ferry out there."

"Hey, you're the man with the answers," Raydel said. "Let's go for it."

Paulie and Raydel had little trouble finding a furnished two-bedroom apartment on Isla Margarita. It was named Playa el Agua. It was a series of two-story, sand-colored, adobe buildings with red terracotta roofs. It was landscaped with bougainvilleas and cactus. The complex even had a swimming pool for the residents. The owner was asking $70 a night rent but readily agreed to take $1800 a month if Paulie and Raydel agreed to lease it by the month. It was perfect.

For the first few days, Paulie and Raydel chilled out and familiarized themselves with their new environment. "You did good," Raydel said. "I'm going to really enjoy this. I don't know why I didn't discover this place years ago."

"Because you didn't have a windfall of cartel money to live off of," Paulie reminded him. "I'm going out for awhile. I need to call my mother and see if she got a package I sent her."

When Paulie returned to the apartment, his good mood had turned sour.

"You know that package I sent my Madre," he said. "Well, she doesn't have it. Catterina called her and convinced her that I wanted her to hold it instead. My Madre sent it to Catterina."

"So what was in it that was so important?" Raydel asked.

"Oh, just everything I need to keep the cartel from ever putting heat on us." Paulie then explained about the diary, and how he gave him the upper hand on many dangerous cartel figures. "I was going to use the diary if they ever decided to play hardball on the missing drugs."

"Well, hopefully, like you said, we are about as under the radar screen as we can get ... even from the cartel. You're sure we won't be extradited back from here if the shit hits the fan?"

"Positive. Besides that, we haven't even been charged with anything. About the only thing they extradite people for in Venezuela is bigamy," Paulie said sarcastically, "and I haven't married your ugly ass. It's not my week for boys. Why'd you ask?"

"Oh, no reason. I guess I just wanted some reassurance," Raydel said.

"I can't call Catt and rake her over the coals – especially since I don't know if she knows just what kind of dynamite she now controls," Paulie said, changing the subject. "If she hasn't gone to Miami, she won't know what's in that PO Box. And I sure as hell don't want her to know where I am, especially since I don't know what game she's playing."

"Would it break your heart if she got in trouble?"

"I wouldn't enjoy it. After all, she *is* my sister," Paulie said, "but if it was ever her or me, she better watch out ... especially if she thinks she can put the wood to me. If that's the case, her ass is grass, sister or no sister."

"It's sad that family is so meaningless nowadays. Where's that old blood bond?" Raydel said. "Well, this boy still believes in loyalty. If I can help out, you damned well know I'll do it. You've certainly been a good pal to me."

"That's what friends do for each other."

To himself Raydel thought, *I'm sure glad I was able to get out of Key West before you could find out what a dog-eat-dog world it is for both friends and family when the chips are down.*

CHAPTER 34

Federico Figurosa a/k/a Freddie Figgs squirmed as he shifted his weight back and forth in his chair. Omar Perillo glared at him, waiting for him to speak.

"I haven't been able to find Paulie Lopez yet," Freddie reluctantly admitted.

"Why not, cerote?" Perillo demanded.

"I can't explain it exactly," Freddie said. "The boat captain he was working for fired him. I went to his house in Coconut Grove. He'd cleared out of there. I tried to find him in Key West – no luck. I got a tip he might be on a houseboat on Garrison Bight in Key West. I broke in the boat and searched it – the occupant, whoever he was, had cleared out. I went to Rick's, a bar on Duval Street, where a friend of his worked – the friend had just quit his job at Rick's with no notice. That idiota must have dumb luck, ESP, or an accomplice to be this elusive."

"I want results not excuses if the Latin Kings wish to continue to be our distribution arm," Perillo said. "Do you want me to go back to Señor Soltero with these lame explanations? He don't like to be embarrassed with his superiors. I can pretty much guarantee you what his reaction will be, and it's not going to be one you'll like. He gets overtures constantly from other gangs who would like to step into your shoes. Besides, it is not good for business to let a fierro like Lopez rip you off and get away with it. How'd you like that talk to hit the street?"

"You haven't said anything we don't already know. Paulie does have a sister in Key West. Her name is Catterina Knoll. She's married to a local boat dealer. I'm told sister and brother are very close."

"Then why don't you use her to smoke Paulie out?" Perillo said.

"Do you give a shit if she gets hurt?"

"I really don't care what happens to her as long as no one can track it back to here. She can die, for all I care. I just want to send a message to any other bueno pa nada that we're not to be taken lightly. Comprendes?"

"Comprendes, and remember my comrade:
'Cowards die many times before their death
The valiant never taste death but once,
Of all the wonders that I yet have heard,
It seems to me most strange that men should fear,
Seeing that death, a necessary end,
Will come when it will come'," Freddie said.

"Get your valiant ass out of here, see that death comes to deserving knaves, and restore my respect in the Latin Kings," Perillo said. "I expect more than lame excuses or rhymes the next time we meet."

CHAPTER 35

Anthony Newlon walked into the Key West Police Department and asked to see the officer on duty. Sgt. Smith came out and introduced himself and led Newlon back to an office.

"What can I do for you?" Smith asked.

"I'm a member of the South Florida Symphony," Newlon began.

"What instrument do you play?"

"Cello. I'm also a music collector with a large CD collection. I collect all genres of music as a hobby. I'm sure I probably have one of the largest CD collections in the Keys. I patronize the Salvation Army Thrift Shop on Flagler Avenue. You can get used CD's there for anywhere from twenty-five cents to a dollar. Also, many times you can find vintage CD's which are now out of print. It's my hobby."

"I hope you're not in here to report that they sold you a defective CD," Smith said half-seriously.

"Oh, no," Newlon said. "When you buy their CD's, you know they're used and might be defective."

"So what are you reporting?"

"I got a couple of John Taglieri CD's home the other day. I don't know if you're familiar with him. He's the lead singer for The Durtbags. They're the house band at Rick's on Duval. I was pretty excited to find one of his older CD's – his *Leaps Of Faith* album. I've looked for it for awhile. Anyway, underneath the CD was a homemade disc. For the fun of it, I decided to play it and see what was on it. It turned out to be a woman who appears to be confessing to a crime. I think she's local and with another man, and I don't think she knows she's being recorded. I thought I should bring it down here. Do you have anything to play it on? I brought my Walkman in case you didn't."

"I've got a CD player on my radio," Smith said. "Let me close my door, and we'll listen to it together."

Smith put the disc on, and it began to play. Catt Knoll was talking to an unidentified man and began to rehash the plot they had devised to extort funds out of her husband. It seemed apparent to Smith from her tone and comments that this might be unguarded bedroom talk that was being secretly recorded. No names were called. Smith found himself wondering if the woman's companion was recording it with an I-phone or if a third party was recording it unbeknownst to either the woman or her lover. It only took a few sentences before Sgt. Smith tied it to the Knoll kidnapping. When it had played through, Smith asked Newlon if he would object if he called Chief Wanderley into the office and replayed it for him.

"So you think this is an admission of a crime?" Newlon asked.

"I think it's very possible. That's why I want the Chief to hear it."

Walter came in the room and introduced himself. Smith replayed the disc.

Damn-it-to-hell! I can't believe we don't have that money yet. I know my husband made arrangements for the ransom. Brother has a boat picked out. He said he found a used one up in Broward which is perfect for our need but that if he isn't able to put some money down on it soon, it's going to get away from him though. I just don't think I can take it if we got this close to being able to smuggle mom and dad in from Cuba and then it fell through. They have wanted to come to Florida for such a long time. They're getting older, and I don't know how many years they have left. Now at least we'll be able to spend those years together. Lord, I wish my husband had been more understanding. Cheap bastardo. Then we wouldn't 'a had to go through this charade.

Catt droned on and on. This was almost too good to be true, Walter thought. This was the solution to the case Captain Hillary had been working so hard trying to nail down. And now it had just been dumped into his lap. Even if it didn't call names, it gave them the details they needed to arrest Catt Knoll and get her to admit who her accomplices were.

"Do you mind if I keep this disc?" Walter asked.

"That's why I brought it to you," Newlon said. "Does it concern a specific crime that you're aware of?"

"I wish I could comment, but unfortunately I can't," Walter said, "but you've done a great service to your community by bringing it in. I want to commend you for being such a responsible citizen."

"Hot-diggity! I just knew it was important. I feel like I'm on a true crime reality TV show."

After Newlon left, Wanderley called Captain Hillary and told him about the windfall. Hillary said he would come right down to the station.

After listening to the bootleg recording, Hillary said, "I can't believe after all the legwork and time I've put in this case – including ripping a whole day out of my schedule to go to Miami – and you just fall into the evidence I need."

"We've both been in this business long enough to know that you never rule out luck as an investigative tool," Walter said. "I don't remember the source, but a quote comes to mind. It goes something like this, *it's never luck or fate, it's God's perfect plan.*"

"Well, God was sure on our side on this one. I was wondering what to do next since both Paulie Lopez and his buddy, Raydel, seemed to have conveniently disappeared, and I haven't been able to rattle Mrs.

Knoll into a confession. So you want to take this ball and run with it?"

"As a professional courtesy, I was going to let you do it if you want to," Walter said. "As you just said, you've got a hell of a lot more time invested in this affair than I do. I'm the one who just had the dumb luck. Can you imagine being stupid enough to let something incriminating get out of your possession?"

"No one ever said criminals are the smartest people in the world," Hillary said. "Otherwise, you and I'd be looking for a job. And I guess the perfect crime seldom exists. More often than not, they make some stupid mistake and become their own worst enemy. Well, I guess I'm off the see the infamous Mrs. Knoll."

"Good luck."

"My friend, you gave me the luck I need."

When he got back to his office, Captain Hillary called Catt Knoll and asked her to drop by the Cudjoe Sheriff's Substation. She agreed to come.

When Catt Knoll came in the substation, the receptionist brought her back to Hillary's office. He asked her to be seated and closed his door.

Hillary had a copy of the incriminating disc already loaded in a radio CD player.

Without elaborating further, he said, "I want you to hear this" and hit the *play* button.

Catt heard her own voice on the recording, outlining all the facts she had until now denied or misrepresented. She knew immediately when and where the conversation had occurred. It had happened that day on Garrison Bight on the houseboat after she and Raydel had made love. She had been frustrated that the ransom hadn't been paid and that they had not been able to conclude the whole matter. Now she didn't listen to the CD word for word. She was too busy reliving that day in her mind. She remembered the afternoon she vented to Raydel. Had he recorded the conversation so he could blackmail her, or was it Paulie who was intending to do so? Or maybe it was both of them? Why? Because they didn't trust her? Hadn't she played ball from the beginning and done everything asked of her? Was Paulie just using her and then dumping her in the creek if it became necessary, or was a greedy Raydel double-crossing both her and Paulie? She remembered from a previous meeting with Hillary that he had said someone had evidence proving her involvement, but he had never told her who the person was. Was it Paulie, or was it Raydel? Well, in either case, two could play that game.

I've got Paulie's diary. I bet Captain Hillary would love to see that.

The incriminating CD finished playing. Catt just sat there with her head bowed, looking at her feet. Hillary let her sit and stew for about a minute. It was the longest minute of Catt's life.

Finally he said, "Well, what do you have to say about this recording?"

"It was all Paulie's idea. He made me do it." She began to rattle. "He had to get the cartel off his back or die. He swore if I helped him this once, he'd never have any dealings with them again. That he'd go clean. He told me unless I helped him, he'd leave our parents in Cuba until they died. Can't you see he didn't leave me any choice? And Norm had sworn he would never jeopardize himself by helping. I'm not a criminal or bad person. I was truly a victim. Can't you see that?" Catt began to cry and bury her face in the palms of her opened hands.

"Mrs. Knoll, you have committed a felony. No matter what your motives, I can't just let this matter slide. It's not my job to judge your guilt or innocence. My job is to apprehend law-breakers. Then after that, the courts decide these matters."

"But I'm not a criminal. I'm not a bad person. I don't think I can stand to go to prison," Catt said as she continued to sob.

"As I said, that's not for me to decide."

Well, this is not going well, Catt thought. *It's time for me to switch gears and play my trump card, Paulie or no Paulie.*

"What if I could help you catch some really bad guys?" Catt suddenly blurted out. Her tears went away as suddenly as they had come. "On TV, if someone helps catch a big criminal, they're forgiven for what they've done."

"What are you talking about?"

"I've got documentation which can help you understand the cartel's operation. If I could help you catch them breaking the law, would you just let me get by with probation? I'm going to pay enough as it is. When all this comes out, my marriage is over. I won't have any money or any friends anymore. My family is gonna disown me for disgracing them even though I did it for *them*. I'll have to move and start all over. Isn't that punishment enough for something I was forced to do?"

"That's not for me to decide, Mrs. Knoll," Hillary said. "If you show me what you have, I'll see that it gets into the proper hands, and they'll decide what to do with it."

Catt then told Hillary about Paulie's diary, and how it came into her possession. She then lied and said she had to retrieve the diary from a friend in Miami who was keeping it for her. Catt refused to disclose the third party's name or address and insisted on recovering it alone so as not to involve this person. Reluctantly, Hillary gave her a deadline to return to his office with the diary. He emphatically told Catt her failure to do so meant any potential deals would be off.

CHAPTER 36

Even after this short time span, Raydel Medina was getting a little bored. Isla Margarita was a great place for a getaway, but he wasn't sure it was where he wanted to spend the rest of his life hiding from either the authorities or the cartel. Truth of the matter was that it was a little dull down here. He hated to admit it, but he missed his job in Key West. He missed the excitement of working at Rick's, missed his customers and friends, missed the girls he used to pick up, missed Key West's funky festivals, and missed barhopping in Old Town Key West when he was off of work. Key West was home; Isla Margarita was an idyllic vacation spot, but Raydel hated to think he was possibly exiled in Venezuela over the long run. Especially since it wasn't because of problems of his own making; he was just a friend trying to help a friend. Well, maybe he could still help his friend, Paulie.

Raydel had been encouraged when Paulie had said, "if it were ever her or me, she better watch out ... especially if she thinks she can try to put the wood to me ... her ass is grass, sister or no sister." Now he just had to figure out an excuse to get back to Key West and squeeze that diary out of Catt Knoll.

Paulie'll probably object to me putting the squeeze on his sister so I just won't tell him until after it's done. If I tell him at all. Maybe I'll just save that diary to use as a bargaining tool in case of a rainy day ... But I ain't got to decide the question now. It's always good to have options.

Raydel watched TV while he waited for Paulie to return to the apartment. When Paulie walked in, Raydel called out to him, "You got the hongries?

Wanna go get somethin' to eat?"

"Yeah, man. Sounds like a good idea."

"I'm tired of all this local shit," Raydel said. "How 'bout we get some good old gringo food?"

"What you in the mood for?"

"Pizza. I've been told about this joint on Avenida Aldonza Manrique called Las Mejores Pizzas de Margarita. They say the pizzas are good, and they're cheap."

Paulie agreed that sounded like a plan, and within minutes they were on their scooters headed for the restaurant. Las Mejores was an open-air restaurant with a long, dark green canvas awning which protruded from the building out over the sidewalk. Imprinted on the awning in large white letters was "PIDA PIZZA". It also announced that the restaurant made deliveries and gave a phone number. Under the awning were off-white resin-topped tables with aluminum legs. Each table had green, webbed, aluminum chairs. From the sidewalk they could see more tables and a wall-hung flat-screen television inside as well. Framed posters covered the interior walls. An L-shaped ceramic tile counter separated the restaurant from the pizza ovens.

"You wanna go inside or outside?" Paulie asked.

"Let's sit out on the sidewalk so we can watch the local poontang walk up and down the street."

A waiter took their pizza order and brought them each a bottled Polar beer. Conversation ceased as they watched the pedestrians pass by. The waiter brought out a thin-crust pizza with ham and cheese slices, bacon, diced tomatoes, mushroom, and thin slices of a course ground fatty local sausage. Paulie and Raydel ordered another Polar and dug in.

"You were right," Paulie said. "Sometimes you just can't beat some good old pizza."

While he was eating his second slice, Raydel said,

"Would you mind if I disappeared for a few days?"

"What's up?"

Raydel formed his fingers into an "o" and poked at the hole with the index finger on his other hand. He leered and said, "Oh, I met this sweet young thing I want to get next to for a few nights. I wanna a little company softer, warmer, and more compassionate than a ugly hard-leg like you." He laughed at himself.

"Oh yeah? Where'd you meet someone?" Paulie asked. "Local talent?"

"I ain't telling you all my secrets so you can try to snake her," Raydel said. "This is my secret stash. You can go find your own. I'll tell you all about it when I get back. If you're good, maybe I'll get her to send back some panties for you to sniff." He laughed at himself again.

"So when's this liaison scheduled for?" Paulie asked.

"Sometime later this week. I'll let you know."

"Don't do anything I wouldn't do," Paulie said and winked.

On the way back to the apartment after lunch, Raydel thought, *well, that turned out to be easy. Now I'll just drag my ass back up to Key West and get some stuff accomplished. If I get lucky, maybe I can get laid while I'm there, but one thing I can guarantee is that it ain't gonna be Catt Knoll after what I have to say to her.*

The day before Catt met with Hillary, Raydel arrived back in Key West. It felt good to be home, even if it was only going to be for a few days. He got a motel room out near the "Y" in New Town. The next morning he went to Walgreen's and bought a cheap CD player and some batteries. Then he drove his rental car to Catt Knoll's house on Cudjoe Key, let himself into the house, and waited. Surprise would be his best weapon. Catt walked in, preoccupied about getting the diary back to Hillary until she saw Raydel sitting in her living room leering at her.

"What're you doing here? ... Fucking creep," she said, almost not being able to get the words out. She slammed the door. "Get the fuck out of my house, or I'll call the cops."

"No, you won't," Raydel said. "If you do, you're going to be real sorry. I just wanna talk. And if you don't talk to me, I'll talk to people you don't want me talking to."

Before Raydel could rise, Catt ran to the kitchen and grabbed a butcher knife. "Stay away from me. I mean it, you double-crossing low-life." She motioned Raydel back into the living room with the knife. He had the CD player in one hand.

Before Raydel could say a word, Catt said, "I can't believe what you told that sheriff's deputy. When I see Paulie and tell him, he's going to beat the shit out of you."

"Number one, Paulie can't beat the shit out of me, and he knows it. Number two, you're not going to be seeing Paulie anytime soon, and number three ... the..."

"Where's Paulie? What've you done with him?"

"I can't tell you where he is, but he's fine. You'll have to take my word for it. But as I said, you're not gonna be seeing him for a long time. Back to what I was saying before you so rudely interrupted, number three, the detective caught me off guard. I had to say something, but since I haven't been here to corroborate my story, and since he doesn't know where Paulie is, he ain't got nothing. Hear me? Nothing – just a bunch of hot air which I can deny."

"So why're you here?"

"You've got something which belongs to Paulie, and he wants it back," Raydel said. "And don't think you can lie to me and deny it. Paulie talked to your mother, and she told him you got her to send his letter to you. Your mom still doesn't know you were lying, but me and Paulie do. I'll tell her what a lying bitch she raised as a daughter if I have to. Now, gimme it."

"Go fuck yourself and the horse you rode in on," Catt said.

"Before I take you up on your kind offer, I have something I want you to listen to." Raydel pulled the slim-line jewel case with the CD out of his pocket, put it in the CD player and hit play.

For the second time that day Catt heard her voice coming through the speakers and again relived that fateful day on the houseboat on Garrison Bight. Why had she felt inclined to talk about the abduction? She listened again as she incriminated herself, described the conspiracy, and left no doubt as to her part in it. As she listened, she turned ashen and dropped the knife, almost hitting herself on the foot.

"Where'd you get that?" Catt asked after she got her breath back.

"I recorded it in case I ever needed it," Raydel said. "I was pretty sure I couldn't trust you. And, baby-cakes, I was not going to risk taking the fall for something you and Paulie cooked up. My part in this was helping my friend out. Well, that's still what I'm doing."

"But you're on the tape too," Catt said.

"But no one knows where Paulie and I are, and they're not going to. Even if they did, they can't get to us. Plus, I'm just an accessory at best, and I won't even be that. I'll tell them I didn't know until it was too late what you and Paulie had cooked up. I was just giving you a place to stay to help out a friend. And when I did find out y'all were doing something illegal, being an honest person, I did what a good citizen should do. After I had a chance to think it over, I decided what you were doing was wrong, and that it was my duty to report it to the police," Raydel said. "I think I can sell that story if I have to."

He paused to let his words sink in before continuing.

"The cops do know where you are, however, dear one, and this tape leaves no doubt that you were in the plot from the get-go. Now, what's it going to be? You gonna gimme me what I want, or do you want me to turn this taped confession over to both the cops and your husband?"

Catt went into her bedroom and took the envelope with the P.O. Box number and the key and silently handed it to Raydel.

"Did you get Paulie's diary out of the box?" Raydel asked. Catt shook her head.

"You're not lying to me, bitch, are you?" Raydel said.

Before Catt could answer, Raydel continued, "I'm not going to give you this CD right now. I'm gonna to drive to Miami and retrieve that diary. If it's not in the post office box, when I get back, I'm gonna hurt you bad. And then I'm going to send a copy of this CD to your husband. Finally I'm gonna mail a duplicate copy anonymously to Captain Hillary. No second chances. Comprendes?"

Catt knew she was beaten. She wasn't worried about the disc being mailed to Captain Hillary. He already had a copy. She just didn't want Raydel to kill her. Yes, she was beaten. She went in the bedroom and returned with the diary. She handed it to Raydel; he threw the CD on the coffee table.

Before turning to leave, Raydel said, "I need to use your head to take a whiz."

While in the bathroom, he inventoried the medicine cabinet to see if there was anything which might be useful to him if he were forced to return. He came out zipping his pants. "It's been a pleasure doing business with you, Mrs. Knoll, but if you tell anyone I was in Key West, I swear on the Bible, I *will* kill you."

While Raydel was in the bathroom, Catt picked up the butcher knife again and held it behind her. She took a sideswipe at Raydel, but he sidestepped the blow. He backhanded her, and the knife flew across the room.

"Not too smart, Mrs. Knoll, but I'll forgive you just this once."

Raydel stood there and stared Catt down. She said nothing in return. She fidgeted, finally broke eye contact, and looked at her feet. Satisfied he'd made his point, Raydel turned to leave. On his way out, he said, "Oh, you can keep the CD player in case you want to listen to your premier performance again."

Raydel laughed and then closed the door behind him.

Now how am I going to a make a deal with Hillary? That diary was my ace in the hole.

Catt began to cry. This time her crying was real. She decided to drive around awhile while she sorted out what she should do next. She didn't want Hillary to catch her at the house and demand the diary which she now couldn't deliver. She wondered if she should tell him it had been stolen and by whom.

Why didn't I make a copy of the thing while I had a chance?

CHAPTER 37

Federico Figurosa aka Freddie Figgs kissed his wife goodbye at the front door and backed out of the driveway. She waved him goodbye, and he rolled down his window and yelled back, "Have a great day, dear." It looked like a perfect day to drive to the Keys. The sun was shining, and gentle clouds floated above the interstate. He was sure he would have a good day, but it was not going to be such a good day for Paulie Lopez's sister, Catterina. He was sure of that. It was nothing personal. He was just doing the job Señor Perillo had assigned to him. If he didn't do it, someone else would be dispatched instead. Paulie should have done the job he was paid to do instead of trying to get cute. These people never seemed to learn.

Freddie had over a hundred miles to drive. He put on some soothing music to compliment the lovely day. Soon Pepe Urquiaga, Cesar Gonzmart's vocalist, was singing *So In Love*. He had bought this CD at the Columbia Restaurant in Tampa after he had completed another assignment for Señor Perillo there. He regretted he had never heard Gonzmart perform since Gonzmart had played the Columbia during the sixties.

Too bad they don't play music like that anymore, Freddie thought as he drove. Also t*oo bad I'm not going to Tampa rather than the Keys. I'd plan on staying the night, splurging at the Columbia ... or maybe try to get a ticket to the Tampa Bay Symphony ... and then drive back to Miami in the morning.*

The miles started to melt away. Before long Freddie was in Homestead, then Florida City. He jumped off the turnpike at its dead-end and cruised down the ramp onto US1. He stopped and bought a cup of café misto and two pastelito de guayabas. The guava pastry and the Cuban coffee went together perfectly. He always enjoyed the reverie of driving to a job alone. That way he didn't have to make small-talk with someone; he could just relax and enjoy the scenery. He didn't need backup for this assignment; it was only one housewife, for God's sake. He debated with himself as he drove which persuasion method he would use on Catt Knoll if it became necessary.

We'll see what resources are available when I get there.

By the time he got to the Seven Mile Bridge, Freddie was ready for some peppier music. He had to get himself psyched up for the job ahead. He decided some Latin boogaloo would be perfect so when the Gonzmart CD had finished, he put on Joe Bataan's *Subway Joe.*

Well, I took the subway downtown one day just to find me some

Chinese food, and as I sat down and looked up – what did I see-

There was this little girl, sure looking good.

It took him back to the period he had spent in New York before he got married. Those were sure some good times. He sometimes missed New York, but Miami was sure a better place to live year-round.

When Freddie was got to Ramrod Key, he began to watch his GPS. The Knoll house didn't appear that it would be much of a challenge to find. By now, Freddie was mentally prepared for the job ahead. When Freddie drove onto Cudjoe Key as he turned to go to the Knoll residence, he saw something mildly disturbing, the Monroe County Sheriff's Substation.

Damn, she would have to live behind that. I sure hope she's not right behind it.

He relaxed again when he saw she was several

blocks away.

This should be fine, he thought, *but I'll have to make sure whatever method of persuasion I choose to employ doesn't cause too much noise. This neighborhood might actually be an advantage. No one will expect someone to be daring enough to cause a problem this close to the fuzz headquarters.*

Freddie drove the street once to look over the Knoll residence as well as the neighborhood. All the neighbors appeared to be at work.

Excellent. No nosy neighbors.

There didn't appear to be anyone home at the Knoll residence.

Good. I'll just let myself in and wait on her.

He also saw what appeared to be a vacant house a few doors down.

Also good. Now I can park down the block so she won't see my car in her driveway when she returns. This is working out better than I expected.

Freddie put on his disposable rubber gloves, checked for an alarm, then let himself in, and relocked the door.

Glad there's no pets to contend with.

He checked Catt's freezer. It had ice cream in it. That would be perfect for his plan. He found an ice cream scoop and scooped some into a Tervis tumbler. He made sure he washed the scoop when he had finished. After all, his mother had taught him good manners. He then located her coffee pot and coffee and brewed a pot.

Perfect. I thought I might have to heat up water, but now I'll have a standing reservoir of a hot liquid.

When he was satisfied his preparations were completed, Freddie made sure the rope, nylon zip ties, and the duct tape were out where he could access them easily and decided which dining room chair he would tie her to. He got it out from behind the table and left it in the middle of the kitchen floor. Now he was ready. The only thing missing was Catt Knoll. Freddie turned the lights back off and found a comfortable chair near the door. He would grab the woman as soon as she walked into her house.

Freddie didn't have long to wait. Catt returned from her drive. She still didn't know what to do about Paulie's diary. She had about decided to tell Hillary that she had been burglarized by an unknown thief. Freddie saw her drive up through the front window so he donned and adjusted his mask, and waited next to the door. Catt unlocked the door, not suspecting a thing until Freddie grabbed her arm and clamped a gloved hand around her mouth. He manhandled her and forced her into the kitchen. Freddie roughly plopped Catt into the dining room chair and quickly secured her hands with the zip ties and taped her mouth. He tied her to the chair with the rope and made sure her legs were secured as well. He then turned up the volume on Raydel's CD player/radio which he had turned on but muted it before her arrival. Freddie was a professional who had his craft down almost to a science. When he was satisfied with his work, Freddie pulled up a kitchen stool in front of Catt and sat on it, one swinging foot dangling in the air.

"Mrs. Knoll, my employer would like to know where your brother, Paulie, is. If you tell me, I will not hurt you. If you don't, I will make things very unpleasant for you. I'm going to remove the tape from your mouth so you can talk." Freddie pulled some brass knuckles out of his pocket and put them on. He turned the radio up again slightly. "But if you scream, you are going to be a dentist's best customer. Nod if you understand and agree."

Catt nodded. Freddie pulled the tape off. Catt

gasped, "That hurt."

"I apologize. It was necessary. Now, please answer my question."

"I don't know where he is. I swear I don't," she said.

"That's not the answer I wanted to hear. What you've seen so far is my lovable side. You do not want to see my other one. Now, shall we try it again?"

Catt started to cry. "I ... I ... don't know, I swear. If I did know, I'd tell you."

"I wish I could believe you, but it looks like I'm going to have to escalate this situation to make sure you're being truthful. One last time before I do. Where is Paulie?"

"He didn't tell me where he was going or for how long. Please believe me."

Without saying another word, Freddie went to the coffee pot and poured a cup of black coffee. He put the cup in the microwave for a few seconds to make it was hot enough. While it was heating, the phone rang. He did not answer it. The caller did not leave a message. Freddie then pulled the ice cream he had already scooped into the plastic tumbler earlier out of the freezer. He squeezed Catt's cheeks hard, forcing her mouth to open in an "o". He squeezed again to force her teeth apart and then packed handful after handful of cold ice cream into her open mouth. Before it could melt, he poured the hot coffee in on top of it.

Catt heard her teeth begin to crack as the hot coffee met the freezing ice cream. A searing pain shot through her head. Freddie held his hand over her mouth to keep her from expelling the incompatible combination of hot and cold. Catt's mouth throbbed so badly that she thought she would die.

Freddie then spoke again, "Now, wasn't that fun? And that's only round one. I have some even better surprises waiting if you don't tell me what I was sent to find out."

"I swear ... I'd tell you ... if I knew," Catt gasped, "but I d-d-don't. One thing I can tell you though is that you'll most likely find Paulie wherever Raydel Medina is. They fled together. But Raydel is in town. He came to visit me earlier today."

"Now, we're getting somewhere. Why didn't you tell me this before?"

"He didn't tell me where he was st-st-staying."

"Was Paulie with him?"

"I don't tink so." Catt was beginning to have trouble making her words.

"Why'd Raydel visit you?"

"He said I had sometin' which belonged to Paulie."

"And did you?"

Catt nodded, her teeth continuing to throb.

"A book telling the partic-lars of his dur-drru-drug dealing."

"And did you give it to him?"

"Yeth. He b'ackmailed me with somethin' I don want my hubband to see."

"And what was that?"

"It was not 'in' – important."

"It was apparently important enough to convince you to give him what he wanted. Now, are you going to show it to me, or do we have to go to round two. Each round gets progressively worse. I'm a trained professional who can go ten rounds if need be."

"Tha' disc ... the homemade one over on tha' shelf."

Catt pointed.

"This one?"

She nodded again. Her mouth felt like it would never stop hurting. The phone rang again. The caller hung up before it could go to the answering machine. The man waited for it to stop ringing before he spoke again. His voice sounded conversational and friendly.

"Thank you, Mrs. Knoll for the help you've provided. I'm going to take the CD with me. If Raydel Medina is still in Key West, I *will* locate him, and what I have for him when we do meet, will be much worse than our little session today. Oh, yes. Much worse. 'For in that sleep of death what dreams may come'."

Freddie smiled sadistically as he planned his encounter with Raydel.

"Now, just to show you I'm not such a bad guy, I'm going to untie you from the chair. I'm going to leave your hands secured and re-tape your mouth. You should eventually be able to free yourself. I'll be long gone by then, but we may be in touch again soon. Have a nice day."

Freddie paused before he left, "Oh, a final thought. 'Ay, but to die, and go we know not where; To lie in cold obstruction and to rot.'

"If I find out, you've withheld any information; the consequences will be dire indeed. In fact, my employer has not placed a limit on how far I am allowed to go. You're a very attractive lady who is too young to die – especially for a debt you did not incur, but 'he that dies pays all debts'."

CHAPTER 38

After her tormentor left, Catt Knoll sat and sobbed uncontrollably. Her cracked teeth continued to throb. Before all this started, she had had an idyllic life – a doting husband, a nice home, a luxury car, money to do pretty much anything she wished to do and the time to do it, and community respect. And all this in a paradise most people longed to visit, even if only once, but had little chance of being able to move to until they were old and frail, if ever at all. Now she had an estranged husband, a lonely house, and a cloudy future. She might even soon be a convicted felon. All because of one of Paulie's harebrained schemes. How could she have let herself be sucked into the vortex of this tornado? And now she had to wait for someone to come rescue her. She felt she wanted just to die.

After Catt quit hyperventilating and wading in self pity, it occurred to her that no one was scheduled to visit her. She was all alone. Who knows when she would be rescued! She might starve to death first. She pictured herself dying of thirst and hunger while she defecated on herself. The thought seemed so scary and disgusting she began to wail again. Once she regained her composure, Catt decided if she was going to survive this ordeal she was going to have to depend on herself. Thank God the monster had had the human decency to untie her from the dining room chair and give her a fair chance. Catt managed to stand and work her way over to the kitchen counter. She managed to pick up a paring knife and after some effort cut the zip tie holding her hands. It was clumsy to use the knife, and her wrists almost looked like those of a self-abuser by the time she had freed herself.

Catt sat in Norm's recliner until her heart quit pounding and tried to decide her next course of action. Rational thinking was difficult with her teeth continuing to send stabbing pains to her brain. Her first decision – she would not call Captain Hillary. What good would it do? He wouldn't believe her again anyway, and he would never catch this guy. The man was a professional and had too big a head start. Besides, she didn't even know what the guy looked like. Plus he wore gloves. The man had referred to an employer. Just who was this employer anyway? One of Paulie's drug connections? A boat company he had worked for and maybe screwed over? Someone else she didn't even know about? The man mentioned getting something back that belonged to his employer. What was he talking about? The more she thought, the more she realized how little she knew about Paulie's affairs. She had been Paulie's pawn. She only knew that Paulie's dealings more often than not were shady and that he dealt with unsavory, dangerous people.

Catt thought about calling Norm.

No, that wouldn't work. After everything that's happened he'd never believe me anyway. She cried again as she thought of her destroyed marriage.

The truth of the matter is the only person I have in the world is Paulie, and I can't depend on him, even if I did know where to find him.

Another sharp pain jolted Catt. She got up and went to the bathroom to look for a painkiller. She found some OxyContin pills in the medicine cabinet. They had been prescribed for Norm several years ago when he wrenched his back. She mixed a vodka and tonic and took two pills. It wasn't long before the pain began to subside. After half a bottle of vodka she began to mellow, but then the vodka ran out. She needed to get more before nightfall. She'd drive to Key West. The fresh air and getting out of the house would do her good.

The booze and the drugs hit her like a ton of bricks after she got in the car. The last thing Catt remembered was buying two more bottles of vodka at Walgreen's liquor store and driving back across the bridge onto Stock Island. For some reason Catt didn't understand, she detoured by Prestige Boats and pulled into the parking lot. It was after 4 PM when she arrived. As she tried to get out of the car, she slipped on the pea-rock, lost her balance and toppled onto the ground. She tried to get back up but found herself unable to stand. Arlene, the clerk at the front counter came out for a smoke-break and saw her. Arlene rushed back to the warehouse, where she found Norm talking to his parts man.

"Norm, you need to come out front," Arlene said in a low voice after she motioned to him to come over. I think your wife is out front. It looks like she's passed out on the parking lot."

"Oh, shit," was all Norm could think to say.

He followed Arlene out front. Catt was struggling to stand but still having no success at regaining her feet. Finally Catt was able to grasp the door handle and pull herself up. She teetered and almost slumped back down as Norm and Arlene reached her. As Norm tried to stabilize Catt, he noticed the two vodka bottles on the front seat. He shook his head in disgust. With each of them taking one of Catt's arms, Norm and Arlene walked her slowly into the building and then into Norm's office. They let her slump on the navy Naugahyde couch. Norm thanked Arlene and then asked her to leave them alone.

Norm closed the door before he asked Catt, "What are you doing here? You're drunk."

Catt began to babble incoherently about men being after her. About men wanting to torture or kill her.

About being afraid to go home alone. Her rants were meaningless to Norm. He noticed the deep scratches on her wrist and wondered if she had tried to harm herself. He thought it was a wonder she had managed to get to Prestige Boats without killing herself or someone else. His stomach came up in his throat as he thought about the potential liability or bad publicity. He assured Catt, however, he would not let any harm come to her. This seemed to settle her down, and she lapsed into a drunken catnap.

When he was sure his wife was under control, Norm flipped through his Roll-A-Dex and called Gina Panullo. He hoped like hell he'd be able to get through to her.

Gina was the home duty nurse and sitter who had looked after Norm's mother after she had lapsed into dementia. Gina was a thirtyish, very attractive brunette and single mother. Her daughter, Samantha, had been born border-line retarded. Gina had been dismissed from Fisherman's Hospital in Marathon for some mysterious reason several years back. Something about ethics and not having a patient's best interest at heart. It was all vague. There had also been some narcotics missing from the hospital in her department during her tenure there. Nothing was ever proven, no charges were ever filed, but Gina was blackballed in hospital circles. She chose to become an independent home nurse and sitter. Gina claimed her dismissal was political and had refused to discuss it when Norm brought it up. Norm hired her at first because she was the only person available at the time, but she had worked out very well. In fact, Norm and Gina had become very fond of each other and met occasionally at Two Friends in Key West for happy hour.

They often seemed to end up talking about Gina's private life. Once they got to know each other better,

Gina told Norm about her money problems. She had commented in passing that she was willing to do almost anything to become solvent again. She and Samantha's father had never married. Samantha was an unplanned baby. When the doctors told her Samantha had a borderline IQ, her boyfriend had broken up with her. She had hired an attorney she couldn't afford, and the court had ordered child support. At first the money came in sporadically and then not at all. She had been forced to return to court on multiple occasions just to get that. The former boyfriend, who had no record of drug abuse, died unexpectedly from an overdose of a prescription medicine after an especially bad spat. Because of a lack of evidence to the contrary, his death was ruled accidental. She had told Norm about the incident one day at Two Friends. Shortly afterwards, she said, her problems at Fisherman's Hospital had begun, culminating with her losing her job. Now as a private duty nurse she and Samantha barely got by. Recently Norm had used Gina as a shoulder to cry on about the kidnapping and had confided in her that he had moved out of the Cudjoe Gardens house while he and Catt tried to sort matters out between them. Gina had been sympathetic.

"Gina. This's Norm; I need a favor if you don't have another obligation tonight."

Norm described Catt's drunkenness and her paranoid rantings.

"If I can get my wife home, will you spend the night there tonight and make sure she remains OK? I'll gladly pay your going rate. In fact I'll throw in something extra since I'm calling at the last minute. I'm afraid she's going to hurt herself, if she's left alone. It's a miracle no one was hurt or she didn't get picked up when she drove to Stock Island."

"Only if I can bring Samantha with me," Gina said. "I can't leave her alone, and I won't be able to make baby-sitting arrangements for her on such short notice."

"Of course," Norm said. "I hope Catt's erratic behavior doesn't upset the child."

"I'll take care of that," Gina said. "Do I need to bring any sedatives?"

"Bring whatever you think you'll need. I'm leaving within thirty minutes for Cudjoe. I'll meet you there. I've got treatment ideas I need to talk to you about as well, but we'll do that at my house."

"Is this only for one night? I need to plan ahead."

"I think so," Norm said. "I think she'll be OK when she sobers up. By the way, she might be on some kind of narcotics or pills as well. She seems too far gone for it to merely be alcohol."

Norm arrived at the house on Cudjoe Key and managed to get Catt inside.

Thank God the house is on ground level, he thought, *and I don't have to try to get her up a flight of stairs.*

He tucked Catt into bed.

Norm looked around the silent house. This was the first time he'd been back in it since he moved out to think things over. He relived those days of worrying about his wife's fate. In his mind, he replayed his visit to Will Black's office to arrange the funds for her release and how the forced realization of these gains would add to his already existing tax problems. He cringed as he thought about having to deal with that usurious roach who owned the pawn shop and how he had been forced to roll over and take whatever lousy deal the slimy bastard offered. And then how close he had come to simply losing the money. He remembered sitting by the phone waiting for the next contact from the kidnappers. The more Norm thought about the whole matter, the more enraged he became. He'd been right not to forgive and forget. And his beloved wife, who was supposed to stick by him through thick and thin, condoning it all? Unforgivable! He'd been right to move out. Reconciliation was out of the question. Within minutes, Norm had worked himself into a state.

Norm saw the rope, duct tape and severed zip tie in the kitchen. One of the dining room chairs was in the middle of the floor, and the drawer containing kitchen knives had been partially spilled. He briefly wondered just what had been going on here in his absence. Had she actually had a visitor? Were his wife's drunken tales partially true?

That sorry, good-for-nothing Paulie must be back, he thought. *But why? After all, the plan to sweat money out of me failed. If Paulie has any sense at all, he will have gotten as far away from here as he can get. Away from both me and the law.*

Norm picked up the mess in the kitchen, put the chair back where it belonged, and walked into the bathroom. He immediately saw the open bottle of OxyContin on the counter, and realized that this must be what his wife had supplemented the vodka with. He walked out in disgust. The front bell rang. It was Gina and Samantha. Gina was carrying an overnight suitcase and a black medical bag. He let them in, and they briefly hugged. He turned on the TV to entertain Samantha before taking Gina into the bedroom to see the semi-comatose Catt. Gina quickly took Catt's vital signs and said she thought she would be OK when she sobered up. Norm walked Gina into the bathroom and showed her the open pill bottle on the counter.

"You can use these bedrooms," Norm said and showed Gina the guest bedrooms. "Samantha can use this one unless she wants to stay with you. Let's walk back on the patio. As I mentioned on the phone, I have some possibly unorthodox suggestions concerning my wife's treatments I'd like to bounce off of you."

After checking to see that Samantha was all right, Gina went out to the backyard. They talked for about fifteen minutes before they returned to the house. Norm checked on Catt again.

As he walked to the door, Norm asked, "Do I need to show you where anything is before I leave? There's food in the fridge and the freezer. I'll run to Dion's and get some chicken if you want me to."

Gina assured him everything would be all right.

"Then I'll see you tomorrow morning. You have my cell phone number if you need me. I'll stop by here on my way to work. If the matter we discussed is not practical and she's returned to normal, I guess you can go on home. I'll understand, and neither of us will ever bring the matter up again."

The following morning, Norm stopped by the house as he had said he would. Catt was groggy but more alert. She was insistent that she did not need Gina's assistance that day. Gina assured Norm that matters were under control. Gina gave Catt a business card and told her to call if it became necessary. Norm left for work.

Captain Hillary sat in his office looking at the CD Walter had gotten from the cellist. He was sure he had Catt now and was not going to let her get away. He could virtually taste success. Hillary decided overnight had been long enough. It was time for a wrap. When Hillary got to the Knoll home, he saw Mrs. Knoll's car in the driveway as he hoped. He got out and knocked on the door. No one came. He noticed the bell and rang it. Still no answer. He walked around the house and looked in the sliders. He could see the inert figure of Catt Knoll on the floor. The slider was unlocked, and he let himself in. Hillary knelt down and felt for a pulse. There was none.

He checked for signs of breathing. Nothing. He had waited too long. He should have pulled the trigger with what he had and not waited on the diary. Now the woman was dead. He immediately called the situation in and asked for backup.

Fire Rescue arrived within minutes. The EMT confirmed Catt's death. Hillary immediately cordoned off the house and made sure that he did not touch anything in it. It wasn't long before the Medical Examiner and the Crime Investigators Unit was there. The next several hours were spent examining the house and yard. Photographers took pictures of everything that seemed relevant. There would be no second chance to examine the death scene. It appeared Catt had died from a drug overdose, but he would have to wait for the official results from the Medical Examiner. He saw an empty OxyContin bottle on the kitchen counter, as well as three empty vodka bottles. He also noted that each of the guest bedrooms had a mussed bed which appeared to have been slept in recently. Fingerprints belonging to several different people were taken.

Well, so much for my big bust, Hillary thought. *I should have taken what I had instead of reaching for the moon.*

He wondered if it was a suicide or homicide.

Was there simply too much at stake, or did she fold under the pressure?

He called Chief Wanderley and told him of this latest twist in the Knoll case. When the investigation was completed and all personnel had left, Hillary made the phone call he least wanted to make. It was time to call the next of kin.

"Mr. Knoll? Detective Hillary. I'm sorry to have to report to you that your wife if dead."

"Whaaa...!" Norm said. "It can't be. She was alive when I went by there on my way to work this morning.

When did it happen? How?"

"I can't answer either question definitively yet, Mr. Knoll. I'm waiting on a report from the Medical Examiner's office, but it appears to have happened this morning from a possible drug overdose. She was found on the family room floor."

"Who found her?"

"I did, sir. I came to your house to try to conclude some matters concerning your wife's abduction and found her. She was already dead when I got there."

"But I hired someone to stay with her last night," Norm said. "In all honesty, Captain, I haven't been living in that house recently."

"Would you want to tell me why you moved out?" Hillary asked. "Had she been having a an ongoing problem?"

Norm Knoll then went over the events of the day before.

"Can you give me the name and contact information of the sitter who stayed with Mrs. Knoll?"

"Sure I can," Norm said. "It's someone I've used before. This woman used to look after my mother when she had dementia." He gave Hillary Gina's name and phone number.

"Did I understand you to say that your wife told you she'd recently been threatened?"

"Yes, but she wasn't clear about who or why. She was extremely inebriated at the time. I wondered if it didn't have something to do with that sorry no-account brother of hers, Paulie Lopez. If you find him, I'm sure you'll find the answer to a lot of these questions."

"We've been wanting to talk to him, but he seems to have gone underground for the time being," Hillary said.

"That piece of shit is the root of all our problems. What should I do now?"

"Nothing for the time being. I'll let you know when

the Medical Examiner's office releases the body."

"Thank you. Oh, I almost forgot. When I was over at the house yesterday, I found a cut zip tie, some rope and some used duct tape. I threw it in the kitchen garbage. It's probably still there. Also one of the dining room chairs was sitting in the middle of the kitchen floor. I don't know why it was there, but I put it back where it belonged."

"I'll check the garbage again before I leave here," Hillary said. "Thank you for mentioning it."

The items Knoll had cited had already been found and had been noted by the investigative team. Hillary's next call was to Gina Pannullo.

"Ms. Pannullo. My name is Captain Dan Hillary. I'm a detective with the Monroe County Sheriff's Department. Would you have time for me to come over and talk to you? I believe you may have information relevant to a current investigation."

"And who'd that be?" Gina asked.

"A Mrs. Catterina Knoll."

"What could I tell you about her?"

"I'll give you more information when we meet. Do you have time to see me this afternoon?"

"Only if you come here. I've got a small child sick at home and no one to leave her with."

"I understand. Please give me your address, and I promise not to take up any more of your time than is necessary."

CHAPTER 39

Deputy Hillary drove to Stock Island to meet with Gina Pannullo. She lived in a manufactured home on Maloney Avenue. As he turned onto Maloney, he suddenly remembered why that address was ringing a bell in his head. It had been the scene of a Christmas Eve incident which had been broken up by Deputies Moran and Collier. A man had been playing Xbox games on his front porch about 1:30 AM when a group of men had shown up and had begun throwing bottles, cans, and Christmas decorations at him. Some of his friends in the trailer heard the commotion and came out to help. A melee ensued which had to be broken up by the deputies. They ended up making arrests for battery, criminal mischief and resisting arrest. The Xbox player was taken to the Lower Keys Medical emergency room where he received five stitches in his head.

Hillary saw Pannullo's trailer on the right. It was the typical affordable rental housing the Keys had such a love-hate relationship with. The dented, some-what rusty trailer had been mounted on a permanent pad less than two feet off the ground. The old air conditioner hummed as it hung out of the aluminum window. Inexpensive white plastic latticework had been installed to hide the pad. A small makeshift wooden porch had been added outside the front door. Three prefab wooden steps led up to the porch. The tiny lot was devoid of landscaping except for a scrawny pink frangipani about the same height as the trailer, a Christmas palm between her trailer and the adjacent unit, and a creosote power pole. The yard was covered with weed-grown pea-rock. A corroded manhole cover protruded from the ground behind her car. It was not his definition of paradise.

Hillary climbed the steps and knocked on the door. A barefoot, attractive brunette in a t-shirt and short shorts answered his knock. Hillary introduced himself, flashed his creds and she invited him in. The worn, inexpensive furniture looked perfectly at home in this setting.

"Ms. Pannullo, are you aware that Mrs. Knoll, your charge yesterday, has died?"

Gina looked shocked and hesitated before she answered, "No, I wasn't. My God, what happened to her?"

"We don't have the ME's official report, but it appears she may have died from a drug overdose."

"She was alive when I left yesterday morning. When did it happen?"

"We are still establishing a time of death. Would you mind giving me a synopsis of the time you spent with her?"

"Of course. I got a call from her husband yesterday afternoon telling me his wife was at his office extremely inebriated. They have not been living together recently. He was afraid for her to spend the night alone in that condition, so he hired me to stay with her. I've worked for him before. I watched his mother during her declining days. My daughter and I met them back at their home on Cudjoe. We put her to bed and she slept through the night. Norm ... I mean Mr. Knoll ... came by on his way to work this morning. His wife seemed functional so he told me I was relieved of duty. I fixed her some breakfast and left shortly after Mr. Knoll did. I needed to get my daughter to kindergarten. Mr. Knoll said he'd call me if he needed me further. I haven't heard from him, so I assumed everything was back to normal. Obviously I was wrong."

"So she appeared to be fine this morning when you left?"

"Yes, sir. She was shaky and probably hung over, but Mr. Knoll and I both thought she was fine."

"Did you see anything unusual while you were staying at the house?"

"I saw an OxyContin bottle on the bathroom counter. I put the lid back on and left it there since it was none of my concern. Is that what killed her?"

"Possibly. As I said, we're still waiting for the M.E's report as to cause and time of death. Is there anything else you can think of that you should tell me?"

"No, but now that I know she's dead, I'll give it some thought. It wasn't an issue with me until this moment. Do you think she killed herself?"

"I really don't want to speculate on that issue. Here's my card. Please give me a call if you think of anything else relevant to the case."

"Of course I will. I want to do anything I can to cooperate with you. And please give my condolences to Mr. Knoll."

"I'm sure he'd appreciate that."

The following day Hillary got the Medical Examiner's report. It showed that death occurred from an overdose of OxyContin. The OxyContin time-release tablets had apparently been crushed and consumed with Catt's coffee. The releasing of the entire dosage of the drug into her system at one time instead of gradually had proven to be toxic. The time of death was sometime during the morning shortly before Hillary had found her on the floor. The ME ruled her death to be the result of an accidental narcotic overdose.

~ ~ ~

Dan Hillary and Walter Wanderley sat in the chief's office sipping coffee.

"Do you think the ME got it right?" Chief

Wanderley asked.

"Not only no, but hell no," Hillary said. "There's too many things you and I know about this case that didn't come out in this investigation into Mrs. Knoll's death."

"My opinion as well."

"Her rantings the day before her death about men wanting to harm her could very well have been more than just narcotic induced paranoia," Hillary said. "We did find Raydel Medina's fingerprints in Mrs. Knoll's house. We also found both Mr. Knoll's, Mrs. Knoll's and the sitter, Gina Pannullo's, fingerprints on the OxyContin bottle, but Gina had already told us she handled it to put the lid back on it when she found it on the bathroom counter."

"Has Raydel been in Key West recently?" Walter asked.

"Yes," Hillary said. "His passport was used to enter the Key West airport while Mrs. Knoll was still alive."

"But not exit again?"

"That is correct," Hillary said. "He may still be in town."

"Where was he flying from?"

"Caracas, Venezuela."

"Wonderful. Venezuela is hard enough to deal with when you have a convicted felon. You're sure as hell not going to stand a chance of getting to a person who is simply a 'person of interest.' Maybe old muscle-bound Raydel isn't so dumb after all. What about his buddy Paulie?"

"We found where Paulie used his passport weeks ago to fly to Cancún. Raydel had gone there as well."

"Do you think they're together, or do you think they split up?"

"Who knows," Hillary said. "It doesn't surprise me that they fled together. I was a little surprised to find Raydel's fingerprints in several rooms of the Knoll residence. We find no signs of forced entry at the Knoll house."

"So if he was there on this trip, she most likely let him in," Walter said. "Confirms our theory that if she had a visitor, it was most likely someone she knew."

"That's my conclusion. Besides her, there was only one other person who we know had a key to the house, and that was Mr. Knoll. Recently they've been separated, and he's been living in an apartment."

"I'm not surprised. If my wife ever pulled the stunt his wife did, we'd be separated too."

Hillary nodded in agreement.

"What about this sitter – Pannullo woman?" Walter asked.

"She says Mr. Knoll came by the next morning on his way to work, and the two of them decided Mrs. Knoll could be safely left alone. He discharged her at that point. She says she fixed breakfast for Mrs. Knoll, and that she and Mr. Knoll left at the same time. Pannullo says she had to get her daughter to kindergarten. All that checks out. She said Mrs. Knoll seemed fine when she left. Mr. Knoll told the exact same story."

"But you say the OxyContin residue was found in Mrs. Knoll's coffee cup?"

"That's correct, and Ms. Pannullo's fingerprints were found on the cup. But she's already admitted she prepared the breakfast and set out the dishes, so we expected to find her prints on the cup. Mrs. Knoll could have crushed up the OxyContin in the cup herself after Pannullo left in a suicide attempt. We haven't been able to find what was used to crush the tablets. There was no suicide note."

"So once again, you have nothing definitive," Walter said. "Have you checked into Ms. Pannullo's background?"

"Yes," said Hillary. "It wasn't completely clean. She's a single mother raising a mentally challenged daughter. She was dismissed from Fisherman's Hospital in Marathon for seemingly some ethical questions. Her supervisor was a Navy wife whose husband has since been transferred to another naval base. We haven't been able to talk to her. The file was vague. Fisherman's did have a problem with some missing narcotics in Pannullo's department, but their investigation didn't turn up any specific suspects and no charges were ever brought against anyone. I did think it was strange that their problem didn't reoccur after Pannullo's dismissal, but the investigation could have just scared the living shit out of whoever the perp was."

"Once again, nothing definitive," Walter said. "Just red flags."

"She was telling the truth about having worked previously for Mr. Knoll. She was the private duty nurse and sitter for his mother when she had dementia."

"And what about brother Paulie's supposedly drug dealing history?"

"We're still working on that but have nothing right now, Hillary said. "If he was mixed up with drug pushers, we both know anything is possible. Those boys are brazen animals who'll do pretty much anything if someone crosses them. Oh, I did confirm that Mrs. Knoll's parents are indeed in Cuba."

"So what you're saying is that we're pretty much stuck with the ME's conclusion unless new facts come to light."

"I'm afraid so, but I'm not ready to file this case away."

"Neither am I," said Walter. "Somebody's going to make a mistake, and when he does, we're going to nail his ass."

CHAPTER 40

"I haven't seen much of you in the bank recently," Betsy Black said as she sipped her coffee with Chief Wanderley.

"Well, I used to not appreciate the Steven Seagal quip, 'It's a lot harder now to be a police officer than what it used to be,' but I'm beginning to think he had a point."

"I've been reading about Catt Knoll's unexpected death," Betsy said.

"Off the record, unexpected to most people, but not as unexpected as you might think."

"The stories I read said the official cause of death was an accidental overdose of a prescription medicine."

"That's what the ME decided since he didn't have enough evidence to say anything else," Walter said, "but you and I both know the woman was playing fast and loose, and some of her playmates might not have been the most savory people in south Florida. I wouldn't be a bit surprised if some of her brother's drug connections didn't play a part in her demise. These people and their entourage don't pay nice, and they don't play fair. What to us is unthinkable doesn't bother them one bit. I'll give you an example we just had in Key Largo. It involved one of the Dade County hot-mamas who runs with the Latin Kings. She walked into the funeral home to view the corpse of her rival. While viewing the body, she went into a rage and sliced off both of the deceased woman's breasts and took one of her toes as a souvenir as well. She and the corpse wore the same size shoes, so she stole the dead woman's shoes on top of that. I'm telling you, these sociopaths don't think like you and I do."

"That chills me to the bone," Betsy said.

That's because you're normal. Deputy Hillary suspects Paulie Lopez might have had dealings with the Latin Kings."

"Yikes. I never knew the brother, but Catt Knoll always seemed so straight and normal," Betsy said. "I guess you never know. Have you talked to Paulie?"

"Hillary tried to, but Paulie seems to have conveniently left the country. As I said, right now, with what I have to work with, I'm going to have support the ME's conclusion, but that doesn't mean that I'm going to close my eyes to new evidence which might show him to be in error."

At the same time Walter and Betsy were talking, another meeting was going on at Will Black's office. This one between Will and Norm Knoll.

"Betsy and I are so sorry about your wife," Will said as he showed Norm into his office. "Is there anything we can do?"

"Thanks for asking, but no, I can't think of anything," Norm said. "As you can imagine, I'm still pretty shell shocked. I knew the abduction had affected Catt both psychologically and physically, but I guess both the doctors and I underestimated its impact on her. I'd hired a sitter to be with her, and I stopped by to check on her on my way to work that day. She seemed fine."

"Stopped by on your way to work?" Will asked.

"Oh, yes," Norm said. "I guess you didn't know, but Catt and I had been living separately while we tried to work some things out."

"I'm sorry to have brought up a sore subject," Will said. "I didn't know."

"Well, it wasn't something we broadcasted," Norm said, "but let's get to my reason for being here this morning. As much as it still hurts, business must go on.

I need to fill out the paperwork to claim the death benefit on Catt's life insurance policy. I also need to change the beneficiary on my IRA."

"I suspected that was the reason for this meeting," Will said. "I had Barbara assemble the forms which you need to file."

"Will I have to pay taxes on the money?"

"No, the policy was purchased with after-tax money, so you're fine on that count. Also since you were the owner of the policy, it won't even be included as an asset in Catt's estate."

"Fuckin' hallelujah! I've had enough tax issues recently to last me a lifetime. ... IRS bastards. I guess I have about two million coming to me?"

"Not exactly. A million is more like it," Will said.

"What about that double indemnity clause I paid extra for?"

"I'm afraid it doesn't apply in this case."

"But the Medical Examiner ruled that it was an accidental drug overdose."

"The way double indemnity works is that it excludes deaths caused by suicide or the person's own gross negligence. One or the other is sure to be the ruling of the insurance company."

"Bastards! Always set up things which sound good, but don't give you a dime when you need it," Norm said.

"Only 5% of the deaths that occur in the U.S. are classified as accidental. That's why the coverage was so cheap."

"I should've known it was too good to be true. Well, let's file the paperwork, and get this thing moving before they find an excuse not to pay that either. How long's it gonna to take?"

"I hope it won't take long. The cause of death seems pretty cut and dried. You do have a death certificate, don't you? I'll fax the documents and overnight the originals to try to speed things up. Do you want the proceeds sent to you at home or just deposited in your account here?"

"Here will be fine," Norm said. "You'll let me know when you get them?"

"Of course. They'll go into your money market fund. I'll start to work on a proposal on a better way to invest the funds for the longer term. Money market funds don't pay a whole lot. They're just a good safe place to put money while you're trying to decide on the other alternatives available to you," Will said.

"Fine. Whatever. Now let's get on the paperwork so I can get to work."

CHAPTER 41

Will Black's assistant, Barbara, picked up her phone and answered, "Will Black's office. Barbara Danise speaking."

"Barbara, this is Norm Knoll. I don't want to bother Will about this minor item, but would you check my account and see the insurance money came in?"

"Of course, I'll be happy to. Wait a second while I pull up your account. Nope, not here yet."

"Thanks."

Two days later.

"Barbara. This is Norm Knoll. I hate to be a pest, but would you look and see if the insurance money hit."

"You're not a pest. Just give me a moment. Nope. Don't see it."

"Thanks."

The following Monday.

"Barbara. Norm Knoll. Is Will available? If so, please connect me with him."

"Norm, he's on his phone. May I have him call you back?"

"Certainly. I'm at work."

Will returned Norm's call. Norm answered on the first ring.

"Norm. Good morning. Will. What can I do you for?"

"Is my money in?"

"I checked before I returned your call. Still waiting."

"Do you think you ought to call them and make sure there isn't a problem?"

"Oh, I'm sure it's just going through their system. Insurance companies don't do anything in a hurry. They're some of the stodgiest bureaucracies on earth."

"Would you call anyway? Just for my peace of mind. If there's a problem I want to know about it."

"I'll call and get back to you."

"Thanks."

Later that day.

"Norm. Will. I talked to the company. Doesn't seem to be a problem. Payouts at this level have to be approved by a committee. It only meets on Wednesdays."

"Ass-wipes. They sure take their time when they're playing with somebody else's money."

"I wish I had some control," Will said. "This is not uncommon. These things just take time. Do you need some money?"

"It's not that. I just have to go out of town for a few days and wanted to get this matter put to bed before I have to leave."

"If you don't mind my asking, where are you headed?"

"The Martin County Boat Show. I plan to be gone for almost a week."

"When is it?"

"In a couple of weeks."

"I promise you. I'll stay on top of this," Will said.

"Thanks."

The funds were wire transferred into Norm's account early the following week. Will called Norm and told him the deposit had hit."

"Are they good funds, or is your company going to put some kind of bullshit hold on it?"

"Oh, they're good funds. It was a wire transfer not the usual insurance company bank draft. Do you want to get together so I can show you my ideas on how to integrate these funds into your portfolio?"

"Not now. I'll get back to you. I'm getting ready to leave town for the boat show I told you about. I'm going to visit some friends on the Treasure Coast while I'm there. I'm leaving this weekend," said Norm.

"That's great. After everything you've been through, getting out of town and having a change of scenery should be good for you. I hope it's a good trip. I'll talk to you when you get back."

Will came in the following Monday morning and began to prepare himself for the coming week. Barbara printed out a money market run for him and circled items she wanted to bring to his attention. One item she circled was Norman Knoll's account. The account balance was down $500,000. Will brought the activity screen up on his computer. Norm had written a check to the IRS for the entire $500,000.

Wow, Will thought. *He never mentioned this to me. I've heard Norm cuss the IRS a few times. I thought it was just the typical taxpayer anguish we all go through from time to time. I guess there was more to it than just that.*

Will and Betsy used the same CPA Norm did. Will gave him a call.

"Reese. Will Black." He then got the usual small-talk preliminaries out of the way before getting down to business.

"Reese. I don't mean to be nosy, but, off the record, has Norm Knoll been having tax problems? He's been really antsy about getting that death benefit on his wife's life insurance policy. He called me on several occasions while it was being processed to see if I could speed things up, and then when the money finally did come in, he immediately wrote a check to the IRS for half a million dollars. He's gone out of town so I can't ask him about it. And by the way, this is not just nosiness. His account is collateralizing a line of credit with our firm. He hasn't used it, but if he did and the IRS then froze the account, my firm would be at risk."

"Will, I understand your concern. Normally I wouldn't comment, but since you and I know each other pretty well and I know you'll be discreet with anything I say, I'll answer. Yes, he did. This money was a very timely windfall for him. He's been audited for the last several years, and the IRS was beginning to put some serious heat on him. He'd run out of appeals and if he hadn't brought himself current, the situation you envisioned could have become a reality. Do I need to say more?"

"I hear you loud and clear," Will said. "Thanks for giving me a heads-up. And by the way, we never had this conversation."

"I wouldn't have said anything if I thought otherwise," Reese said. "Have a nice day, and tell your wife I send my regards. We need to get together soon and bend an elbow."

"Yes, we do."

Wednesday morning, Barbara came into Will's office.

"The Knoll account is down another hundred grand," Barbara said, "and there's some debit card charges on it as well."

"No wonder Norm was so evasive when I tried to schedule an appointment to talk about investing the new funds. At the rate he's going, there aren't going to be any new funds to invest," Will said.

Will brought up the account. A check made out to G. T. Pannullo had cleared for $100,000.

What the hell – who's that?

There was also a dinner and bar debit card charge for $124.19 dated the same day at the Roostica restaurant on Stock Island.

Stock Island? Norm's supposed to be in Stuart all week attending the Martin County Boat Show. Pretty long drive from Martin County to Stock Island. This dog don't hunt.

CHAPTER 42

"Remember the song, *The Streak*?" Will said as he sipped a cup of coffee and ate a piece of toast.

"Yeh, I do. Boogie-dy, boogie-dy," Betsy said in a deep southern drawl, imitating Ray Stevens. "You haven't been streaking around Key West have you?"

"No, but I think someone else has," Will said. "This is your action reporter covering a disturbance at the Stuart Boat Show. I wus just goin' down thar to git Ethel a snow-cone when he come out of the concession stand – naked as a jay-bird. Streaked all the way to Key West. Mooned Ethel and gave that shameless hussy a free shot."

"What in the world are you talking about, Clyde?" Betsy asked.

"What I'm talking about is how Norm Knoll can be in Stuart and Key West at the same time." Will went on to fill Betsy in on how Norm had told him he'd be attending the Martin County Boat Show all week; yet he'd still found time to have a luncheon on Stock Island.

"I'm beginning to see what you mean," Betsy said. "I don't think the Miss Budweiser power boat could accomplish that one. You're talking about four hours-plus in driving time."

"Each way. That's some serious boogie-dy boogieing. There's nothing about that situation which seems to be right."

"I assume you're referring to the whole situation with Norms wife. That seems to've been resolved."

"No, not just that," Will said. "I managed to get her life insurance death benefit paid to him. He had ants in his pants the whole time it was pending."

"Well, that is a lot of money. When's the last time

we saw a million-dollar windfall?"

"The last windfall we got was your bonus in Jamaica," Will said, "and you're right, it wasn't that much. I guess I'm a little chapped because I worked my butt off putting together a presentation for Norm to invest the funds, and then when the insurance money hit; the dough started flying back out the door before the ink was dry on the check. If he knew he was going to spend the proceeds, why didn't he simply tell me he had other plans and save me all that work? I consider that inconsiderate. I had several hours invested in that proposal."

"Well, I hate to remind you, but it's not the first time he's done something like that to you. He insisted on you giving him ideas on restructuring his account and then took $200,000 out of it days later."

"But that's when the ransom demand came in. We both know he didn't see that bullet coming," Will said. "But he damned well knew he owed the IRS half a mill. I got a call from a compliance officer. The whole matter hit compliance's radar screen."

"Well, you're going to have to just put on your big-boy pants, call him, and discretely find out what's really going on."

Will called Prestige Boats later that morning and asked for Norm. The receptionist took a message. He didn't hear back. He called again and left another message with the receptionist. On Will's third call he was finally put through to Norm.

"Will, how are things in the world of high finance?" Norm asked.

"Great. I was calling to ask you how the boat show went."

"That thing keeps growing every year. It's not as big as the Miami or Lauderdale shows yet, but it's only five years old. It's certainly worth my time since it takes place in the spring and the big boat shows in south Florida aren't until later in the year."

"I was hoping we could get together when you returned and I could share some of my investment ideas with you, but it looks like I'm going to have to rework my proposal since you've expended some of the funds."

Norm's voice sounded hesitant. "Yes, I had some things come up. The IRS's been questioning some of my personal tax returns, and my accountant advised me maybe we ought to settle up with them and move on instead of continuing to fight an uphill battle. The bastards have all the advantages on their side, and us little guys down on Main Street don't have a Chinaman's chance in hell against them ... even when they're wrong. Sons-a-bitches. I don't know why us hard-working entrepreneurs have to support every low-life the Federal government wants to give away money to. We're the backbone of this nation, not the ones sponging off of it."

By this time, Norm's voice indicated he had worked himself into a state. Will made a few neutral comments and waited for Norm to calm back down.

"I haven't felt right about this economy," Norm continued. "If the government keeps soaking the producers to transfer wealth to the non-producers and the government doesn't balance its budget, sooner or later this stock market is going to take a tumble."

"I noticed you wrote a check for $100,000 out of the account," Will said when he thought Norm had completed his rant. "Was that for an alternate investment idea?"

"Well, yes and no. It was business," Norm said. "I came across an opportunity at the boat show which was too good to pass up. I met someone willing to sell a Sea Ray 350 Sundancer with two Mercruisers for $100,000.

This cream puff had less than 200 hours on it. That's a hell of a deal. Needless to say, somebody else was going to be all over that honey in a hurry if I didn't take it right then and there. That boat made the trip to Stuart worthwhile. I should be able to flip it for over $200,000."

"Congrats. Good for you. Boats *are* your business," said Will. "You certainly should know a steal when you see one. So do you want me to come up with some suggestions for the remaining part of the insurance settlement?"

"Let me get back to you on that," Norm said.

"I'll be ready whenever you are," Will said. "We'll just leave it at that."

CHAPTER 43

When Will got home that night, Betsy asked him if he had had a chance to call Norm Knoll.

"Sure did. Took three calls to finally get him on the phone. Made me almost wonder if he were avoiding me. That guy can sure blow hot and cold," Will said.

"I told you that," Betsy said. "So tell me about your conversation."

"I think he's lying like a carpet," Will said. "He told me the hundred grand check was for a deal he ran across at the boat show on a used boat which was simply too good an opportunity to pass up, and he had to use funds he could get his hands on immediately so this steal wouldn't get away from him which makes sense since he's a boat man and knows boat values."

"OK, I'll buy that," Betsy answered.

"He also has a business which he can use to detail the boat to make it look new and then flip it for a maximum price. Per Norm, he can flip it and double his money on it in nothing flat. I can't do that for him in the stock market."

"Everything you're saying makes perfect sense," Betsy said. "So why's he a liar?"

"Because, as I told you yesterday, the same day he bought the boat in Stuart, he used his debit card to take someone to lunch at Roostica on Stock Island."

"Really. You sure he didn't buy the boat from someone on Stock Island?"

"He specifically said he bought it at the Martin County Boat Show," Will said. "He made a big deal about the fact that running into this bargain made the whole trip to Stuart worthwhile. He was also very emphatic about the importance of being in Stuart all week since the boat show there precedes the ones in south Florida by months. Why would he lie to me?"

"A valid question. For some reason, it seems he didn't want you to think he was in the Keys on that particular day. Did he say anything about the half-million-dollar check to the IRS?"

"He owned up to that one. He ranted and raved about what assholes they are, and how he was being treated unfairly," Will said. "I already knew he had IRS problems thanks to Reese, our mutual CPA. Norm's had several audits on his income tax. He said Reese had advised him to quit battling them and just pay the taxes. Apparently Norm was one step away from having the government attach everything he owned."

"I'm glad he got that straightened out," Betsy said. "Since WB is his banker, we could've been drawn into the middle of the whole mess. I'm glad I avoided that bullet. I've got an idea."

"I'm listening. Are we still talking about the Knolls, or did you have something more personal in mind?" Will said and winked.

"I'm still on business, but we can discus the other later. I know Roostica has security cameras. If you could see the footage on that day you might find out two things. One – if Norm was really there, and two – who was with him?"

"That's an excellent suggestion. Coach John Wooden once said, 'whatever you do in life, surround yourself with smart people who are willing to argue with you.' I'm sure glad I surrounded myself with you, even if you can sometimes be cantankerous," Will said. "I guess the question becomes, just how do we get access to that video?"

"Maybe if I explained our quandary to one of our law enforcement friends, he'd become equally curious about your magical client," Betsy said.

"As many hours as they've spent on the Knoll quandary recently and as many questions that have been left unanswered, I'm sure we could pique their interest rather easily. Why don't you bounce this off your coffee drinking buddy, Chief Wanderley?"

The following morning Betsy called Walter Wanderley and suggested he stop by the bank for a chat concerning the Knolls. He quickly agreed to pay her a visit. When he arrived, Betsy filled him in with a brief overview.

"I agree that the Roostica footage would be most interesting to view. I'll get right on it. I don't think access will be a problem. Bobby Mongelli is a pretty decent guy. But this might be better off going through Captain Hillary. He's been a lot more involved in the Knoll case than I have. Bobby is just as likely to make the tape available to Hillary as he would be to me, and whatever's on it might be more meaningful to Dan than it'd be to me. I'll give the captain a call."

"Would he allow Will to watch it with him?"

"I don't see why not. I'll ask Dan about it and tell him I'd consider it a personal favor if he would allow Will to be there."

"The next time I hear someone call you a pig-cop, I'll tell them you're not a swine but a cuddly manatee," Betsy said.

"I'm not sure I want to be either one," Walter said. "Are you hinting that I need to shed a few pounds? Well, no more doughnuts."

"I heard that," Margaret said, poking her head in the door. "Mrs. Black may not want doughnuts, but I do."

"Like you really need them," Betsy said. Margaret stuck out her tongue.

Wanderley explained the discrepancy to Captain Hillary, and Hillary easily obtained Roostica's security tape for the day in question. He invited Will to join him to view the footage.

Hillary fast-forwarded until he recognized Norm Knoll and then slowed the speed back to normal. Norm was sitting at a table with an attractive brunette younger than he was. Fortunately, they were facing the camera. As they watched, the couple ate pizza and talked. Will and Dan couldn't hear what was being said, but it appeared to be a lively discussion. Each smiled at times as they discussed whatever it was they were talking about. Norm patted her hand. When they had finished eating, the waitress asked if they needed a box for the left-over pizza. Both declined. After the table had been cleared, Norm pulled out his RST checkbook and wrote the woman a check. She looked at it and beamed. They briefly toasted by clinking their water glasses together. They then walked out of the restaurant, his arm on her shoulder.

Hillary was the first to speak. "I know who that woman is. That's Gina Pannullo."

"Who's that?" Will asked.

"The private nurse and sitter Knoll hired to watch his wife the day she got totally shit-faced drunk," Hillary said. "This nurse had previously looked after Knoll's mother when she had dementia. Knoll called her to stay with his wife the night before she died because she was out of control, and he was afraid she might hurt herself. He's been living in an apartment while they tried to work out the issues they were having, and he was afraid for her to stay by herself. He came by the house the following morning and discharged Pannullo on his way to work. He said his wife was sober and acting OK. Mrs. Knoll purportedly OD'ed that morning after Pannullo and Mr. Knoll had left. Maybe he's just writing her the money he owed her for watching out after his wife."

"Now I know who G.T. Pannullo is," Will said. "I saw a check clear Knoll's account made out to her. I just didn't know who G.T. Pannullo was. The check sure wasn't for one night's baby-sitting service. The check was for $100,000. Knoll told me it was to pay for a used Sea Ray he bought at the Martin County Boat Show that same day. That's why I brought this whole matter up. I couldn't figure out how he could be in Martin County and Monroe County at the same time."

"$100,000! That definitely was not for one night's service as a care giver," Hillary said. "If that's what they make, you and I are in the wrong business."

"Before we jump to conclusions, may I make a suggestion?" Will said. "You can check boat registrations to see if Ms. Pannullo ever actually owned a boat, can't you?"

"Of course."

"She may have really sold Knoll a boat," Will said, "and for some obscure reason, he's not being forthright about it. Maybe he was trying to screw the IRS. Maybe hide the transaction from his wife. Who knows; maybe he didn't go to the boat show at all but was shacking up with the nurse, and he didn't want his estranged wife to find out about it because she could use the affair to squeeze him for money in a divorce proceeding. It could be something as simple as one of those things."

"You're right," Hillary said. "There could be a simple explanation for this whole thing ... and I might be more inclined to go with one of those theories if Mrs. Knoll hadn't ended up dead."

"I'm sure there's more to this whole matter than meets the eye," Will said. "We just don't know what the something is."

"If I were at liberty to share everything I know about this case," Hillary said, "you might realize just how close to the truth we might be getting. My compliments on your astute observation and diagnosis. It's not just everyone who would have noticed Knoll's conflicting stories and then would've taken the trouble to give us a heads-up. We might possibly have never stumbled on Knoll's mistake without your help."

"As John Brown said about Jack Sparrow in *Pirates of the Caribbean*, 'Just doing my civic duty, sir.'"

CHAPTER 44

Captain Hillary invited Chief Wanderley to come up to the Cudjoe Key Sheriff's Substation to view the video tape he had gotten from Roostica. The Chief gladly accepted his offer.

After they watched the tape together, Hillary commented, "I'm sure glad Will Black was here to view this with me the first time. Otherwise I'd never known the size of the check Knoll wrote and the reason he fabricated for giving it to Pannullo. I would have just assumed he was paying for one night's nursing services. Since then, I made my inquiry with DMV. They have no record of a Gina Pannullo ever owning a boat of any kind."

"I'm not totally surprised. If I'd been sitting here alone watching this tape cold for the first time, I never would have suspected that much money was passing hands, and even if I did, I wouldn't have guessed the reason," Walter said. "I know it was a little irregular to have a civilian present when you previewed that tape, but the Blacks aren't average civilians. They've assisted me on several occasions in solving challenging cases. Also keep this in mind; it was not my idea to request the Roostica tape; that idea originated with the Blacks."

"Yep, it's luck you've got such a good relationship with them," Dan said. "I'll take a little luck any day I can get it. So now that you've watched the video, give me your feedback."

"My feedback is this," Walter said. "We know Norm Knoll is a liar, but we don't know to what extent. Just because he lied, doesn't mean he's a killer or even an accomplice. We just know he's not the angelic husband he's pretended to be since this whole mess started.

We've known his wife was dishonest for a long time, and we know her brother and his associates are creeps who probably should be rotting in jail. We know she was running with a rough crowd. Now I guess we know that husband and wife probably deserved each other. I'm a firm believer in the adage 'where there's smoke there's fire', but right now, until we get more, we're still playing with matches."

"So, you got any suggestions?"

"As a matter of fact I do," Walter said. "I'd love to get another crack at Knoll's house to see what info it may still be hiding, but I'd rather that he didn't know that I'm doing it. Also since we now have reason to broaden our suspect list to possibly involve women, I'd also like to bring a woman's perspective into the equation. I've got a woman on my staff named Sylvia Hernandez. She's smart and an up-and-comer. Before she was a cop, she had her own house cleaning service. Now that we know more about what we might be looking for, I'd like to get Sylvia in there pretending to be a maid. That way she'll have plenty of time with no one distracting her to see if she can uncover something your boys missed the first time around."

"How do you propose getting her in there?"

"I've already been working on that," Walter said. "My proposal is that we involve the Blacks again. They've already been involved with this case on several occasions. I'll ask Betsy to call Norm Knoll. Betsy's story will go something like this. 'I know Catt was a housewife and kept your house immaculate while she was alive, but someone else will need to take over those duties going forward. I know a reliable maid service which will come in at a reasonable price and keep your place clean. She'll come in as often as you need her. I know this woman and have complete confidence in her. She's honest, bonded, and you won't even have to be there while she's working. When you get home in the afternoon you'll have an immaculate house.' Do you like that script? I've already run it by Mrs. Black. She says she has no problem with helping us out."

"So you're just going to lie to Knoll."

"Turnabout is fair play. The SOB's been lying to us. If he's not guilty of anything, he's got nothing to worry about. If he is, then he's going to get what he deserves."

"I'm willing to give it a try if you are," Hillary said. "I really don't want to show our hand until we've got more evidence to support our allegations. Let me know how it comes out."

"Let's just hope Betsy Black can sell the deal to get Sylvia in," Walter said.

Betsy called Norm and paraphrased Walter's suggested script.

"Norm, I'm sure your house has got to be a mess without Catt there to keep it clean. I can just imagine what kind of shape all those cops must have left it in after traipsing all over the place."

"Yeah, I'm not much of a house cleaner," Norm answered. "I've been meaning to try to call someone, but I seem to keep procrastinating about it."

"I know someone who's good, reliable and reasonably priced."

"Really? Do you think she has time to clean for me?"

"I'm sure she does," Betsy said. "Do you want me to give her a call? Her name is Sylvia Hernandez."

"Is she legal?"

"Oh, sure. She's an American citizen," Betsy said, "and she's bonded. With your permission, I'll give her a call."

"Oh, hell yes," said Norm, "I really appreciate it. I owe you one."

"You don't owe me anything."

Betsy called Walter and reported her success.

Walter told her to call Norm back and see if the following Tuesday morning would work. Norm would be at work so Sylvia would have the run of the house for as long as she needed that day by herself. Norm signed off on the date, and Betsy got him to drop a house key by her office.

Tuesday arrived. Norm had expressed his reluctance to open his house to a stranger so Sylvia went by before Norm went to work and introduced herself. Norm gave her instructions and showed her where he kept things. Soon she had the house to herself. Sylvia started in the bedroom, stripping the beds and putting the sheets in the washing machine. Nothing seemed unusual there. Next she went through the kitchen. She looked in the cabinets, inspected the refrigerator, and checked for unwashed dishes.

Mr. Knoll isn't a complete bachelor slob, she thought. *The sink's not full of dirty dishes and glasses; the garbage isn't overflowing; there aren't pizza boxes everywhere.*

She tidied up the kitchen, washed off the counters and stove, and checked the containers in the fridge for spoiled items or items, which didn't look like they belonged.

Nothing green and disgusting in here.

Next she started in the bathrooms. She checked under each sink and looked in each medicine cabinet. The medicine bottles all seemed to contain what they were supposed to. Just as she was about to close the medicine cabinet door in the guest bedroom, she noticed a toothbrush on the shelf. The butt-end of it had a white powdery residue on it. She carefully picked it up with a piece of tissue paper. When Sylvia lightly tapped it on the counter, more white residue fell from the bristles. She touched a damp finger to the residue and tasted it. It didn't taste like either toothpaste or baking soda. It had a medicine-like taste that was slightly sweet. She put it in a zip-lock for further analysis. Sylvia finished cleaning Norm's house. Nothing else seemed unusual.

When Sylvia was leaving, she snapped the lock on the sliding glass patio door. She pulled on it and it still opened. She snapped it again and pulled. It still refused to lock. She noted the fact that the lock appeared to be broken.

If someone wanted in, they wouldn't have to break in.

She left the door unlocked and returned to the police station.

"So'd you turn up anything of value?" Walter asked.

"I only noticed one thing that I think the sheriff's team may have missed," Sylvia said, "and that may be absolutely nothing." She pulled out the zip-lock with the toothbrush and gave it to the chief. "Would you have the lab test this? It's got some sort of residue on it which I couldn't identify. Also tell them to be careful handling it. It may contain useful fingerprints." She then reported the broken lock on the slider.

The following day, Hillary called Sylvia and told her he needed to meet with her.

"Congratulations. You were right about that toothbrush. The residue on both ends was OxyContin mixed with Splenda. As you're probably aware, Mrs. Knoll died from an overdose of OxyContin. She also had Splenda in her system. My guess is someone used the butt-end of that toothbrush to muddle OxyContin and mix it with Splenda. Then they used the bristle end to sweep it out of whatever container they had mixed it in. Did you find a container which looked like it had residue in it?"

"No, only the toothbrush."

"I'm not surprised. The person remembered to

wash the container but apparently forgot to wash the toothbrush. I'm guessing the Splenda was in there to hide its presence or maybe make it more palatable so it'd go down easier."

"Like to put it in coffee or tea? So do you think Mrs. Knoll did it herself in a suicide attempt," Sylvia asked.

"Maybe, but maybe not. You were also right about being careful not obliterate any fingerprints. The fingerprints on the toothbrush are not Mrs. Knoll's."

"So who did they belong to?"

"The nurse, Gina Pannullo."

"Whoa! Well, that was the bathroom the nurse was using when she stayed overnight. But what motivation would the nurse have to give Mrs. Knoll a lethal dose of OxyContin?"

"That's a damned good question. Now that I have something to work with, I think it's time to put the squeeze on Ms. Pannullo and try to find out. Sylvia, you've done a terrific job. I've been telling people in the department you were and up-and-comer, and you've proven me right. Your performance on this case *will* be noted in your file. Good work."

"Thank you, sir."

CHAPTER 45

Captain Hillary assembled the deputies for a special staff meeting. He handed out photos of Raydel Medina.

"This person's name is Raydel Medina. He may currently be somewhere in Monroe County. He's a person of interest in the Catterina Knoll investigation. I need you to locate him for me. Until recently he was a bartender at Rick's on Duval Street. His last known address was a houseboat on Garrison Bight. After our initial interrogation, he left the country for Cancún and then Venezuela. His passport records show he recently returned to Monroe County via the airport. I've got no record of his leaving again. He's a body builder so gymnasiums are a possible way to trace him. He likes to hang out at local bars as well. There currently is no warrant for his arrest, but I have reason to believe he may have been involved in Mrs. Knoll's kidnapping. He's been known to associate with some disreputable people. One of his longstanding friends, Mrs. Knoll's brother, Paulie Lopez, is a possible suspect for selling illegal narcotics for the Latin Kings. OK, men, go find him for me."

That same morning, Walter Wanderley had a similar meeting with his staff and passed out Raydel's picture. He dispatched them with a similar message, "Find Raydel Medina for me."

Not knowing that both the police department and the sheriff's office were trying to find him, Raydel was keeping a low profile under an alias in his motel room on South Roosevelt near the "Y" in Key West. He rationalized the need to monitor the news of Catt Knoll's death for a few days before departing so he could report the events completely and correctly to Paulie when he returned to Isla Margarita. He felt little reason to be alarmed. The newspapers said her death had been ruled an accidental drug overdose. The real reason he wanted to stay in Key West for a few more days was that he was simply not ready to return to exile before he had to – even if it was in a Latino paradise. After recovering that damaging diary from Catt Knoll, he felt he deserved a little R&R. Besides that, he wanted to familiarize himself further with the diary while he still had it in his hands. After all, knowledge was power. Raydel wouldn't have felt so smug had he known that he had been spotted in Key West, and that his presence had been reported back to Omar Perillo. Omar had ordered an e-mail with Raydel's picture sent to bartenders who the Latin Kings used as small-time cocaine retailers. It offered a reward for any Raydel sightings. He had dispatched Freddie Figgs to find him as well. Perillo still wanted to locate Paulie and settle the Latin Kings' score with him.

Raydel Medina was not used to confinement. It wasn't long before he began to get cabin fever in his motel room. He knew better than to risk exposing his presence in Key West. He knew too many of the service people who worked the Old Town joints. But he rationalized that he was not known in the county. He could have a fun evening at Mangrove Mama's, the Boondocks or Looe Key Tiki Bar without being recognized. After seeing that Looe Key had a Middle Keys entertainer playing from five to nine, he decided to go there. After all, if he didn't like it, the Boondocks *was* right across the street. Sounded like a plan.

Raydel arrived about six o'clock. The bar was already hopping. A white-haired guitarist was playing a song entitled *Take That Cell Phone and Shove It*. The crowd obviously agreed and cheered to show their support. Raydel ordered Appleton dark rum on the rocks. He also asked for a menu. When the bartender brought his drink, he asked who the singer was.

"That's Joe Mama," the bartender said. "He lives up in Marathon and performs mostly up there, but we get lucky and get him down here every once in a while. He's been around here longer than I have."

Perfect, Raydel thought to himself. *I bet he's never played Rick's or any of my other Key West watering holes. Ideal.*

He looked around the bar and didn't see a soul he recognized or who looked likely to recognize him. Raydel began to relax.

Perfect for unwinding.

A drunken local woman clumsily attempted to strike up a conversation with Raydel. He tried ignoring her but when she persisted, he asked the bartender where the men's room was. The bartender pointed to a freestanding building behind the tiki-hut. When Raydel returned, he made a point of unobtrusively moving to the other end of the bar.

No use causing trouble.

When Raydel went to the restroom, the bartender pulled a picture from beneath the bar. *Yep, same man,* he thought. *I'll pick up a little easy walking around money.*

He quickly dialed his cell phone. Freddie Figgs picked it up after two rings.

"Yes."

"Sir, this is Mickey at Looe Key Tiki Bar. The man the Latin Kings are looking for is in the bar right now."

"Is he getting ready to leave?" Freddie asked.

"I don't think so. He's in the head right now. I think he's going to order dinner when he gets back."

"Good. I'm near. I'm on my way. Is the motel full?"

"Not even close."

"Get me a door key to one of the back rooms and give it to me when I get there. And don't say a word to a soul. You've got a reward coming if you play this right, but I don't want to think what would happen to you if anyone ever found out I was there. You with me?"

"I understand."

Freddie grabbed his already-packed hostage kit and a small ice chest before jumping into his car. He calculated he was probably twenty miles away from the Looe Key Tiki Bar. He had one stop to make on the way, a convenience store, to buy a gallon of ice cream.

That strategy worked out pretty well with the Knoll broad, he thought. *If there's a coffee maker in the room for me to use to get hot water, I'll do the same thing to this asshole and watch his teeth shatter as well. If not, I've got plenty of other backup persuasion methods at my disposal.*

Freddie smiled sadistically as he thought about the coming confrontation. He enjoyed this part of his job.

~ ~ ~

"Take over for me," Mickey said to one of the other bartenders. "I'll be back in five."

He walked over to the dive shop. Looe Key Tiki Bar used the desk clerks at Looe Key Dive Shop as a motel front desk. It closed at 7PM. He got there just as the clerk was getting ready to lock up.

"I've got to take a crap something awful," Mickey said to the clerk, "and I'm not about to do it here where all those drunks have pissed all over the floor."

"I don't blame you," Tom, the clerk, said.

"You go on and close up. Lock the door," Mickey said. "I've got a key. I'll let myself out and lock it up again when I'm finished."

"Works for me. I'm ready to get the hell out of here. It's been a long day," Tom said. "Fire an aft torpedo for me."

"This log's for you," Mickey said. "Go on and get outa here so I can get something down on paper."

Mickey went in the restroom and listened for the door lock to snap. Then he came out and inspected the key pegboard. He selected a downstairs key well away from any room which appeared to have a guest. He locked the dive shop front door and returned to the bar.

"Where'd you go?" the other bartender asked.

"Had to squeeze out some brown soft serve," Mickey said. "Thanks for covering for me."

~ ~ ~

Freddie Figgs stood in front of the bar since there were no bar stools available. Mickey saw him and worked his way down to where Freddie was standing.

"Estancia merlot," Freddie said and handed Mickey a twenty. Mickey poured the wine and got change for the twenty out of the cash register. He handed it back to Freddie with the motel key in the middle. Freddie saw Raydel eating an order of hot wings. As soon as a bar stool became available, he sat and nursed his beer, all the while watching Raydel out of the corner of his eye. Raydel seemed in no hurry to leave. He continued to knock back straight Appleton's on the rocks. Freddie could tell he was beginning to get tipsy.

Joe Mama began to wind up his last set. Raydel paid his tab and staggered towards the back entrance of the tiki-hut and then stumbled uncertainly across the irregular, pitted pea-rock parking lot. Freddie followed. When Raydel got to his rental car, Freddie looked around for witnesses before giving him a controlled whack on the head with his leather sap. Raydel collapsed and dropped the keys. Freddie pushed him into the car. Freddie retrieved the keys, drove the car the short distance to the motel and located the room. He unlocked the door and helped

Raydel into the room. He quickly secured Raydel to a chair with duct tape and stuffed a wash cloth into Raydel's mouth. Raydel was beginning to come around. When he saw Freddie, his eyes opened wide with fear.

"Good evening," Freddie said pleasantly and took the washrag from Raydel's mouth. "My employer's been looking for you."

Raydel looked momentarily confused, and then a light seemed to go off in his head.

"You ain't looking for me," he said. "You've got me confused with Paulie Lopez. I'm not Paulie."

"We know that, but you can tell us how to locate Paulie ... And you *will* tell us how to locate Paulie."

"But I don't know where he is."

"That's the wrong answer," Freddie said as he shook his head and sighed. "I've never understood why people so often choose the hard way when the easy way is so much simpler. I also might add, less painful. Mrs. Knoll didn't believe me either. So needless, so needless."

Freddie sat in silence as his comments sank in. He looked at Raydel almost as if he felt sorry for him. Finally he said, "I'm going to heat some water in the Mr. Coffee. If your memory doesn't return by the time it's brewed, I'll have to try to help it along. You've got a few minutes to think it over, but not long. And there will be no second chances." He turned on the coffee maker and began to draw water from the tap.

Raydel began to piss on himself. He also began to think; *maybe I can get out of this mess alive without totally dumping my friend in the creek.* He also had another thought, *I'm living off of Paulie's stolen money, and if that money goes away, I won't have anything to live on. Well, I ain't got nothin' to lose by trying.*

"I don't know where Paulie is, but I do have something else I can offer you if you let me go."

Freddie motioned for Paulie to continue.

240

"Paulie kept a diary of his dealings with the Latin Kings. His sister stole it from him. I got it from her. If you lemme me go, I'll give it to you."

"Do you have the diary with you?"

"No, but I can put my hands on it real easy."

"Where is it?"

"I can't tell you that until I know we have an agreement."

Freddie opened his ice chest and took out the gallon of ice cream.

"What're you gon' do with that?" Raydel asked nervously.

"You'll see momentarily." Freddie retrieved the hot coffee pot and set it on the table next to them. He then pried Raydel's mouth open with a spoon and began to stuff it with cold ice cream. Raydel's cheeks bulged out, and he tried to keep from puking as Freddie continued to stuff his mouth. Within moments, Freddie had over half a gallon in his mouth. Then without saying a word, Freddie began to pour the hot water in behind the ice cream. Raydel's teeth began to shatter. He tried to scream, but Freddie clamped his hand over Raydel's mouth while he bound it with duct tape. Raydel's bowels let loose. Freddie gave him a blank stare; he might as well have been watching a toothpaste commercial.

When he was satisfied the ice cream and water had done its work, Freddie calmly said, "When I take this tape off, you will tell me where that diary is. You will also tell me where to find Paulie Lopez. Otherwise, I have more tricks in my bag, and they will make what you have just endured look like a stroll in the park. I tried to tell you there are hard ways and easy ways; I just don't know why people never seem to believe me. Maybe I should work on my communication skills. Have you ever seen the imaginative things which can be done with a simple pair of pliers? I'm going to pull off the tape now. If you scream, I'm going to hit you with my leather sap. Understand?"

Raydel nodded. Freddie ripped the tape off in one motion. Raydel's teeth hurt so bad he hardly noticed the new pain from his stinging lips.

"The Best Western, man! The Best Western on Sout' Roosevelt!" Raydel immediately blurted out.

"Which room?"

"Tuh – o – tuh."

A pain shot through Raydel's mouth after his attempt to reply.

"Where in 202?"

"It's in muh sui'case in the closet."

"Is the suitcase locked?"

"No."

"Where's the room key?"

Raydel winced before replying.

"In muh p-p-pants pocket."

"Thank you. I'll be back within an hour. I'm going to have to make sure you don't get into any mischief until I return. Since I won't be here to supervise you, I'm going to have to truss you up pretty thoroughly. Now, where's Paulie? We can either talk about that topic now, or we can cover it when I get back. Your call. All I'll say is, I get more irritable the closer I get to my bedtime."

"He's near Vens-s-uela at a place called Isla M-margarita."

"Where on Isla Margarita?"

Raydel gave him an address.

Freddie straightened up the room, repacked his hostage kit, put it in his car trunk, and drove to Key West making sure he obeyed the speed limits. He donned his disposable gloves and let himself in to room 202. The diary was right where Raydel had said it would be. He turned around immediately, drove back to Looe Key Resort, and parked his car as close the room as possible. He looked around and saw he had the parking lot to himself. He untied Raydel enough to walk him out to the car. As he had Raydel propped up against the side of the car, Freddie gave him a shot with the hypodermic he had in his jacket pocket. The hypo contained a custom cocktail of cocaine, strychnine and a sedative Freddie had designed for such occasions. Raydel collapsed, and Freddie loaded him into the back seat. He then took the room key back over to the tiki-bar, silently got Mickey's attention, laid it on the end of the bar along with two one-hundred-dollar bills and turned and left.

Freddie drove the unconscious Raydel down a deserted road on the Gulf side until the road dead-ended into some mangroves. He knew he needed to offload Raydel soon. After ten to twenty minutes the drug cocktail would begin to kick in. Once there, he put on his gloves and unloaded his unconscious cargo. Freddie waited for the cocktail's effects to begin. Within five minutes, Raydel's body muscles began to twitch as the muscles started to spasm. It started with the head and neck and spread to every muscle in the body. The spasms began to increase in intensity, and Raydel's backbone began to arch.

It shouldn't be long now, Freddie thought.

He had administered a strychnine/cocaine death on many occasions. He knew from experience Raydel would die either from asphyxiation or exhaustion from the convulsions.

There is no antidote. I could leave now, but I might as well watch the fun for a few more minutes, he thought. *Too bad I won't be able to see the grand finale, but that'll take a couple of hours.*

He knew that the slightest stimulus would intensify

the convulsions. He found a stick and poked Raydel
with it to enjoy watching his reactions.

"I offer you a final thought before I depart:
'Go thou, and fill another room in hell.

That hand shall burn in never-quenching fire,

That staggers thus my person. Exton, thy fierce
hand

Halth with thy king's bloodstain'd the king's own
land.

Mount, mount, my soul! Thy seat is up on high;

Whilst my gross flesh sinks downward, here to die.'"

When he tired of watching and poking Raydel,
Freddie pushed the twitching body out into the
mangroves.

Freddie didn't realize until he got back on US1 just
how tired he was. It was getting late, and he had a long
drive to get back to Miami. He just wanted to get home.
His shoes had been on so long they felt like they were
growing to his feet. He had been away on business now
for several nights, and he just wanted to see his family.
He waited until he got back to Marathon to fill the car
and to get some coffee and a snack for the drive back.
Freddie put on the same Latin boogaloo CD he had
been playing on the way down.

*This should be peppy enough to keep me awake on
the drive back.*

Soon the Joe Cuba Sextet was playing *Sock It To
Me.*

Freddie Figgs laughed to himself as he drove and
ate the Goya vanilla wafers he had bought.

*Well, I didn't lie to Raydel. I told him I wouldn't
torture him anymore if he told me what I wanted to
know, and I didn't. At least I waited until he was
unconscious. He just didn't ask the right question. I
never told him I wouldn't kill him. He should have
known I couldn't leave him alive to warn Paulie Lopez*

or tell someone I had visited Paulie's sister. That was just common sense. I shouldn't have told Raydel about visiting Mrs. Knoll, but it didn't make any difference anyway since the plan was to kill him all along. Señor Perillo is going to be pleased I got that diary. I bet that was a dangerous document he didn't even know existed. If I get a bonus, I'll get tickets to take the wife out to see Romeo and Juliet while it's in town. Hell, I'll take her out anyway. Then I'll tell her while she's in a good mood, that I might have to go to Venezuela on business for a few days.

When Freddie got home, he was exhausted, went straight to bed and slept soundly, satisfied with a job well done.

CHAPTER 46

Walter Wanderley gave Dan Hillary a courtesy call. "Dan. This is Walter. I've got something to report on Raydel Medina."

"Your ears must've been burning. I was getting ready to call you. Have you found our bad boy?"

"Well, sort of," Walter said.

"The reason I was getting ready to call you is we sort of did too. You give me your sort of, and I'll give you mine."

"We found where Raydel's been staying, but we haven't found Raydel," Walter said. "The desk clerk at the Best Western on South Roosevelt recognized the picture, but that's not the name he registered in. He called himself Carlos Marcello."

"Like the gangster?"

Like the gangster," Walter said. "The name didn't mean a damned thing to the desk clerk."

"Why am I not surprised?" Dan said. "It's a pitiful commentary on modern life, but the American public doesn't know shit about shit. He probably could have used the name Ted Bundy or Douglas McArthur without raising any eyebrows."

"Just think, that's the same informed public who are electing our country's leaders and offering opinions on policy matters. The concept of 'one man, one vote' is rather frightening."

"Just so you don't think the KWPD is superior to the sheriff's department, I'm going to match you tit-for-tat. You found a room; we found a car, but we didn't find Raydel either. Deputy Kohout got a call from Looe Key Resort saying that a car had been abandoned in their parking lot. She went over to check it out and

247

found out it was rental car. And guess what, the lessee was our boy, Raydel."

"So he rented a room under an alias but a car under his real name."

"I'm sure he didn't have any choice. The car rental company would have demanded to see a valid driver's license."

"But you didn't find Raydel?" Walter asked.

"No Raydel," Hillary said, "but my deputy Linda had the picture we handed out. She showed it around the waitresses and bartenders in Looe Key Tiki Bar on Ramrod. One of the bartenders remembered the face. Seems like Raydel came in there the night Joe Mama was playing. Raydel sat at the bar and drank rum on the rocks and ate wings while he listened to the music. The bartender said Raydel was alone and stayed to himself. Even avoided some drunk woman lush who tried to hit on him. Bartender said he paid his bill and left. And that was all there was to it. Linda took the picture over to the dive shop, but they said he hadn't registered to stay in the motel. He's just disappeared."

"Just like at the Best Western," Walter said. "He's never checked out. His things are still in the room. For some reason, his suitcase was left open on the bed. Desk clerk said they didn't give Raydel much thought since he hadn't caused any trouble, and he'd paid through the end of the week. Any helpful prints on the car?"

"Nope. Only his. I guess we're going to just have to keep on looking for him," Dan said.

"Us too. I'm sure he's going to turn up somewhere. If he abandoned his rental car, how's he getting around?"

"Damned if I know. He must be riding with someone else."

Later in the day, Walter's phone rang.

"Found Raydel."

"Oh yeah? Where's that?"

"In the back country off Big Torch," Dan said. "Deader than a door nail. A fisherman snagged him with his hook."

"Look like someone offed him?"

"Don't know yet," Dan said. "I don't think the body was necessarily beat up. No apparent broken limbs or bruises or anything. I'll let you know as soon as they tell me."

Dan called Walter the following morning.

"Official cause of death was cocaine laced with strychnine administered intravenously. The only sign of trauma was that his teeth had been shattered. That's weird since you would think that if someone hit Raydel in the face, his lips and all around his mouth would be bruised."

"Boy, that's a gruesome way to die. Someone didn't like him at all. But there are certain similarities to Catt Knoll's death," Walter said. "She died of a drug overdose, and her teeth were shattered as well. She also had no bruising around the mouth, lips or cheeks."

"Almost seems like both got involved with the same person."

"Maybe, maybe not. Her death was from OxyContin that could have been self-administered. His was definitely not self-administered," Walter said. "Keep me in the loop as you learn more."

"Will do."

249

CHAPTER 47

Walter opened his e-mail. It contained a message from Dan Hillary.

Walter immediately dialed Dan's cell phone. Dan picked up.

"Walter, thanks for calling. As we both know, communications from third world countries concerning American citizens are not as efficient as we'd like. They're especially bad in hostile countries like Venezuela. We've found the American embassies in some of these remote places to be far more efficient and reliable communicators than local law enforcement. Sometimes when an American dies in their jurisdiction, local officials simply make a cursory record of the event and have the body destroyed."

"It's a sad commentary, but I know firsthand what you're saying is true. They might not even attempt to contact a next of kin," Walter said.

"Since we knew Paulie Lopez had flown to Caracas, I sent an e-mail to our embassy there requesting they keep me apprised if there were any future news concerning him. This morning they were kind enough to respond. Paulie Lopez is dead."

"Another one bites the dust. What happened to him? Another drug overdose?"

"You hit it right on the head. Overdosed on cocaine mixed with strychnine taken intravenously," Dan said.

"Where?"

"In an apartment he was renting on Isla Margarita. In case you're not familiar with it, it's an island just off the Venezuelan coast."

"Can't ignore that distinctive M.O. You've got to be one mean, callous M.F. to use it."

"That's for damned sure, and know what you're doing. Now, you ready for the finishing touch? Paulie's teeth were shattered," Dan said.

"He took a beating as well?"

"Nope," Dan said. "His teeth were simply shattered from some kind of undetermined trauma with no other bruising."

"Do we have a serial killer on the loose?"

"I don't think so," Dan said. "I believe we are dealing with a professional killer who has an affinity for using the same methods time after time. Probably because they have been effective for him."

"Or he just enjoys them. I've got an idea," Walter said. "We need to reassess our strategy and do nothing going forward. At the rate we're going, everyone in this case is gonna drop dead, and we won't have to be concerned about any of it."

"You think you're being funny, but the way things are going, the case may turn into an academic exercise."

"Or a way to bring the Latin Kings down," Walter said. "It's got their fingerprints all over it. We sure have a whole lot to have nothing. We've got that confession on CD with Raydel and Mrs. Knoll candidly discussing the kidnapping and confirming that one of the reasons for it was to get Paulie off the hook with the Latin Kings. We know Paulie was a cartel mule who had stolen some of their money, and that the ransom money was partially to pay off what he owed 'em. We also know that when the score was settled, they planned to resume using Paulie as a mule, and he was to captain a boat they had an investment in."

"Tell me about it. I remember all those facts. They were some real zingers, and if everyone involved hadn't died, I was going to use them to put the whole sorry lot of them away," Dan said. "After all the work we both put in, we deserved that resolution. Maybe Thomas

Jefferson was wrong when he said about the harder you work, the luckier you get."

"Yeah, after all that, you would think we'd have a perp. Do you think Mr. Knoll was involved?"

"I still doubt it. I continue to think he was a victim, but I'd sure like to find out the real reason why he wrote his sitter a check for a hundred g's. She must be great in the sack," Dan said.

"You jest my friend, but there apparently is a lot more to their relationship than we know about. By the way, are you going to contact Paulie's next of kin?"

"All I know about them is their name is Lopez, and they live in Cuba – probably on a very limited income. If there's any other kin, I don't know about 'em. Besides that, the Venezuelan authorities disposed of the body after doing their cursory autopsy so even if the Lopez family could afford to bury him, there's nothing to bury. We're lucky the locals were able to tell us as much as they did."

"Ain't that the truth. Ask the husband anyway when you see him. Surely he knows how to contact his in-laws in Cuba," Walter said. "If my child died, I'd at least want to be told about it, even if there was nothing for me to do."

CHAPTER 48

Captain Hillary called Norm Knoll at Prestige Boats. "Mr. Knoll, may I come by for a few minutes this morning? I've had some new developments concerning your wife's brother, and there's still some things concerning your wife's death which are unclear in my mind. I can come at your convenience."

The two men agreed on a time mutually agreeable to both of them. Hillary was there promptly at the appointed time.

"Mr. Knoll, I'm afraid I have some bad news concerning your wife's brother, Paulie Lopez and his associate. Both are now dead. As you know, both were involved in the plot to kidnap your wife."

Norm sat there as if he didn't believe what he was hearing. Finally he said, "Where? How?"

"We've been looking for Mr. Medina for some time to follow up on our initial interview with him. He had quit his job and apparently gone abroad. He recently returned to Key West under an assumed name and has been living in a New Town motel. We're still unclear just what brought him back. His body was found by a fisherman floating off Big Torch Key. Our autopsy shows some trauma to the body similar to that experienced by your wife but shows the primary cause of death to be cocaine and strychnine administered intravenously. Were you in touch with him while he was in the city?"

"No, I wasn't. I didn't even know he was here."

"May I ask you where you were Tuesday night?"

"I worked until we closed. I'm always the last to leave since I have to lock up. I went by Hurricane Harbor for happy hour and decided I didn't feel like cooking. So I stayed and had dinner. After that, I went on home and watched TV until bedtime. In fact, if you'll give me a minute, I'll show you my credit card charge from Hurricane Harbor. I've still got it here in my wallet."

He produced the credit card receipt.

"Would you make a copy of that receipt for me? I'll get back to you if I need any further clarification."

Norm ran a copy of it and handed it to the captain.

"We've received a report that Paulie Lopez is dead," Hillary said. "He had also left the country shortly before your wife died. His body was found in an apartment on an island off Venezuela. He also had experienced some trauma, but the cause of death was ruled to be a poisoning homicide from an intravenous drug overdose."

"I guess what goes around comes around," Norm said. "He'd been peddling that shit for years. I guess one of his druggie buddies finally got to him."

"We don't know," said Hillary. "The information is incomplete. What we do know is because of a brief communiqué from the American embassy there. What kind of next of kin does he have?"

"Catt was his only sibling. Both of their parents are alive, but they live in Cuba. They don't have any money. If you need someone to bring the body back, I'll pay."

"That won't be necessary. It was disposed of by the Venezuelan authorities, but someone does need to tell his parents. Are you in touch with them?"

"Not really. I haven't even told them about Catt. I barely know them. If I gave you their phone number in Cuba, would you get someone to call them?"

"If you wish, even though you should be the one doing that," Hillary said.

"I just don't think I'm up to it."

"May I change the subject for a moment?" Hillary

continued. "I've had a report that you have spent $600,000 of the million dollars of the proceeds from the life insurance policy on your wife."

Who told you that?"

"I'm not at liberty to disclose my source, but it is a reliable one."

"Big fucking brother looking over our shoulder reporting our activities to the government. Is there no such thing as privacy anymore? We're turning in to one big socialist state. It's not America anymore – just a communist country." He began raising his voice.

"I'm not here to debate politics, Mr. Knoll," said Hillary. "I just want to make sure these expenditures don't relate to your wife's case. I was hoping you would clarify them."

"If you must goddamn know, I settled a claim with the IRS – bastards – I didn't owe it, but the little guy can't fight city hall, and I spent a hundred grand on a deal on a used boat at the Martin County boat show. You know, I *am* in the goddamn boat business," Norm said. He was starting to get angry.

"Mr. Knoll, the day this check was written you were not in Stuart. We have security footage of you and Ms. Pannullo having lunch at the Roostica on Stock Island. The film shows you writing a check and giving it to her at the table. The check is also made out to G.T. Pannullo. That's a lot of money for one night's nursing services. Our investigations also show that according to the DMV Ms. Pannullo has never been listed as the registered owner of a boat in Florida. Now, do you wish to amend your explanation and explain it more fully?"

"No, I do the hell not. My affairs are no business of the government's. I don't have to justify everything I do to you or anybody else."

"You'll have to admit, if you were in my shoes, wouldn't you wonder about these things too?"

257

"Wonder all you want. I have a right to my privacy. I don't have to explain what I do to anyone. My personal affairs are private, and they're gonna to stay that way. I've done nothing wrong. So, Captain, unless you have some concrete reason to suspect me of wrongdoing, I'm terminating this conversation right now. I'll remind you, *I* was the victim in this case, and now you're trying to twist things around and make me into a crime perpetrator. Bullshit! It ain't going to happen."

"I'm not trying to make you into anything that you're not, Mr. Knoll," Hillary said. "I'm just trying to get to the truth, and my attempts to do so lead me to explore all angles. If you can think of anything which will help me get to the truth, will you please call me?"

Norm just sat and glared at the captain.

CHAPTER 49

When Hillary left, Donna, Norm's secretary, came into his office with the mail and a couple of pink "while you were out" slips. He curtly thanked her in a flat monotone. He absentmindedly flipped through both, not paying close attention. He vaguely realized that he was sweating and that his jaw muscle seemed sore. His mind was still replaying the conversation he had just had with Captain Hillary. He had another thought.

It's a good thing I kept that ceramic bathroom tumbler which has the OxyContin residue and Gina's fingerprints on it. I will use it to divert suspicion away from me if the cops try to blame me for Catt's death. I've enjoyed what Gina and I have had together up until now, but I've been through enough. I'm not taking a murder rap for anybody.

Norm regained his focus on the incoming mail when he noticed a letter from the Internal Revenue Service. He momentarily became short of breath as he looked at it. He hated those bastards. They had recently gouged him for $500,000. What was this – a thank you note from the President? Bastards! Rubbing it in? He certainly deserved a thank you plus some. He quickly tore the envelope open. It was a notice that the IRS was now questioning the last four tax returns from Prestige Boats. Wasn't it enough they had put him through hell on his personal returns? Now the Nazi bastards wanted to take his business away from him.

Norm slammed his desk drawer shut and dialed Reese Leffew, his accountant, his fingers punishing the number buttons as he dialed. The receptionist told him that Mr. Leffew was away from his desk.

"Then find him," Norm rudely growled. "I'll hold." The accountant came on the line almost immediately.

"Reese, the bastards are at it again."

"Is this Norm?"

"Who the hell do you think it is?"

"Norm, calm down. Who are the bastards you're referring to?"

"The goddamned IRS! Who do you think I'm talking about – the fuckin' Easter bunny?"

"Tell me what's going on."

"They're after my business returns now," Norm hissed into the phone. "They want to audit four years returns. I just paid the SOB's as much as many people make in a lifetime."

"What are they questioning?"

"They think I've falsely reported taxable wages for some of my employees."

"If you'll remember, I questioned you about the same issue. Were you doing so?"

"Well, sometimes they did me free favors not associated with the business, and sometimes when they needed money, I'd give them a loan."

"Did they repay those loans?"

"Of course not. Like I just said, they were good employees who did me favors occasionally. You know, one hand washes the other."

Reese sighed. "Norm, the IRS will say you intentionally under-reported salaries paid to employees in order to reduce payments to the government, and if these loans were never paid back, they really weren't loans at all. They could have a pretty good case."

"So you're saying I'm going to have to come up with some more money to pay those Nazi assholes just because I'm a nice guy who takes care of the people who work here?"

"We could be talking about more than tax money. We could be talking about fraud. That's a felony. Let me read you something out of one of my tax guides. 'It is a felony to conspire with other people to defraud the United States government in the ascertainment, computation, assessment and collection of employment taxes.' That's pretty clear."

"I wasn't trying to do anything wrong."

"Send me everything you have gotten from them, and let me look at it. I'll see what I can do to put a spin on the situation in your favor. This does *not* look good, but the good news is that it takes the government a long time to prosecute these cases."

"Like how long?"

"There was a case I was involved in similar to this in Islamorada. The investigation took over four years from the time the client's records were seized, and it hasn't come to trial yet. Keep in mind, your records haven't been seized, you're still in the initial inquiry stage."

"What's the worst case scenario for the guy in Islamorada?"

"Five years or so in a Federal pen."

"Wonderful, as if I didn't have enough shit in my life," Norm said.

"Tax fraud is a serious matter. What do you think sent Al Capone to prison? I can name a few others too who got in trouble – like Martha Stewart and Willie Nelson."

CHAPTER 50

Captain Hillary had scheduled an appointment with Gina Pannullo the same morning as his appointment with Norm Knoll. If she and Norm were conspiring or comparing notes, he didn't want to give her any more time than necessary prepare a pat, canned story.

As he drove to Stock Island to meet Pannullo, he thought about how defensive and upset Norm had gotten. He'd never seen Norm's short fuse before. He knew Norm had been through a lot recently, but he couldn't understand Norm's totally stonewalling the questions about the $100,000 check unless he had something to hide.

And it sure seems that way, Dan thought as he drove. *It's not everyone who pays a sitter that kind of serious dough – even if she is a nurse.*

He was hoping he'd get luckier when he confronted Gina.

Hillary turned onto Maloney Avenue. Gina's rusty, beat-up trailer looked the same and just as depressing as the last time he had been here. He parked and walked through the weeds to the tiny front porch. She answered after the third rap and invited him in.

"Good to see you again," Hillary said as he held out his hand to shake hers.

"Are you still investigating Mrs. Knoll's death?" Gina said. "I thought it was ruled to be an accidental drug overdose."

"It was," Hillary said, "but there's still some things about it which bother me. I was hoping you might be able to help clear them up so I can close the file on this matter once and for all."

"I'll certainly do what I can."

"We found a used toothbrush in the medicine cabinet of the bedroom you stayed in the night you spent the night at the Knoll residence. The butt end of it had both OxyContin and Splenda residue on it as if it had been used to possibly crush the OxyContin tablets and then mix them with the Splenda. The brush end also had the same residue on it. Your fingerprints were on the toothbrush. Could you explain how this came to be?"

"Partially," Gina said without hesitation. "I brush my teeth every night before I go to bed. I need to rinse my mouth after brushing. There was a small, white, ceramic tumbler with a pewter base on the counter. It looked dirty. I wasn't sure what had been in it, but I certainly wasn't going to put water in a dirty container and then rinse my mouth with it. I found a toothbrush in the medicine cabinet and used it to scrub the tumbler clean before I rinsed with it. I stuck the toothbrush back in the medicine cabinet. I guess I forgot to wash it off. I didn't know what was on it until you just told me."

"We didn't find a tumbler matching that description in the bathroom," Hillary said.

"I really don't know what happened to it," Gina said. "I used it that night and then again the following morning. Someone must have taken it out of there."

"Obviously," Hillary said, "but you did not dispose of the tumbler or put it in the dishwasher or anything like that?"

"No, I left it right on the counter where I found it."

"It would seem that the overdose Mrs. Knoll took might have been dispensed from that tumbler," Hillary said. "There's another matter troubling me as well. I hope maybe you can shed some light on it too."

"And that matter is?"

"Mr. Knoll wrote a check to you for $100,000 a few weeks after Mrs. Knoll's death. That's a rather large check for sitting services. We have a security tape showing you and Mr. Knoll having what appears to be a very jovial luncheon together at Roostica before he wrote you a check at the table. Would you mind telling me what that check was for?"

Gina was not so quick to come up with a glib answer to this question. Her shoulders tightened, and she seemed to turn slightly ashen. When she finally spoke, her voice had a false bravado. "Mr. Knoll bought a boat from me."

"I've checked with DMV. They have no record that you have ever owned a boat."

"This is a private matter between Mr. Knoll and myself. I don't wish to discuss it with anyone else."

"It looks awfully suspicious when that amount of money changes hands for an undisclosed reason."

"I guess it'll just have to look suspicious then. I have no further comment."

"If these are wages, I'll have to report that fact to the IRS."

"Then you'll just have to do what you have to do. I have no further comments on the matter. It was a private affair."

"Is that your final word on the subject?"

"Yes, it is."

Hillary waved at Gina as he drove away and tried not to show his disappointment.

That's twice I've been stonewalled today. Sure makes me want to know what that hundred grand was all about, but I don't know how to force it out of either of them. One thing's for certain, they've both moved up my suspect list.

As she watched Hillary drive down the street, Gina was lost in thought as well.

That fuzz may cause me some problems before it's all over, but answering questions would cause me more problems yet.

Gina's mind reverted to other thoughts after Hillary left. She was determined that she would not spend the rest of her life in this second-rate trailer park. She was willing to do whatever it took to give herself and Samantha a better life. She thought about the pressure Hillary must be bringing to bear on Norm Knoll, and what she would do if Norm tried to shift blame to her. Her thoughts went back to that day at Two Friends when Norm had first demanded a concession from her. He had informed her politely that he simply could not afford their present arrangement to look after his mother. He said, however, he'd devised a plan which would bring the costs back into line. Instead of her billing him for nursing and sitting services which were not beneficial to him tax-wise, Norm had told Gina that he wanted her to invoice Prestige Boats for lettering and sign painting services to put names and numbers on the boats people purchased from him. He would pay her and deduct her services as a business expense. This would reduce the dealership's profitability while making her services tax deductible. He had told her that if she were unwilling to make this concession, he would have to make other arrangements for his mother's care. He had even gone so far as to have printed a letterhead for her new "business" on some blank invoices. All she had to do was submit her usual billings on these invoices instead of her regular ones. He would see that she got paid, no questions asked. Gina had reluctantly agreed to do as Norm had demanded rather than risk losing critical income at a time she couldn't afford to do so.

Gina smiled as her next thought came into her mind.

What Norm didn't know is that I kept copies of every invoice and every check. I also documented each conversation we had on the topic. I'm not sure what the penalty is for tax evasion, but I do know it is a felony. If push comes to shove and Norm even hints he might try to shift any blame to me because of that $100,000 check, I'll simply threaten to turn my entire file over to the authorities. And I'll do it too, Norm honey, if you make me.

CHAPTER 51

Dan Hillary called Walter Wanderley and suggested they have breakfast and talk. They decided to meet at Mangrove Mama's since it was a compromise drive for each of them. Dan got to the restaurant first and decided to eat breakfast in the open courtyard behind the main building. He ordered a cup of coffee and a glass of water while he waited. Walter arrived a few minutes later. He walked in the front door and looked around. When he didn't see Dan, he walked through the building and looked in the protected open-air bamboo area. Dan saw him and waved him out onto the open courtyard adjacent to the back-building containing the bar. He motioned for Missy, the waitress, to bring Walter's coffee. After some friendly banter, Missy took their breakfast order.

"So how'd it go with Mr. Knoll?" Walter asked.

"Not so well," Dan said. "He first tried to lie to me about the check, but when he found out that story wasn't going to fly, instead of trying a second line of bullshit or getting flustered, he simply clammed up and told me to mind my own business. He didn't seem to care that his attitude elevated him on my list of suspects. Of course, he was already on it anyway, if for no other reason than he was the recipient of his wife's life insurance proceeds. But he didn't seem to care. He just got pissed and told me to fuck off. And he's right. I can't make him tell me what I want to know. That alone is not enough reason for me to arrest him and then take him in and then try to sweat the truth out of him."

"You're right. That's not enough to arrest him, especially with all the conflicting evidence we have. You'd never get an indictment. You'd just end up looking like an idiot."

"And he knew it," Dan said.

"What about Gina Pannullo?"

"Pretty much the same thing happened with her," Dan said. "I brought up the toothbrush with the OxyContin residue and the fact that her fingerprints were on it. She said that she'd used that ceramic tumbler to wash her mouth out with after she brushed her teeth. She said it looked dirty, and she used the only thing she could find in the medicine cabinet to clean it with before she filled it with water. She said she didn't have any idea what was on the toothbrush at the time. It looked clean to her. When I asked her what happened to the tumbler, she said she had no idea – that it was there when she left the next morning."

"I don't know if her story's true, but it sounds plausible," Walter said. "What did she say about the check?"

"Same thing Knoll did," Dan said. "That it was a private matter - none of my business, and I could fuck off. I told her if it was wages, I'd report her to the IRS. I told her about the security tape from Roostica. Neither fact fazed her."

"This case has certainly gotten complicated," Walter said. "Let's summarize. Even though we both think the official conclusion about Mrs. Knoll's death is incorrect, we have nothing. We can't prove anything against Paulie or Raydel, and even if we could, they're both dead – victims of their own unsolved homicides. What evidence we do have against them concerns the kidnapping, not Mrs. Knoll's death. We can't charge Mrs. Knoll with a crime since she's already dead. You've certainly got to wonder about the Latin Kings' role in the whole affair, but we don't have anything concrete against them either. We don't have any evidence which will hold up against Mr. Knoll. He obviously wasn't part of the original kidnapping, and it's not a crime to be an insurance beneficiary. We know Knoll had IRS problems, but that's a separate, unrelated issue and one that existed a long time before this case ever started. If anything, the money which was siphoned off from him during the abduction reduced his ability to settle with the government. There was no way at the time to predict her unexpected death, and that it would lead to a windfall which would allow him catch his taxes up to date. Gina Pannullo had a perfectly legitimate reason to be at the Knoll residence, and her actions were in line with what she was hired to do. The only big red flag we have is that $100,000 check, and we can't force either of them to tell us what why it changed hands unless we can find some other form of leverage on either one of them or unless one of them out of greed, fear, or spite dumps the other person in the creek."

"That's an extremely good summary," Dan said. "At this point, someone apparently has pulled off the perfect crime unless some new evidence comes into our possession."

"That's the size of it. We may have to file this case as unsolved unless additional facts come to light to help us out. We may have a cold case on our hands."

"I hate to have to admit it with all the work we've got into it, but I'm afraid you're right. It looks like the bad guy or guys won."

"I wouldn't call three people dead winning," Walter said. "Let's just say they're currently ahead on points."

"For the time being, I'm going to need to move along to new cases," Dan said.

"I am too, but I'm still going to keep an eye open for a way to reopen this case."

"Then, we're in agreement. Let's finish our breakfast before it gets totally cold and then go after some bad guys we *can* catch and prosecute," Dan said.

"Amen, my friend. I hate cold grits."

EPILOGUE

Norm Knoll and Gina Pannullo sipped their drinks and enjoyed the Little Palm Island ambiance. Norm had gotten the weekend getaway package for them to rekindle their relationship.

"You look stunning tonight," Norm said.

"You look dashing yourself," Gina said. "When I saw that silk sport jacket in the Saks catalog, it looked like you, and I had to buy it. I can't wait to get you out of it later."

"You got just the right size too," Norm said. "It required no alterations."

The soft strains of the solo pianist gently wafted across the room playing the familiar strains of *The Christmas Song*.

"I always love this time of year," Gina said. "Everything is so special. It makes you feel like dressing up and celebrating. Look at these Christmas decorations. Have you ever seen anything more beautiful? I could never understand Scrooge. Another year's almost over, and this one has certainly been special. Thank you for arranging this weekend."

"It's the least I could do since we haven't been able to see each other for six months. And I thought this would be a perfect place for us to get reacquainted without the prying eyes of Key West being on us. I don't mind telling you, I was a little bit nervous when that Captain Hillary continued to probe and ask questions. He was getting a little too close for comfort. I sure as hell didn't want him to see us together for awhile after that and realize we were more than employer and employee. I just wanted him to lose interest in Catt's case and go away."

"Yes, I felt the same way," Gina said. "I don't know why he couldn't just take the coroner's decision and live with it. Why'd he have to go on and on like a broken record?"

"Because he's a nosy goddamned cop. That's why," Norm said, "and that's what cops do. I shouldn't have written you that check out of my brokerage account, but I honestly couldn't think of another way to distribute the money. If I cashed a check for a hundred g's, it certainly would have attracted attention, and I didn't have any other accounts to transfer that money into which would've been less visible. If I'd made the check out to cash, it probably would have attracted even more attention, and you might've had a problem cashing it anyway. I was hoping they'd buy the boat story since the Martin County Boat Show was going on at that time."

"I'm not an expert in moving money around either," Gina said. "I'm not sure how I would have done it if the situation had been reversed."

"So we did the right thing. We stonewalled," Norm said. "The cop may not've liked it, but there wasn't a damned thing he could do about it but bitch. I'm glad you had enough presence of mind to stonewall him just like I did. Fuck him and the horse he rode in on."

"Do you think it ever occurred to him that you were paying me to terminate your wife?"

"I don't know and don't care what he thought as long as he couldn't prove anything. I wasn't planning to add him to my Christmas card list anyway."

"It's lucky that Catt's brother muddied the water with his problems. That certainly was timely," Gina said. "And it's also fortunate your wife had that OxyContin in the house. It saved me from having to use one of the medications I had previously gotten from Fisherman's Hospital. It was *so* simple to add a lethal dose to her coffee. She was so hung over that morning she never even commented on tasting anything unusual. All she tasted was the Splenda. And it was easy to circle back by there after I took Samantha to kindergarten and wash out her coffee cup before the excitement started. I forgot about that toothbrush though."

"You did a good job of explaining your mistake away. Good thinking on your feet. Catt brought this shit on herself," Norm said. "I never would have thought of doing harm to my wife if she hadn't gone along with that no-good brother of hers and tried to shaft me first. It's all that sorry Paulie's fault. I would've found another way to pay off the IRS, but when she pulled that kidnapping and extortion crap, the gloves came off. It became dog-eat-dog."

"As the gloves should have come off, and let that bitch-dog get eaten," Gina said. "She never suspected you and I had formed a relationship while I was caring for your mom."

"Nah, she was too self-absorbed to even notice."

"So where do we go from here?" Gina asked.

"How would you like to be the second Mr. Norman Knoll?"

"Is that a proposal?"

"Yes, it is. I think you and I are very compatible."

"And you're willing to become a father to Samantha?"

"If that's what it takes to get you."

"Let's finish dinner and consummate this partnership," Gina said.

"I was hoping you'd say that."

The pianist played a soft medley of *Have Yourself A Merry Little Christmas* and *Jingle Bells* as Norm and Gina walked out arm in arm.

~ ~ ~

Monday when Norm returned to work, he called an insurance agent he and Gina had met at Two Friends. It was not his usual agent. This young man was young

275

and trying very hard to get established with a small, independent insurance company. Since a small company had to work harder to get business, Norm hoped it would have lax underwriting policies. Norm also reasoned that since the agent was just starting out, he would be hungry and do whatever it took to get new business on the books. It was also a plus that the agent was a person who did not run in Norm's usual social circles. Norm had sold insurance himself when he was in his early twenties, and he knew that the odds were against the kid making it as a sales rep.

That's fine. Just what I'm looking for, Norm thought. *All I want is for this patsy to get a policy on the books. This'll be a one-time deal. Then if he blows out of the insurance racket, even better. He won't be around to look over my shoulder. He won't even remember who I am and what's more, won't care. The main thing is I'll have a life insurance policy on the books in case I need it in case my tax situation worsens. That policy on Catt sure came in handy.*

Norm went to Two Friends that afternoon hoping the agent would be there for happy hour. He saw him sitting at the bar alone.

Perfect.

"Jerry, would you mind joining me at this table?" Norm asked. "I've got something I need to talk to you about." They walked over to a table out of earshot of the bar.

"Jerry, I'm going to get married soon, and I want to give my wife a present. I'd like to buy a million-dollar term policy on her. I don't want her to know about it."

"I'd need to get her underwritten," Jerry said. "Is she in good health?"

"Excellent. I want this kept confidential, or there's not going to be any deal."

"That might be a prob-problem..." Jerry stuttered.

Norm could see him calculating the commission dollars in his head. Norm knew he had him. He suspected Jerry badly need a commission. What Norm did not know was that Jerry hadn't sold a policy all month, and his sales manager had been reminding him of that fact daily.

"I was going to give you first shot at the ticket," Norm said, "but if you can't handle it, I'll get someone else."

"No, no, no, no," Jerry said, sounding panicky in spite of himself. "Just give me a second to think about the best way to get it done."

Norm waited for Jerry to speak.

"We could do an electronic application. That way she won't have to sign it. And you did pick the right time of year to buy insurance – December. Normally underwriting would ask for blood work and maybe a physical, but right now the company is pressured to get as much new business on the books before the end of the fiscal year as they can, and sales is putting pressure on the underwriters. Bonuses for everyone are at stake. Underwriting will then often overlook things and take shortcuts when the insured is a younger person, especially if I tell them you guys are traveling for the holidays and won't be back for awhile, but that I've got your money in hand so we can book the policy as this year's business. I guess you do know there'll be a two-year contestability clause in the policy if something does go wrong?"

"Yeah, I know that. I used to sell insurance a long time ago," Norm said. "No biggie. She's healthy as a horse. That's not a deal breaker for me. I'll give you the whole first year premium up front. Today if you want it."

"OK," Jerry said. "Let's give it a try. I think I can get this through the system."

My sales manager will go to bat for me, Jerry thought. *If I don't make my numbers for the year, it looks bad for him too.*

He went out to his car and returned with an application. They filled it out on the spot.

Norm congratulated himself on the way home.

If Gina turns out to be disloyal like Catt was, I'll have an additional option, he thought.

The following morning, Jerry got another call at his office.

"Jerry, my name is Gina Pannullo. I don't know if you remember me, but we met at Two Friends. I'd like to talk to you about taking an insurance policy out on my fiancée. It's got to be a secret. It's a wedding gift. Do you think you can help me?

Jerry smiled to himself.

This is my lucky day. Maybe I'll make my goals this month after all and get that sales manager off my ass.

"Why yes, Gina. I think I might be able to handle that transaction. How much insurance did you have in mind?"

"Oh, say a million dollars."

"An excellent figure. When do you want to get together?"

"Today works for me."

One way or another, I'm telling this goddamned raggedy-ass trailer goodbye forever.

Thank you for reading. Please review this book. Reviews help others find Absolutely Amazing eBooks and inspire us to keep providing these marvelous tales. If you would like to be put on our email list to receive updates on new releases, contests, and promotions, please go to AbsolutelyAmazingEbooks.com and sign up.

About the Authors

David Beckwith is a three-generation native of Greenville, Mississippi, with a BBA and an MBA from Ole Miss. His parents owned an independent cash commodity trading firm which also cleared securities trades through Goodbody & Co. David spent 40 years in the securities business, the first half of his career with Bache & Co. and its successors, the second half with Morgan Stanley. He retired as a Senior Vice President with approximately $500 million in responsibilities. For 25 years he has served as an adjunct professor at five different universities.

His first book was a narrative nonfiction work published by the University of Alabama Press in 2009 entitled *A New Day In The Delta*. The Mississippi Institute of Arts and Letters chose it as the runner-up for nonfiction book of the year. The book is often compared to Pat Conroy's *The Water Is Wide*.

David's wife Nancy earned a doctorate in finance and was the largest commercial lender and underwriter for Florida National Bank/1st Union/Wachovia, a member of their President's Club, and a board member. Also she served as the provost of the Brookley Campus for the University of South Alabama.

David and Nancy started writing the Will and Betsy Black Adventure Series in 2010. The protagonists of this series are a married couple somewhat reminiscent of Nick and Nora Charles of *The Thin Man* Series or Jonathan and Jennifer Hart of *Hart To Hart*. Their unique hook was that like the books' protagonists the authors were also a happily married couple.

Moving to Key West, the Beckwiths were tapped to write a book review column for the Key West *Citizen* which David continues to produce on a weekly basis.

ABSOLUTELY AMA⚡ING eBOOKS

AbsolutelyAmazingEbooks.com
or AA-eBooks.com